Lock Me Out

USA TODAY BESTSELLING AUTHOR
C. HALLMAN

Copyright © 2023 C. Hallman

Editing by Kelly Allenby

All rights reserved.

No part of this book may be reproduced in any form or by any electronic or mechanical means, including information storage and retrieval systems, without written permission from the author, except for the use of brief quotations in a book review.

To everyone who waited for this book to come out.

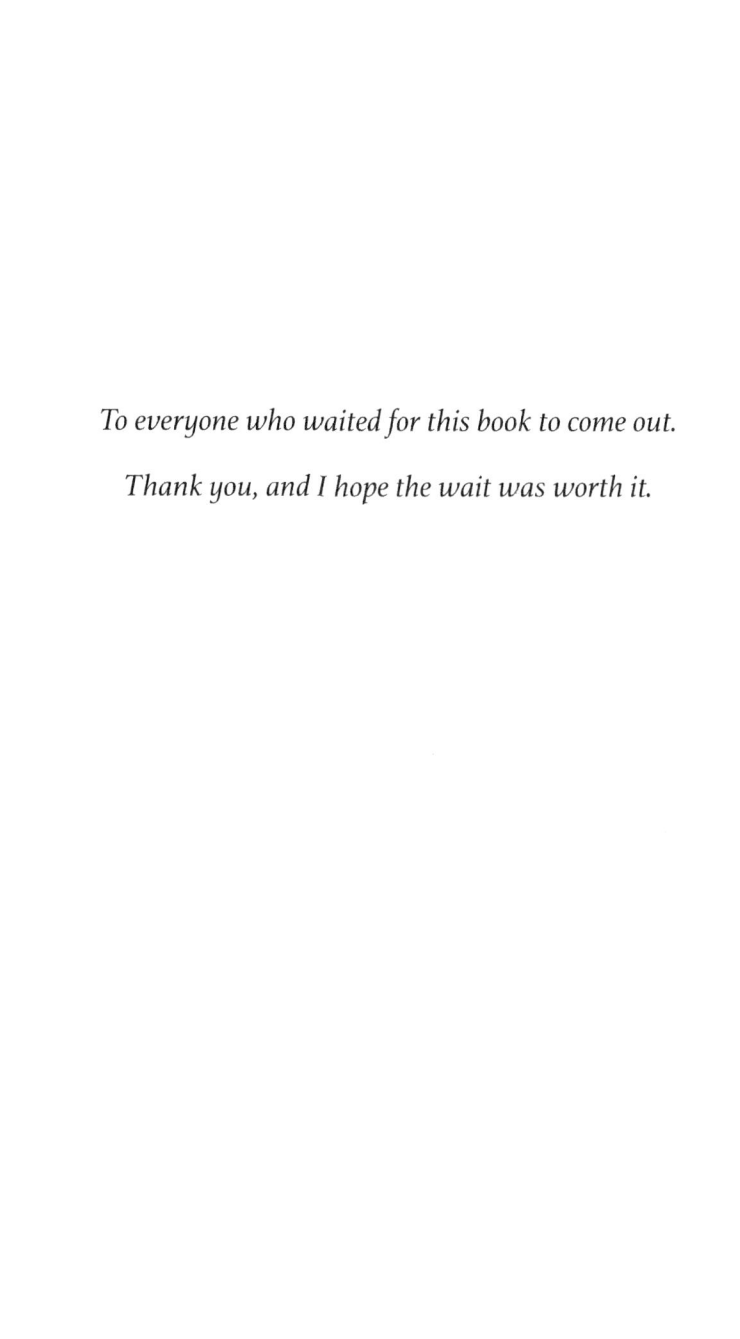

Thank you, and I hope the wait was worth it.

1. COLT

"Get the fuck out of the way!" I punch the horn with my fist, making it blare loud enough that Leni winces in the passenger seat. I see her over there, and I'm even sorry for upsetting her, but I can't find it in me to apologize. Besides, I know she understands. This is what I've waited for these past six months since finding Mom in the hospital and moving her closer to us so I could be with her when this day finally came. Until now, I wasn't sure it ever would. It wasn't until we got the call not more than twenty minutes ago that I believed it was possible for my mother to wake up after being in a coma for years.

"Colton, she's awake. Your mother woke up a few minutes ago." I was deep asleep when the phone rang, but by the time I heard those words, I was wide awake and already out of bed. Leni stared at me in a mixture of dread and confusion as she sat up, scrubbing a hand over her tousled hair. She finally pulled it all together over the course of the

questions I fired at the doctor, and by the time I ended the call, she was already getting dressed.

Mom is awake. I don't know what life is going to look like for her, but she's awake. That can't be anything but a good sign.

"Maybe slow down a little." Leni's voice is barely louder than a whisper, and it's filled with nerves. But this isn't her mom we're rushing to. It's my mom. My mom, who I hadn't seen in years before she was found in that hospital where Dad stashed her, far away from her sons, the people who actually loved her and needed her. There's part of my soul—what little of it is left—that craves the sight of her. That longs to have her look into my eyes and see me for the first time in too long.

"We'll be there in a minute." I can't slow down. When the asshole in front of me taps his brakes instead of trying to beat a yellow light, I swerve around him, honking, ignoring the shouts through his window as I speed through the light and travel the last block before the hospital comes up.

"You have to try to calm down." Leni's hand covers my leg, and I have to resist the impulse to brush it away like I would a mosquito or a fly—like she's a pest when she is anything but. "You don't want her to see you like this. She would want you to be calm."

She's right. The fact that I almost swatted her away proves that. But she doesn't know how it feels, either. Thinking for so long something was lost forever, then finally getting it back.

I wish Nix was here. That would make it perfect.

My heart is sinking by the time I take a quick right turn into the hospital parking lot. Dammit. He should be here. She should have both of her sons with her, letting her know we never stopped thinking about her, that we've been waiting for her to wake up ever since finding her alive.

But no. One of us is supposedly dead.

A burning coal of resentment lodges itself in my gut every time I think about him and the way the rest of the world is ready to accept the idea of him being gone. Nobody knows him like I do. He's alive. I feel it.

I'm the only one that believes it. Not even Leni gets it. She's content to believe what everyone else does: that he died in the explosion, that it's his body in the grave in the cemetery. I went to his funeral and probably looked like a heartless, unfeeling bastard when I didn't shed a tear while people all around me wept their hearts out.

Leni was one of them, whimpering softly, dabbing her eyes with a tissue and holding onto my arm for support. I gave it to her, but I felt nothing. It was like going through the motions in a nightmare or a fever dream, something that didn't make any sense.

I sort of feel like I'm in a dream now, rushing to the hospital door once I've parked the car in the first available space. Leni has to trot to keep up with me and finally catches up by the time we've reached the elevators beyond the front desk. I've been here so many times, I practically know the hospital like the back of my hand. I recognize the people behind the desk, the security guard sitting with them, and I nod to them before jabbing my finger against the button.

"Seriously, Colt. Breathe." Leni takes my hand, ignoring my tension, running her thumb over the back of my knuckles. "You want her to see you at your best. We don't know how much she's going to remember or whether she knows time has passed. It could be enough of a shock just to see you older than she remembers you."

She's right, isn't she? While waiting for the elevator to arrive, I force myself to take a deep breath. There's no way of knowing right now how much Mom will be able to handle. I need to be calm, gentle, even if I feel anything but as the doors open and we step inside.

Shifting my weight back and forth from one foot to the other, I can almost laugh at myself. I'm so nervous. What if she doesn't remember me? What if she doesn't know me at all? What if she's awake but unresponsive? She had woken up only minutes before the doctor called, so there wasn't much he could tell me about her condition. He probably still won't have a clue. It will probably take time to get to the heart of the damage that was done.

I have to brace myself again as the doors open, taking a deep breath of disinfected air as we step out. Mom's team is hanging around outside the door to her room, muttering things to each other, typing things on their tablets. One of them notices Leni and me as we approach and turns our way, meeting us halfway down the hall.

"I need to get in and see her," I murmur, ready to push him aside if I have to. Dr. Spencer is probably my favorite of all of them. He's honest, he doesn't bullshit me, and I appreciate that. I feel like Mom would appreciate it, too.

That doesn't mean I won't bodyslam him if he doesn't get the fuck out of my way.

The overhead light gleams off his bald head when he shakes it. "Just a minute. Let's touch base before you go in there."

Leni stays beside me, her grip on my hand tightening. There's something about the way he said that which doesn't exactly inspire confidence or hope. My heart drops like a rock, but I force my way through it, stiffening my spine. She needs me to be strong now. Both she and Leni need me to be strong. "Give it to me straight. How is she?"

Offering a faint smile, he claps a hand over my shoulder. "It's not bad at all. I'm sorry if I made it sound that way. It's just that some people, in situations like this, expect to find their loved one exactly as they remember them. That's just not possible when a person has been comatose for as long as your mother has. The fact that she's woken up at all is... Well, I don't like to use the word miracle, but it's close."

"Okay. I'll try to be realistic."

"That's good to hear. She's not able to speak yet," he explains with a sympathetic grimace. "She'll need a little more time and practice. Even then, she's going to need extensive speech therapy, not to mention physical therapy. But she has proven she is alert and aware, is able to nod in response to questions, and we could not be happier with what she's shown us so far."

"That's great news." Leni's breathless whimper tells me she's close to tears, and I pull her against my side, holding her close.

She's right. It is great news.

And Nix should be here, dammit. He's missing all of this. Why the hell won't he come back? Maybe one day I'll be able to understand, but right now I can't imagine forgiving him for missing this. He's going to regret it, the asshole.

"Can we go in now?" I ask. When the doctor nods, Leni takes my hand again, walking beside me as we take the last few steps into the room we've visited countless times in the last six months.

All this time, I've only seen her with her eyes closed, her face slack, lifeless. Now she's sitting up a little more instead of lying back, her head propped up by a pillow, her eyes wide open as they take in the room around her.

And when they see me, they go wider and watery as tears fill them.

It's like being punched in the gut, but in the best way. The shock is almost enough to make me sway on my feet, while my mind tries to make sense of what I'm looking at. Like I'm afraid to accept what I see. "Mom," I whisper, almost laughing when her head bobs just a little, enough that I know she hears me and understands.

And now nothing matters more than being by her side. I cross the room quickly and sink into the chair next to the bed, taking her hand, touching my forehead to the back of it. After everything I've done and all the sins I've committed, I have no right to thank God for anything, but that's what I do. Silently, in my heart, even though I doubt there's any entity that will actually understand. *Thank you. Thank you so much.*

"They told me you can't talk yet, but I know that will come back with enough practice." I'm almost giddy, chuckling when I raise my head. "Can you imagine there would ever have been a time you couldn't talk your head off? You'll get it back. I know you will."

Her eyes search my face, filled with wonder and confusion and so many questions. "You've been in a coma for a long time. I'm sure they told you that already," I whisper, and she nods slightly, squeezing my hand. My mom just squeezed my hand. A sob tries to build in my chest, but I hold it back. I'm so fucking happy; I don't know what to do. It's like getting the biggest, best gift ever, and I have no idea what to do with it. "Do you know why?"

Her eyebrows draw together for a second, and I wish I hadn't asked when I see the pain in her eyes. She remembers. But hey, at least now we know her memory wasn't lost. If she remembers the bad, that means she'll be able to remember the good, too. That's how life works. Good and bad.

"Let me tell you something." Looking her straight in the eye, I murmur, "He's dead. Dad is dead. You never have to worry about him again. He can never hurt you again—he can't hurt any of us. That part is all over. All you have to do now is focus on recovering. And I will do everything I can to help you, I swear. We've got this, right?"

The corners of her mouth twitch in a weak smile, but again, her brows meet over the bridge of her nose. When her lips part, I hold my breath, waiting. Is she going to try to speak? Will she be upset if it doesn't work?

After what feels like forever, she lets out a frustrated sigh and mouths a single word: "Nix."

Obviously, she was going to ask about him. I'm sitting here, practically in tears, but he's nowhere in sight. "Nix isn't here right now. We haven't seen him in a while. He is... away, but it's okay. I know he'll be back." It's only when Leni makes a choked sound behind me that I remember she's even here. I've been so focused on Mom, I didn't think about her. She doesn't approve of what I said, just like she doesn't approve of me refusing to believe my brother is dead. But that's because he's not dead. I know he isn't.

It's safer and better to turn toward her and extend a hand. "Mom, Leni's my girlfriend now. I know that will come as a surprise," I add, turning back to her and watching her eyes go big and wide. "We live together, only minutes from here. We've come to see you so many times, and we'll be back all the time, too. Both of us. I know you must have a million questions."

Mom snorts softly, and Leni and I laugh. Even the fact that she can do that is a win. The sort of win I never hoped for.

She's obviously getting tired, her eyes half-closed and her head sinking into the pillow. There's been more activity in the past hour than she's experienced in years. After promising to be back to see her tomorrow, I kiss Mom's forehead and we leave the room, heading down to the cafeteria since we never took time to eat breakfast, and I'm not quite ready to leave yet. There's too much to process.

I barely feel my feet touch the floor the whole way downstairs. My head is in the clouds. It was a short visit, but it was the best visit of my life.

"You were so great in there." Leni waits next to me while the guy behind the counter scrambles eggs for us. The cafeteria is surprisingly good, with a huge selection of foods. We've eaten more than a few meals here ever since I had Mom moved so she could be close to us.

"It's one of those things where you imagine a hundred times what you would do or say, but then the moment comes and everything you ever thought goes out the window." Leni is the only person I would confess something like that to—well, her and Nix. I don't know what's worse: missing him or hating him for removing himself from my life, all our lives. Upsetting Mom, though I'm sure he never thought she would factor in. I didn't learn until after the explosion that she was even alive and comatose in a Florida hospital.

"I don't know how I would've handled it, so I'm in awe of you," she says. I don't know how she manages to be so supportive and loving sometimes. Like there's this endless well of love inside her. I don't think I deserve it, but she seems to think I do.

A handful of tables are in use, and I glance toward them as we pass with our trays. People in scrubs, grabbing a quick breakfast and coffee. A couple off in the corner, leaning on each other for support. There are so many stories around here—ours is only one of them. Today we are one of the happy stories, sitting together, grinning at each other every once in a while. I couldn't have known when I fell asleep last night that the morning would turn out like this.

Just like I couldn't have imagined watching my house explode one day. An explosion that killed my father and Leni's mom... and someone else, a third body that was never identified, a body close enough to the source of the explosion that it was pretty much completely destroyed. Lazy investigators assumed it was Nix's, and the fact that my brother decided to disappear only strengthened their theory, at least in their own minds.

I don't want to think about that now, not when there's hope and the promise of a future for a woman whose life was almost taken by the man who was supposed to love her. He destroyed her, he almost destroyed Leni, and he got what was coming to him. Now, with Mom being awake, there's the possibility we'll all be able to move forward.

All I need is for my brother to come back and prove I was right all along. That's the only thing that will begin to erase the damage that bastard did.

2. LENI

A SENSE OF HEAVY SADNESS SETTLES OVER ME AS WE ROLL through the tall, wrought-iron gates leading to the place where Mom and Nix are waiting. It's so peaceful here—the kind of quiet that I suppose could be considered eerie, but at times like this, it feels comforting. I like to think of them being at peace here, especially Mom, whose life was so difficult in her later years, after I was injured, and she worked so hard to make sure I had what I needed.

It's so damn unfair that we're never given any warning when our last years will come. James had seemed like a dream come true; the answer to all of her problems. At least she had a little bit of time when she didn't have to constantly worry about how we were going to make ends meet.

Of course, there's no such thing as miracles, and her short-lived freedom came at a heavy price. I almost wish she had never found all that incriminating evidence. I wish, if she had to die, she could've died believing her life was a happy one.

That's where my sadness comes from as we roll to a stop at the end of a row of graves. They're newer on this side of the cemetery—there's one up ahead that looks like it was only just filled recently. By now, the earth over Mom's grave has flattened out until it looks pretty much the same as all the others.

"Are you okay?" Colt's question is maybe a little sharp, a little testy. Being here freaks him out, but he says he understands why I need to do this. Maybe one day I won't feel the need as strongly as I do now, but regular visits help me feel connected.

"Oh, yeah. I'm fine."

"Then why are you sitting here?" he asks while his fingers tap the wheel. "You don't have to get out if you don't want to."

I can only shake my head at the way he misunderstands me. "I wish you could get out of the car with me and visit. That's all."

"You're not really visiting anyone." I wince at his reply, which makes his expression soften along with the tone of his voice. "You know what I mean. It's just bodies in the ground."

I know what he means, but he isn't telling the whole story. Does he really think he can fool me? Like we don't already know each other better than that? "Can I ask you something?" I murmur while my pulse picks up speed.

"Sure."

It's not easy to put into words in a way that won't insult him. I almost wish I hadn't said anything in the first place. All I can do is stare down at the two bouquets in my lap—one for Mom and one for Nix. Mom's favorite flower was always roses, and since I don't know if Nix had a favorite flower, I got roses for him too. I don't think he would care very much either way. Stroking the silky petals, I ask, "Why didn't you tell your mom Nix is dead?"

I hear the sharp intake of breath, but I'm too unnerved to look his way. He'll be angry. Most things about Nix make him angry. He doesn't like talking about his brother, especially since we so clearly disagree over the facts. "Because he's not. So why would I tell her he is?"

I don't know how to get through to him. I don't even know if it's possible. All I know for sure is he won't accept the truth. It's too much for him. I've lost track of the number of times I've wanted to run away from the truth in my life, so I understand. But that doesn't make this any easier.

"Besides," he continues, his left knee bouncing up and down with agitation, "she just woke up from a coma. I'm not going to drop all that on her at once. The man who put her in that coma is dead—she deserves to know that. She deserves to know she's safe."

"Of course."

"But telling her everybody thinks Nix is gone? What if it made her relapse or something? I couldn't do that."

"You're right. I get it." I feel a little dumb for asking, because what he said makes total sense. We have to be careful with her in these early days. She's been through so much. I wonder if it's true what they say, if people in comas can actually hear and understand what's happening around them. Maybe she could. Maybe she understands time has passed. Or maybe she feels like she just woke up from a nap. I guess we won't know until she can speak again.

Embarrassment flashes through me as I leave the car, but it's nothing compared to the weight of grief pressing down on me as I walk the gravel path toward the graves. We're near the edge of the cemetery, and the trees ahead are so thick the late-day rays of sun can't break through. But I turn away from that and toward the marble headstone bearing my mother's name: **Amanda Peters**. I didn't want the name "Alistair" etched in stone. I didn't want her marriage to James following her into eternity, at least as long as this headstone remains intact.

"Hi, Mom." Gently, I place the roses at the base of the headstone. Who takes them away once they're wilted and dead? The groundskeepers, I guess. They must do it discreetly when no one is watching. It's a tiny mercy.

There are a few scattered leaves and dandelions dotting the grass, which I gently pull away and toss aside as I murmur, "Guess what? Corinne's awake. Can you believe it? I honestly didn't think it was possible for someone to wake up after being in a coma for so long. The doctors think she'll be able to recover, but it's going to take a lot of time."

Once the ground is clear, I settle on my knees, sitting back on my heels. For some reason, I feel like I should fold my hands, even though I've never been religious or anything like that. It just feels respectful somehow.

A warm breeze stirs a few red tendrils away from my face, and I close my eyes, letting it wash over me. The sun's rays are warm on my skin, and the delicious scent of the flowers brings a faint smile to my lips. It's getting a little easier every time I visit.

The first time, I kneeled in front of Mom's grave and cried until there were no more tears left in my body. I cried until my eyes were swollen, and I could barely breathe. I was so exhausted that I wanted to lie down on the mound of earth covering her casket and just sleep.

Every visit since then has been a little easier—no, that's not quite right. A little less hard. I doubt it will ever be easy to visit this place and see Mom's name on the headstone. All she ever wanted was something better. Did she always make the right decisions? Absolutely not. But life threw her more than a few curveballs, and that's something I try to keep in mind whenever bitterness starts creeping in.

I'll never forget how devastated she was the day of the explosion—only minutes before it happened, in fact—when she called me in hysterics, horrified, begging for my forgiveness. She told me she didn't know until she found all those photos on James's hard drive.

"I do forgive you," I whisper, patting the ground in front of me. "I really do. Sometimes, when you don't want to believe something, you make yourself blind to it. You pretend it doesn't exist. That's what Colt is doing right now."

Sliding a look his way from the corner of my eye, I see him sitting behind the wheel of the car, staring straight ahead. He won't even glance over here. He won't even let himself look at Nix's headstone. Maybe that would make it all too real for him, and he can't let even a sliver of reality into his thoughts.

"I don't know what to do for him," I admit. It's funny, but it's so much easier to talk to her now. If only it had been this easy when she was alive. "He needs my support, and I want to give it to him, but to him, support means agreeing with this delusion or whatever it is. I can't do that. I love him. I can't just sit here and pretend there's anything normal about this."

Now that I've started talking, I can't seem to stop. It's almost like I'm catching up with a friend I haven't seen in a long time.

"I got another one of those messages yesterday. I haven't told Colt about it yet," I whisper. Even though I know there's no chance of him getting out of the car and hearing me, I still feel like I have to be careful. "Whoever is sending them keeps telling me they know what I did and threatening to go to the cops, but I don't know why they would. Even if the explosion was deliberate, it's not like I was there. Neither was Colt. We had nothing to do with it."

Closing my eyes again, I can feel the heat from the explosive blast that rocked the ground under us and sent a fireball into the air. "I still believe James set the whole thing off. I wish you could tell me whether or not I'm right," I confess in a rush of words and emotion. "I wish I knew for sure, either way. It just seems funny to me that he came home that day after you accessed all that information, and suddenly the house went up in flames. I mean, if I were a monster like him, and I had all that incriminating evidence stored on my cloud, what would stop me from doing whatever it took to protect myself?"

"He probably figured he would escape. Or maybe…" I pause, shivering now as the breeze feels colder. "Maybe he figured it was too late to save himself and didn't want to face what would happen once the truth came out. I guess that makes more sense than anything else. Even though, really, none of it makes sense at all," I conclude. If it did make sense, I'd have to worry about myself, because James Alistair was a demented monster whose mental processes are not something I want to understand.

Once I'm finished checking in with Mom, I visit Nix's grave and perform the same ritual, placing the flowers in front of his headstone. His grave is cleaner than Mom's, free of any weeds or leaves. I'm sure I'm not the only one who visits. It's never easy to lose somebody, but it's especially grim for people our age. You don't expect to lose a classmate at nineteen, especially not in such tragic circumstances.

"Your mom woke up. Can you believe it?" Tears fill my eyes as I position the flowers and lower myself to one knee, my hand resting on top of the headstone. The dates etched there are heartbreaking. Nineteen years of life. That's all he got. He had so much more to give the world. Without his dad poisoning him, he could've been something great. He could've been his own man, built his own life.

My heart is so full it clogs my throat with emotion. I have to look away from those tragic dates marking his short life, my gaze lifting to the trees farther out.

Where something moves.

An icy finger of dread runs up my spine, freezing me in place as though ice is spreading through my body. I know I'm not imagining it. Something is definitely out there—something big. Is there wildlife in this area? My eyes dart left, then right, but I'm alone here. Except for whatever that is in the trees. A bear? No, that doesn't make any sense, but it's the only thing that comes to mind.

A person? Why would they be hiding? Because without a word spoken, I know that's what they're doing. They're hiding back there. Watching.

The last message I received flashes in my mind like a warning: *Watch your back.*

Are they really following me? Whoever they are?

A scream builds in my chest, fueled by rage and fear, growing and clawing its way to my throat. I want to shout at them: *Who the hell do you think you are?*

But instead of screaming, I yelp when a horn blares behind me. Colt. My head snaps around just in time to see him scowling and tapping the horn again.

I whirl back toward the trees, but the figure is gone. Nothing but deep shadows now. There's no point in telling Colt about my fears, since I can't give him yet another thing to worry about when there's so much on his mind. He has no idea about the anonymous emails and texts I've been getting—the longer I go without telling him about them, the harder it is to come up with a reason why I've kept them a secret.

Somehow, I walk slowly and steadily back to the car, even as every nerve in my body screams at me to run. I need to let them know they're not important. Let them know I don't care.

They can't see how I'm trembling inside.

3. NIX

THAT WAS CLOSE. FOR A SECOND, I THOUGHT FOR SURE SHE recognized me.

That's stupid. How would she, with my face covered? Somehow, deep down, I get the feeling she would know. The connection we have—our ugly, dirty connection—would ensure she knew I was the one watching from a distance, lurking in the shadows, watching her every move and trying to understand what she was whispering.

I should stop. I know I should. That's probably what every addict tells themselves before their next drink, their next pill, or the next time they slide a needle into a vein. *Just one last time, and then I'll stop.* I keep telling myself the same thing. But there's a difference between me and those addicts. I don't believe myself. I know I'll have to see her again.

She gets into Colt's car, and they pull away. He's in a hurry, like he can't wait to get out of here. I can't blame him. I don't like coming here either, especially knowing there's a headstone with my name on it up ahead.

It's too bizarre. I'm dead to the world. A ghost walking the streets night after night. Watching her, watching him, watching life go on without me. Like now, stepping out of the tree line only when I'm sure no one will see me. Stepping into sunshine that doesn't touch my face, thanks to the hood pulled over my head.

There are flowers at Amanda's grave—and mine. I step closer, almost surprised to see white roses sitting at the base of the marble slab that bears my name and the dates of my birth and supposed death.

In a way, I did die that day. The Nixon Alistair the world knew ceased to exist once the house went up in flames. He's miles away from the man I am now. The old Nix is barely a memory that gets fainter every day. I can't remember being him when my current life is so completely different.

Why did she leave flowers for me? Her mom, sure, but me? After everything I did to her? Even now, months later, my body responds to the memory. I should be repulsed; I know I should. But the opposite is true. My pulse races, hunger slithers through me, and my dick hardens when I remember the dark pleasure I took from Leni's body. Again and again.

Maybe I deserve to be dead.

I can't hang around here too long. This is a newer part of the cemetery, meaning there are more visitors here than in the older sections. The grief is fresher. Over time, it fades. People forget. Graves get overgrown.

What about the people nobody mourns? Because I'll never mourn my father. I don't even think of him as my father after what he did.

That's why Bradley and I went to the house that day and set the fire.

It was his idea. That's the one piece of truth I cling to, the way I cling to everything else as I leave the cemetery on foot. I've done a hell of a lot of walking these past months, ever since I snuck out of the hospital where everybody knew me as *John Doe*.

I'm supposed to be dead, so I can't just go out and buy a car. Still, I've made enough connections to pick up a used model with cash sometime soon. I doubt Colt could trace my bank activity, so there's no danger in withdrawing cash. He hasn't noticed it so far.

But I can't keep this up forever. I know that. Eventually, Colt will find me, or I'll take one risk too many and be discovered.

He already knows I'm not dead—he keeps emailing me, updating me on his life. Not every day, but a few times a week. I access the messages at the public library. Of all the things I miss from my old life, a smartphone might be the hardest to live without. But it's too traceable. I can't take that risk.

For so many reasons.

For starters, there's Bradley's charred remains lying in my grave. Nobody would believe me if I told them the fire was his idea. I still see his wicked grin in my mind's eye. *"You can teach the bastard a lesson."* I never told Bradley the details of the shit Dad made us do or what he did to Mom, but he knew I hated the son of a bitch.

Even now, knowing Dad's dead and gone, just thinking of him makes my fists clench in my pockets as I walk with my head down and my shoulders hunched. It's become a habit, hiding myself from the world, making it so they don't have to look at me.

If it weren't for the constant craving to see Leni again, I might never leave my apartment. It's not worth risking people seeing me—wincing, immediately looking away. That's the thing about people trying to be kind: they end up being the most hurtful. Someone like me, someone who used to take good looks for granted and revel in the attention he got from girls... the ultimate punishment is people feeling too sorry for me and too disgusted by me to stare too long at my face.

"You're lucky to be alive, young man. If you hadn't been found out there, there's no telling what might have happened."

I'll never forget the agony as I stumbled away from the burning house, fumbling my way through the woods. I had to get away. That was all that mattered—getting away. There was no feeling. I didn't even register my injuries, no more than I noticed the branches whipping against me or the uneven ground that made me stumble and fall to my hands and knees more than once. I just kept going, some instinct telling me to put as much distance between myself and that house as possible.

Looking back now, I know I was in shock. I could barely string two thoughts together after apparently getting out of the house before the explosion, though not soon enough to avoid the fireball that burst from the windows and blew out the back door. I got lucky, even if I didn't feel lucky in the days that followed.

Dark now. So dark. Lights up ahead, traffic sounds. I can barely breathe. Every breath feels like fire in my lungs. And my face, there's something wrong, I know there is. Every breeze that moves across my skin is like a thousand knives slicing into my flesh. I don't want to see it—I don't even want to touch it, afraid of what I'll find. All I can do is keep moving, dragging myself forward, forcing one footstep after another.

It was only when I reached the road that I let myself rest. I had no choice. I collapsed in the dirt along the shoulder, my last conscious thought hoping someone would find me before I allowed exhaustion to win out.

Someone did find me, someone I was never conscious enough to speak to. I woke up in the hospital without any idea how much time had passed until one of the nurses told me the date. It had been two days since the fire.

And according to the news, I was dead.

By the time I reach the sketchy part of town that is now my home, the sun is sinking. Broken glass crunches under the soles of my boots, and a stray cat darts out from between a pair of trash cans as I approach. What was a warm breeze earlier has turned colder, sending ripples of goosebumps over my skin and making me hunch my shoulders higher, my chin close to my chest. Walking around with my hood pulled up gives me tunnel vision. I can't see what's happening on either side of me, which makes it all the more important to listen carefully to my surroundings.

This is my life now. Hiding from the world, protecting myself, wondering how much longer it has to be this way.

The old brick building where my apartment sits is about as grim and depressing as I can imagine. It always stinks of piss, and the walls are paper-thin, meaning I can hear every damn thing happening around me at all hours. But everyone minds their own business. That and a couple of working locks are all I need right now.

A pair of guys who I'm pretty sure live on the front steps day and night jerk their chins in my direction as I walk past. I give them my usual grunt in response before walking through the plexiglass door into the narrow space where rows of mailboxes sit. There's no name on mine—not that I get any mail anyway.

"He came to us with no identification and doesn't give any answers when we ask about his identity. And nobody has called in looking for a missing person."

They think I'm asleep, in a drug-induced haze, which is the only way I can be sure they'll speak honestly while I can hear.

I'm supposed to be dead. Bradley must've been killed, and they figured his body was mine. They haven't said anything about him on the news, so that's the only thing that makes sense.

Dad is dead. Amanda, too. I didn't mean to kill her. She wasn't supposed to die. I'm sorry for that. I'm sorry for Leni. One more way I destroyed her.

I take the stairs slowly, as usual, listening for anyone hiding out further up in the stairwell. Sometimes, a guy who lives here will wait around, hoping to score a little something out of the pockets of someone coming in or leaving. Considering I helped kill my father and stepmother, I can't really give them any shit over it. Everyone does what they have to do to get by.

They probably see me and figure I came from a shitty background, addict parents or something like that. It's easy to make assumptions about a person's past based on the way they look and act today.

I wonder what any of them would think if they knew how I really grew up. The comfort and privilege. I had every opportunity to be better than this, at least on the surface. The rot was underneath, out of sight.

Not that I owe any of them an explanation. Nobody asks questions—and nobody looks too long at me if we happen to pass in the hall. I might as well be living on the moon, away from humanity, even if I can hear them through the walls.

I unlock both bolts on the scarred front door of my third-floor apartment, glancing to the right and left one more time before opening the door and quickly closing it behind me. Once the locks are flipped again, I release a long breath and touch my forehead to the cool wood.

That was a close one back at the cemetery. I need to be more careful, which means not venturing out in the daytime. It would be too easy for Leni to spot me and maybe recognize me.

The thought makes me laugh—softly, bitterly—before lowering my hood and running a hand through my short hair. It's longer now than I used to keep it, covering the random bits of damage to my scalp.

Turning the lights on only makes everything look bleaker. If I cared, I'd get some actual furniture, maybe lamps, to make it warmer and more homey. But who needs comfort? Who needs to pretend life is anything less bleak than it is? Anyway, it's what I deserve. After what I did, the bare minimum is all I should ever have.

Not that I'm super upset about what happened to Dad. Fuck him. It's the memories of everything I did to Leni—and how I ended up destroying her life—all because he wanted me to.

Though really, thinking back on what I saw at the cemetery, she doesn't look like her life has been ruined. And she did leave those flowers for me. Does that mean she's forgiven me? A brief smile touches the corners of my mouth. That's rare nowadays, with pretty much nothing to smile about most of the time. It would be just like her to forgive me. Somehow, that's who she is. Life has handed her so much pain, disappointment, and shame, but she's still Leni.

I don't understand that kind of person and can't pretend to. I carry grudges. I hate, I resent, and I want to inflict pain on those who have hurt me. Sometimes, imagining inflicting that pain is all that gets me through the worst of my solitude—the long, lonely nights spent doing absolutely nothing. Back in the day, there was always something to do: a party, a night out with my brother, maybe someone to hook up with. There was never a shortage of ways to distract myself or reasons to keep going.

Now, all of that is gone. And I have to wonder why I'm still alive while Bradley is dead in my grave.

As far as I know from the internet searches I've done at the library, there haven't been any big stories about him going missing. The family must be keeping it quiet, which, of course, they'd do to keep their name out of the media. Not like they're anything special, but they think they are. In our world, that's enough.

No, not our world. Their world. I have a world of my own now, where what might have once been a big bedroom now serves as an entire studio apartment. A tiny sink, a two-burner stove, and an oven barely big enough to fit a plate inside serve as my kitchen. The bathroom is so small I can barely turn around without bumping into something, and the sofa doubles as my bed. I'm a lifetime away from the sprawling house I blew up seven months ago.

And I'm not the person I was back then, either. Going to the bathroom and catching a glimpse of my reflection in the mirror over the chipped, permanently stained porcelain sink is always a stark reminder. Not that I could ever forget—I can't move my face the way I used to. It really sucks when I forget, and the tightness of my scar tissue reminds me I'll never be normal again.

There's no point in trying to avoid the sight of myself. Instead, I stop and stare straight at my reflection. The left side of my face is mostly what it used to be, but the right? It's a map of twisted scar tissue, still a pale pink that I guess will eventually turn into a ghostly white. A monster, in other words. But then, I always was. Thinking back, going over every ugly thing I did at Dad's command, it all helps me understand that my outside now matches my insides.

And it's even worse than that. I can't kid myself. When I look into my blue eyes, I see the eyes of someone who, if given the chance, would do everything the same. Because as much as I crave something to do, something to make me feel alive again, I crave Leni twice as much. Ten times as much. The feeling fills me, consumes me, makes me toss and turn in a cold sweat. Knowing where she is—with my brother—and that it would be so easy to go to her, to have her again, to satisfy every dark yearning.

Which is why I need to stay here. Away from her. Always.

4. COLT

I've stopped being my own person around school.

The rest of the world sees me as Colt Alistair, Leni's boyfriend, not the kind of guy you want to fuck around with.

But when we get to school, I stop being me. Now, I'm the guy whose brother died. That's the risk you take when you spend so much time with someone who happens to look a hell of a lot like you. People get used to seeing you together everywhere you go. Then all of a sudden, there's only one of you, and every time they notice you're alone, they remember why. They get this sad, almost embarrassed look on their faces.

It happens all the time, even months later. You'd think they'd get used to it by now, but it still feels fresh. At least now, no one says anything. I couldn't handle more questions like, "How are you? Are you holding up? Is there anything I can do to help?"

So now, I don't have to fight the urge to ask if they know how to bring people back from the so-called dead.

They wouldn't believe me, anyway. I can't even get Leni to understand, so why would a bunch of people I don't care about, whose names I hardly remember, believe me? I used to care about the way I was seen around here. There was a time I enjoyed walking across campus, being recognized, waved at, invited to parties, and that kind of thing. It used to matter.

I barely remember being that person now.

The one bright spot in my life is the girl walking by my side. She's a ray of light, almost like she carries her own personal sun inside her and glows from the inside out. I can't believe I ever saw her the way I once did. I can't believe it was ever so easy to hate her, to abuse her. Love changes everything.

But it hasn't changed me. Not completely. There's still a darkness deep inside. The impulse to remind her that she belongs to me when she smiles as we pass a group of people who call out to us. They don't deserve her attention. Only I do.

It's like she hears me as we walk, glancing up at me before color floods her cheeks. "What will you do between classes?" she asks, brushing a strand of red hair away from her face when a gust of wind teases it from her ponytail. The floral scent of her shampoo reaches me and soothes the worst of the boiling, swirling darkness that's always just under the surface, threatening to consume me.

"I thought I would go to the library."

The way she narrows her eyes before tipping her head to the side tells me she doesn't exactly believe my answer. "You've been spending a lot of time in the library lately."

"Have I?" I shrug. "I haven't really thought about it."

"Better be careful." She gives me a gentle nudge with her elbow, a playful smile tipping the corners of her mouth. "I might start thinking you're meeting a girl in there."

Coming to a stop at the intersection where one of the paths leads to the library, I turn to her and take her face in my hands. How is her skin so soft? "That's one thing you never have to worry about."

"I know. I'm only playing." She closes her eyes before I press a kiss to her forehead, forcing myself to memorize the softness of her skin under my lips. How eager she is to accept affection. I carry that in my heart all the time, along with every little thing I've cataloged and memorized about her. Sometimes, those memories are all that keep me from losing myself to the rage. Maybe one day I'll have to process it or whatever, but today is not that day.

As much as I don't like letting her go off by herself, there's no choice but to watch her continue to the arts and sciences complex where her next class is. Once I watch her walk inside, I turn around and head for the library.

Of course, Leni was right. I'm not here to study. Maybe it's wrong to hide this from her, but then again, right and wrong has never mattered all that much to me. We spend so much time together at the apartment, I don't feel comfortable doing my research there. She might see me, get a little curious, and start asking questions. She's not going to like the answers she gets, and I won't like the way she doesn't like it. I'm pretty new to this whole relationship thing, but I know it's smarter to avoid the shit you see coming a mile away. That's why I use one of the computers in the library to dig around.

I don't even know what I'm looking for. A sign, any sign. I have to do something. I can't sit around and accept what everyone else has accepted. I would know if my brother was dead. I never saw the body. There was no ability to test his dental records since he was basically blown apart.

Whoever it was, it wasn't Nix. I don't know who else would have been in the house that day, but it wasn't him. Nix wouldn't let himself get blown up like that. He would've smelled the gas—it was a gas leak that set off the blast. He would've been smart enough to get the hell out of there.

Because otherwise, he did it on purpose, and I can't accept that. The idea of him doing something like that, without at least hinting to me he was thinking about it... it doesn't make sense. That's not him. That's not us. And that's what Leni couldn't possibly understand.

Finally, when my research comes up with nothing as it usually does, I move on to the next step. There's no way to know whether he reads these emails I send every few days, but I have to keep trying.

First, though, I have to look around, make sure nobody's paying attention. This whole thing has turned me into a paranoid freak, always looking over my shoulder, because I know anyone would think I'm crazy or pathetic and deluded if they knew I can't accept Nix's death. Like I'm some emotional basket case who can't accept the truth.

Brother,

When are you coming back? Life is pretty fucking boring without you. I feel like I ask that question all the time, but the days keep going past, and you still haven't said anything to at least let me know you're okay.

Maybe this will get you to show yourself: Mom is awake. We saw her a few days ago. I've been waiting to get back on campus to send you this email and let you know. She's doing well, at least according to her team. I don't think they ever expected her to wake up. Now that she has, I'm not sure I was ever all that confident either. I mean, I hoped. I thought I could make her wake up somehow if I concentrated hard enough, or something like that.

I know she wants to see you. She can't talk yet—it might be a long time before she ever can—but I know. Right away, she wanted to know where you were. Maybe you were always right when we were kids, and you said you were her favorite. It would suck if her favorite never came to see her.

I'm acting like the kid I was back in those days, trying to goad him, but I'm pretty fucking desperate at this point. Whatever it takes, I need him to respond. I would feel it inside if he were gone. I'm sure I would.

She's at the hospital I told you about before, where I had her moved closer to me instead of hiding her out in Florida the way that asshole did. I told her he's gone, and she cried a little, which tells me she still remembers things. I told her you went away because that's the truth. I know it's the truth. You're not dead. I don't know why you feel like you have to stay away. Is it guilt? Are you afraid somebody will blame you for the explosion? You don't have to worry about that.

You don't have to worry about Leni, either. You know how things are between us now. She knows why we did what we did. She doesn't hold it against us.

Even as I type the words, I feel a strange, uncomfortable sensation growing in the pit of my stomach. It's another thing I'm not used to—second-guessing myself. Is that what love is? Trying to do the right thing, and then always wondering if it was right after all? Going over every conversation when things seem off, wondering if you did or said something wrong. If you brought the person you love closer or pushed them away.

I think something is up with Leni, but she is pretending nothing is wrong. You know what a terrible liar she is. She tries to act tough and strong. She thinks she has the world fooled, but we can all see through her. I don't know why she can't be honest with me. I don't know what I have to do to make her trust me. The more she doesn't trust me, the angrier I get. The more hurt she gets. I see that hurt in her eyes—fuck, she might as well punch me in the face when she looks at me. It might be easier if she did.

"Hey, Colt."

My head snaps up at the sound of a voice murmuring my name. A lot of people think they can just walk past and start a conversation when somebody's busy. They're lucky I just jerk my chin in recognition. I'd rather ask them why they can't mind their own damn business. I feel like a guilty kid caught cheating on a test or something, looking around again to make sure nobody's watching over my shoulder as I basically treat my brother like my personal diary. The whole thing is pretty pathetic.

But then they wouldn't understand. If anything, I'm glad for them. Glad for anyone who doesn't have to carry this weight around. Knowing in their heart that things aren't the way they appear.

By the time I send the email, I know what I need to do when we get home later. I need to figure out what the hell the girl who supposedly loves me doesn't trust me enough to tell me.

∼

I'M BARELY able to wait until we're inside with the rest of the world locked away on the other side of the door before pouncing on her the way I've thought about doing ever since I was in the library. She wants to keep something from me? She needs to know she can't do it for long. I have ways of making her talk. I know exactly which buttons to push.

"Oh, so that's how it's going to be." She's giggling, unaware of what I have in mind while I paw at her, holding her against me from behind before she's had the chance to drop her backpack on the floor. When my hand cups her tit, she lets out a soft moan. "You know, I was planning on working on a paper as soon as we got home..."

"That can wait," I whisper in her ear before letting my tongue play over the lobe until she trembles against me. It is so easy to push her buttons and get her hot until she has no memory of why she wanted to do anything but lose herself to this pleasure.

Pretty soon, she's wiggling her ass against my dick. "Tease," I breathe in her ear, and she shivers, moaning softly when I slide a hand inside her T-shirt, working my fingers under her bra cup to tease her nipple. "So that's the game you wanna play? Turns out, I had the same idea in mind."

Only it's going to go the other way around.

"Can I at least get a snack first?" When I squeeze her tit hard enough to make her gasp, it's all the answer she needs. She doesn't put up a fight as I walk us both toward the bedroom, since I want her spread out for me, flat on her back. I want access to all of her.

"Take off your clothes," I murmur, letting her go once we're next to the bed.

"You don't feel like doing it for me?" Sure, keep playing, play while you can. I don't say a word, only stepping back with my arms folded until she gets the hint and pulls her T-shirt overhead. Her jeans come next once she kicks off her shoes.

At first, it's enough just to stare at her body in the light coming in from the window at her back. She's perfect from head to toe, a wet dream come true. Even the scar on her back only sets off the perfection in the rest of her, a small flaw that makes the rest of her shine through.

Holding my gaze, she reaches behind her to unclasp her bra, then just as slowly slides her pink bikini panties to the floor. "Now what should I do?" she asks in a seductive voice, with a smile to match.

"Lie down. Ass on the edge of the bed. Leg spread." She's trembling with anticipation but does as I say, parking her ass on the edge of the bed and lying back with her thighs spread wide.

That's how much she trusts me in moments like this. Doing as I say without asking why. The thought is humbling in a way, but I don't have time for that right now. I can't let myself get lost in the moment.

At first, it's enough for me to run my hands from ankle to hip, teasing her skin until goosebumps rise over it. She giggles and squirms, looking up at me with desire in her eyes. So beautiful, all mine. And it's up to me to fulfill that desire.

Right now, it's also up to her, even if she doesn't know it yet.

There's a wicked gleam in her eyes when I reach into the nightstand drawer on my side of the bed and pull out a magic wand vibrator. "Heavy duty, huh?" Her knowing laughter is edged with anticipation. "What did I do to deserve this?"

If she only knew how right she is, that she did something to deserve this. "You'll find out," I decide to answer as I plug it in. "Maybe I just want to make you feel good."

"You're too good to me."

She won't feel that way much longer. At first, it's enough to start at the lowest level, letting the vibrator's head take the place of the hands that were just touring her legs. "Oh, that's nice," she whispers, a smile tugging at the corners of her mouth. "That feels good."

"Do you think that's good?" When I touch the head to one nipple, then the other, her back arches and a moan tumbles from her lips.

By the time I move further down, watching her contract before reaching her mound, she's writhing slowly, sensually. It's almost enough to make me forget why I'm doing this and take her here and now.

But no. I'm getting answers. Moving up to the next level, I begin running the silicone over the inside of her thighs, watching her juices flow freely, coating her lips, making them glisten. "Yes," she moans, angling her hips to give me better access to her pussy. "Yes, so good."

"You like that? What else would you like?"

"What do you think?"

"You have to tell me, or I won't know what to do."

"My pussy." Her already flushed face goes a shade darker. "Please. God, you're driving me crazy."

"Oh, that's what you want?" Her throaty groan makes me laugh before I ever so slightly touch the vibrating head to her mound.

"Fuck! Yes!" She's lost, completely consumed by her pleasure. "Yes, more!"

That's fine. I'll give her more. I'll give her more until there's no choice but to give me what I want. Upping the intensity, I run the vibrator along her seam, careful not to move too deep, content to play with her while she grinds her hips in slow circles, her hands running over the duvet, her head moving from side to side while she moans helplessly.

I'm content to let her keep going, to watch her pleasure build, to listen as her breathing gets faster, harder.

And when I touch her clit, her hips shoot up off the bed, a broken cry filling the air. "Yes! Yes! God, so close!"

Which is exactly when I pull back a little.

Her green eyes fly open, filled with confusion. "What are you doing?"

"You're not going to come," I tell her, "until you tell me what it is you've been keeping from me lately. And I know you have, so don't bother lying."

"What? Are you kidding? Colt!"

Her protests go silent when I press harder, leaving her drowning in sensation again. "You heard me. Do you want to come? You're going to tell me what I want to know."

"But... I can't!"

"You can't come? That's fine." I go back to teasing her lips, and I'm pretty sure she's on the verge of tears, but somehow, I can't feel sorry for her.

"You know what I mean! There's nothing to say!"

"I don't believe it. You're keeping something from me, and you're going to tell me what it is." Rubbing her clit again, I wait until she's moaning before asking, "Don't you want to come? Wouldn't it be nice? I bet it'll be a good one, too."

Her fists twist the duvet. "You're killing me!"

I'm sure it feels that way. "Nobody ever died from this. Maybe I'll just stop."

"No!" she howls. "Please, let me come!" I've never heard her like this, so full of desperation, like her life depends on me releasing her from this torture.

"Not until you tell me what I want to know. I can do this all day," I warn, holding the toy against her just enough for stimulation, but not enough to take her over the edge. She's a sopping mess, hips grinding, lifting them like that will do anything to help. It only makes me pull back on the pressure even more until she sobs in frustration.

"There's nothing... to tell you...!"

"And I know you're lying. I can always tell when you're hiding something. Why can't you..." Trust me. Believe in me. She can lie back and spread her legs at my command, but she won't let me any deeper than that. She won't let me help her.

"This isn't fair!"

I don't say a word, only moving the vibrator through her wetness, noting the sloppy noises that result. She is that close, and it has to be torture. "It's up to you. I'm actually getting off on this—I don't want it to end."

"Oh, my god!" Her back arches, her face twisting in agony before she finally shouts, "Messages! Threats, it's stupid! That's all!"

My rigid cock suddenly starts to soften. "Somebody's sending threats?"

"Probably Deborah," she whimpers, still fighting to reach the finish line, rolling her hips, trying to get the help she desperately needs. "That's all."

Then she sobs again, louder than ever. "Will you let me come? Please!"

Someone has been fucking with her. "How long?"

"Colt!"

"Tell me."

"Months. I just wanted to ignore it."

That's the thing about Deborah. She won't give up. "You don't keep these things a secret from me from now on. Understood?"

"Yes! God, yes!" I get the feeling she would agree to anything now. She would sell me her soul if I would let her come.

I take pity on her, finally pressing the buzzing wand against her clit until her anguished screams turn to ecstatic shrieks. Then she goes stiff, holding her breath before falling back against the bed with a shuddering cry.

It goes on, her bliss, but I can barely pay attention now. For months, somebody who is probably Deborah has been fucking with her, and she didn't think she needed to tell me? What else is she not telling me? Any thoughts of fucking her now are long gone—I'm not in the mood. I don't know if she even has it in her after the roller coaster I just put her through. She's splayed out on the bed, whimpering weakly.

Tossing the vibrator onto the bed, I sit next to her, my elbows on my knees. "Why didn't you tell me?" I ask, staring at the wall.

It takes a minute for her to answer. She probably needs to catch her breath. "You've already got so much on your mind."

"That's not an answer. You're my girlfriend. I love you. And if somebody is hurting you in any way, I need to know about it. Understood?"

She sits up slowly, sighing. "I understand. I'm sorry I didn't tell you."

And I'm sorry, too, even if I can't bring myself to say it out loud. I'm sorry we started off the way we did. I'm sorry there was ever a reason for her to not trust me in the first place.

I wonder if there's ever going to be a time when I'm able to make up for all of that. If I can ever help her forget the pain I put her through.

Otherwise, I can have her body. She can sleep beside me every night, eat her meals with me, share her thoughts with me. But I'll never really have her. There's always going to be this invisible barrier between us.

I don't know how long I can live with that.

5. LENI

"Hey, are you okay?"

Piper's whispered question pulls me back to the present moment, where she is staring at me while a couple picks a fight with each other on the screen in front of us. The rest of the audience laughs along with the jokes—it's one of those snarky, cleverly written romantic comedies that I would probably enjoy much more if I could concentrate on it. The girl picks up a balled-up pair of socks from under the bed and hurls them at the guy's head after spending most of the movie asking him to pick up after himself. Everybody bursts out laughing.

"I'm fine," I tell her, forcing a smile before reaching for the popcorn. She doesn't buy it, obviously, and I can see her shaking her head from the corner of my eye. Yeah, it would be really nice if I felt like I could tell her what's going on, that I keep getting these messages from whoever is trying to get into my head—and how they keep getting worse.

But what could she do about it? It would just be letting whoever is behind this win, and I'm not going to let them win. They don't deserve it. They're not going to ruin my life.

What I really need to do is enjoy a night out with my friend. This is supposed to be my chance to leave all the stress and drama behind for a little while. As happy as I am to be with Colt, as much as I love him, the air in the apartment can sometimes get so thick it's hard to breathe. Sometimes he gets in these moods where I'm afraid to move too much, like it might set him off.

I know it's not about me, and that he wouldn't take his anger out on me. He just can't accept the truth, is all. He's hurting, even if he would never say those words out loud. He misses Nix. He is sure Nix is alive, and the rest of us are crazy for thinking otherwise. He's carrying a lot of anger and other feelings inside him that he doesn't know how to express. I doubt James was exactly the kind of father who encouraged sharing and talking.

He was too busy being a sick bastard.

As usual, my stomach churns when I think of him, meaning I should stop thinking about him. He's already taken up enough space in my life and doesn't deserve another inch.

Besides, there's already so much going on in my head. Who am I to worry about Colt and what he's going through when I'm sitting here with the feeling that I'm being watched?

I have to be imagining it. I mean, I'm sitting here in a theater full of people—of course, there's bound to be somebody looking at me at some point, right? There are rows and rows of seats behind me. I need to get out more if just going out to a movie with my best friend has me this freaked out.

Grabbing a handful of popcorn, I decide to focus on the movie and ignore the way my skin keeps crawling. I have everything in life, don't I? I have a boyfriend who loves me. I live in a beautiful apartment. I go to school, and even if I don't have a ton of friends, I have Piper. If there's one thing I've learned, it's quality over quantity every time. I could have a hundred shitty friends who make my life miserable and keep me guessing whether or not they actually like me, or I could have one good friend who I know wants the best for me. I have it better than a lot of people do when I look at my life that way.

So why the hell am I sitting here wishing I could run out of the theater because I can't shake the feeling of being studied? Not just watched, but actually studied, like I'm a science project. Who am I to wonder whether Colt needs to talk to somebody about his inability to face the truth when I'm making up an entire story in my head?

A story that makes me look over my shoulder as casually as I can, scanning the seats behind me. What do I expect to find? The Grim Reaper? Somebody holding a scythe? Somebody dragging their thumb across their throat before pointing at me? Maybe a big old sign: "I am going to kill Leni Peterson."

At least my snickering is covered by the laughter of the audience, who are actually paying attention to the movie.

I'm almost kind of sad when the credits start to roll and the lights come up. Once again, I let my inner thoughts get in the way of the present moment. "That was fun. Sometimes you just need something that doesn't make you think, you know?"

"Yeah, you just need to turn off your brain for a little while. Really, I should've stayed home and studied for physics." She groans while gathering up the leftovers of our snacks. "But I literally could not take another second of it. The words were starting to switch places on the page."

"Just don't blame me if you don't get a good grade on the exam." I'm teasing, laughing, while at the same time looking around to see if I can figure out who might have been watching me from one of the back rows now that the lights are up. There are so many people—I didn't think the theater would be this crowded so late on a weeknight. I guess I'm not the only person who wanted to escape reality for a little while.

"You know me," she jokes, waving a hand. "I'll take a nap when I get back to my room and cram a little more until the second before class starts, and I'll end up getting an A."

"I would call that humble bragging, but you're not even being humble about it." We're both laughing as we walk out of the theater with only a few people behind us at this point.

The hallway and lobby are completely choked with people. I guess all the movies got out around the same time, all of the theaters emptying out at once. "Glad I don't have to pee," I mutter, eyeing the number of women heading for the bathrooms.

Piper only groans. "I knew that large Diet Coke would be a bad idea." She shifts her weight from one foot to the other, grimacing.

"Go ahead, I'll wait," I offer, even though I'm pretty sure I'll end up waiting forever at this rate. There's a bench near the hallway leading to the restrooms, so I plop down and pull out my phone to text Colt and let him know I'm going to be home soon.

"I thought something smelled like shit around here. Now I know why."

I look up before I can think twice, more curious than anything else. But I know before I've even made eye contact with the person that nasty voice belongs to who I'm going to find. There's only one person I've ever met who manages to sound so disgusted.

Deborah changed her hair color recently. Now it's a vibrant, almost platinum blonde that shimmers when she shakes her head disapprovingly. "I'm surprised Colt lets you out without a leash."

"Maybe he hopes she won't be able to find her way home." That charming little quip comes from the guy she's standing next to, who I realize after a few confused seconds is Bradley's brother, Dennis. He looks me up and down, just as hateful and smug as the girl he drapes an arm around. "He might as well leave her in town with a sign that says *free to a good home*."

Of course, Deborah laughs like it's the funniest thing she's ever heard. That's how she is. It doesn't matter who she's with. She'll treat them like they're the funniest, most interesting person who ever lived, so long as they pretend to like her. I would feel sorry for her if she wasn't such a disgusting person.

Of all times for Piper to need a bathroom break. I have to sit here while they laugh at me, while the people still leaving the different theaters glance our way in curiosity as they walk past. A few of them look sorry for me, which only makes it worse.

Finally, I can't take it anymore. There's only so long I can pretend not to be bothered. "Don't you have anything better to do?" I ask, and I'm not faking how tired I sound. I'm exhausted by all of this. Why can't she move on?

"Just now? No, I don't. Because I don't like it when people leave trash lying around," she retorts, hands on her hips. "And you are most definitely trash."

"Sorry you feel that way." Because if there's one thing I know she hates, it's when I don't react. That's how bullies function. Taking away the reaction they're looking for is like taking away their oxygen. With a sigh, I turn back to my phone, trembling a little but pretending not to care.

"Everybody knows what you did."

Those are the exact words my online bullies used the last time they sent a message. It takes every ounce of self-control to not react when, really, I want to scream. I want to jump off this bench and pull every strand of fake platinum hair out of her scalp. I might shove it down her throat while I'm at it.

"And exactly what did I do? Since you seem to know so much about me," I reply without looking up. It's actually a shame Piper isn't here to see this. She would be proud of how casual I'm acting.

"Don't be cute," Deborah warns. "It doesn't work for you. And you know exactly what I'm talking about, you little cunt. Where is Bradley?"

Is that what this is all about? Curiosity and surprise make me lift my gaze away from the phone and look at her for the first time. "How would I know where Bradley is? Seriously, why would I know that?"

"For starters, my brother was supposed to be hanging out with Nix the day of that so-called accident at your house." Dennis drops his arm from around Deborah's waist so he can fold both of them over his chest. I wish I could say I wasn't intimidated.

"I heard he went away for the weekend and didn't come back," I reply with a shrug. What the hell is taking her so long in there? Knowing Piper, she's making friends with at least three other women, talking about the movie while they wait in line, complimenting somebody's lip gloss while they're washing their hands.

"Yeah, that's what everybody seems to think, and isn't that convenient for you?" Dennis lifts his lip in a sneer that, no matter how I fight against it, makes my blood run cold. "Just like it's convenient that the explosion was ruled an accident."

"What the hell do you think you're getting at?" I have to ask. "What, you think I'm some psycho mastermind who started an explosion in my own house while my mom and stepdad were in there? Or do you think I'm a stupid piece of trash?" I continue, glaring at Deborah. "Maybe you should make up your minds."

"Maybe you should watch who you're mouthing off to," Dennis warns. His dark eyes are blank, empty as they stare holes into me. "There are all kinds of ways to get a person to admit the truth. Do you really want me to demonstrate them for you?"

It's enough to make my blood run cold. Now I really wish I had gotten in line to go to the bathroom because my bladder suddenly feels too heavy. "Right here?" I ask, faking innocence. "With an audience?"

"Wherever and whenever the hell I want," he replies, and his tone is chilling. Lowering his brow, he sneers, "You just wait and see. You'll never know when it's coming, but it is coming. So enjoy your life while you can."

There's no pretending that's anything less than a threat. Standing slowly on trembling legs, I force myself to look him in the eye. Really, what I want to do is run away and hide, but then that's what he wants, too. "You know, you really shouldn't make threats like that, especially in public. People might get the wrong idea and think you're serious, which I know you can't be."

"Is that what you think? Well, maybe it's what you need to believe," he replies. "And that's fine. Doubt me all you want. I'm going to find out what the hell happened to my brother, what you and Colt did to him—I'm going to make you pay. Wait and see."

"And there I was, thinking the only drama I'd see tonight was on the movie screen." Piper couldn't have picked a better time to show up, draping an arm around my shoulders before snorting. "You sound like a cheesy villain from an '80s movie. Maybe you should start wearing polo shirts so you can pop the collar and really complete the look."

"Fuck off," Deborah sneers.

"What, your man can't speak for himself?" Without waiting for a reply, Piper steers us away from them. "I would tell you to have a good night, but I really hope you don't," she calls out over her shoulder as we walk away while the two of them mutter under their breath.

"They're insane," I whisper as we cross the lobby, now much quieter than before since most people have left.

"I'm sorry you had to deal with that. But they're just assholes, acting like assholes," she decides with her usual confidence. "Trust me, Deborah is so full of shit, I'm surprised her eyes aren't brown."

I can't help the laugh that bursts out of me. It feels good, releasing the pent-up energy like this. "I just don't know why he thinks Bradley has anything to do with me."

"Oh, you know how it is. I guess he doesn't know who to blame or even if there's anybody to blame," she reasons as we cross the lot that has now emptied, for the most part, heading for her car. It's a little chilly, making me wrap my arms around myself before I shiver. "So, what do you do? You lash out. And if you're already an asshole like the two of them, you act like a real dick about it."

She's right, though it doesn't help. They're not just going to magically give this up, and I wouldn't be surprised if I start getting even more messages than I did before. The threats, the warnings, they'll all probably ramp up after what just went down.

And I can't tell Colt about it. I can't. All it would do is give him an excuse to vent what I know is building in him—his frustration when nobody but he believes Nix is still alive. He would take it out on the two of them, and it would get extremely ugly.

Not that I care about them. They could smash up their car on the way from the theater, and I wouldn't shed a tear. I'm more worried about him. I wouldn't want him to get in trouble. No, I can't tell him about what happened tonight or any of it. Because I love him, and I know it would only hurt him in the end.

"Do you feel all right?" Piper sounds concerned as she starts the car, frowning at me.

"I feel fine," I lie, because the truth is, even though I have so many good things in my life, I don't think I've ever felt so alone.

6. NIX

THOSE FUCKING ASSHOLES.

And I thought it was hard staying away from Leni—watching her from afar, being part of her life without showing myself? I thought it took all I had to keep myself hidden from her? I didn't have the first fucking clue.

Because now here I am, standing in the vestibule behind glass doors, watching her walk away with Piper while wondering if anyone would connect her to Deborah's and Dennis's sudden disappearance tonight.

I can hardly believe the thoughts running through my head, but they exist in bright, vivid color. They make my heart beat faster, like I'm anticipating something exciting, something I've been looking forward to. The way other people might look forward to a holiday or a birthday or an anniversary. I'm standing here imagining ending two lives in the most brutal way possible, and I'm excited about it.

But these aren't ordinary people. These are people who go out of their way to make others miserable. People like Leni, who's never hurt them. It was one thing for me and Colt. We had our reasons. Deborah has no fucking reason.

And Dennis? I might feel sorry for him if he wasn't acting like such a complete bastard. If my brother disappeared without a trace, I wouldn't rest until I found answers. There wouldn't be a place in the world I wouldn't look for him. But I wouldn't harass an innocent person in that search, and that's what Leni is: innocent. What the hell can he possibly think she has to do with this? Why would anybody blame her for anything?

Right now, I'm not interested in answers. It's time for a little payback. And since too many people saw them with Leni, that takes a lot of options off the table. But I can't let those fuckers get away untouched.

I don't know where they went. Maybe to the bathroom. Maybe they're celebrating being complete and total assholes. Part of me wonders what would happen if I showed my face. Would they think they were looking at a ghost? No, too risky, even if there's a part of me that craves the shock I know would pass over their faces. Instead, I head outside, where the parking lot is almost empty, and a chilly breeze makes me shiver. I recognize Deborah's car—not that there are many to choose from—and pull out the switchblade I've started carrying as a habit, since my neighborhood isn't exactly safe. When I'm sure nobody's watching, I shove the blade into one of her tires.

The satisfaction is unreal, the act of slicing into something like this. I can't help but do it to a second tire before moving on to the other two, chuckling to myself when I think of how surprised she'll be when she comes out to find that little gift. One day, she's going to regret the things she says.

I genuinely hope I'm the one who makes her regret it.

There's something satisfying about sliding behind the wheel of my car. Of course, it's nothing like what I'm used to—late model, no frills—but it runs. If I want to make sure Leni is safe from Deborah and people like her, I can't keep going around on foot. Nothing matters more than that. According to the last email Colt sent me, it doesn't seem like he knows the first thing about what's going on in her head. But I do now, and the thought sends another rush of satisfaction washing over me. I know something he doesn't. I can help her, try to make up for all the harm we caused.

Taking a shortcut, I'm in time to see Leni get out of Piper's car and hurry into the apartment building where she lives with Colt. My hands tighten around the wheel as I imagine what goes on in there. The life they live together. A life I can't be part of.

For a second, it almost seems like a good idea to get out of the car and go up there. I mean, Colt doesn't believe I'm dead anyway. It wouldn't come as a huge surprise to him.

But it would to Leni. How can I explain it? *Sorry, I figured it was better to stay away so I wouldn't hurt you anymore?*

Because all I want, all I crave, is the pleasure of your humiliation?

This isn't the same as the shit Deborah pulls. We are not the same person; our needs do not come from the same place. I would never do anything to embarrass or hurt Leni in front of other people, and if my thoughts tonight are any indication, I would happily kill anyone who would try to make her feel small or less than. I would happily be her protector until the day I actually die.

But humiliating and using her one-on-one? In private? That is an entirely different story.

I need to get out of here now. The temptation is too much to resist, and I have already resisted it for months. I don't know how much longer my self-control can hold up. Being this close to her is only making it harder for me to stay away. It's for the best that I stay away. I'm doing her a favor.

Maybe I'm just like Dad, after all. I must be. Why else would I drive around imagining all the filthy, vile things I would do to Leni if I had the chance now? I know it's wrong. I know it would really hurt her in the end. But I can't stop thinking about it. I can't.

I know I should, but my mind keeps coming back to the memories. Being inside her—so tight, sometimes to the point of resistance, but I always worked my way inside, didn't I? Eventually, she always succumbed. Even if her mind didn't want me, her body did.

Those memories are all I have to go on now, being in solitude the way I am. They're not the pleasant sort of memories a normal person would look back on. Memories of good times, laughter, happiness. Warm memories of being together. No, I'd rather replay every one of her pained grunts, every one of her groans as she sucked my cock with tears running down her face and saliva dripping off her chin.

I must be exactly like him. Unfixable, broken for good. Maybe it's in my genes, something I can't change. Maybe I'll have to fight against this forever... unless I give in. I could find someone. A prostitute, maybe, some whore who'd be willing to let me do whatever I want so long as I could rid myself of these terrible cravings. It would be easy, and I have the money.

But it wouldn't be Leni, so it wouldn't be the same. I'd probably only end up more frustrated than I was in the first place. No, this is my hell. This is my punishment for what I've done to her. Spending the rest of my life wishing I could do it again, caring too much about her to let myself do it.

It's almost enough to make me want to hit the gas pedal hard. To tear down the street and turn the wheel once the right wall or tree came into view. It's either that or accept the fact that this is my fate. Living in limbo for the rest of my life. Wanting, but not being able to touch. Yearning for something that I know is wrong and should never be.

"Fuck you," I whisper, and I'm not sure who I'm talking to. Myself? My fucked-up father who made me this way?

A glance to my right reminds me there's something else I planned on doing tonight, when it would be late enough that I could get away with it. A bouquet of lilies on the passenger seat. They were always Mom's favorite.

Thinking of her goes a long way toward calming the worst of what's raging in my soul. How can I sit here and think along these lines when she has suffered so much? What would she think of me if she knew the fantasies that run through my head almost constantly?

Colt said in his email he told her I was only away, so she won't be too shocked if she wakes up and finds me in her room. I'll do everything I can to make sure she doesn't, though, because then there would be the matter of what happened to my face. I couldn't explain that without having to explain a lot of other things I'm not sure she could handle—not to mention the time it would take. I need to see her for myself. That's all. After so much time, all the years thinking she was gone forever, I want to see her again. To be in her presence. Maybe the broken, evil part of me will heal somehow.

And maybe I'm a child who still believes in fairytales. Maybe I don't even deserve the comfort of her presence.

The hospital won't be fully staffed at this time of night, meaning it should be easier for me to slip in unnoticed. That's how I managed to escape my hospital in the first place, sneaking out at night when the floor was only half-staffed, if that. I don't understand why hospitals are like that. Do they think people won't have emergencies at night?

Whatever. Right now, it fits my needs. I park a few spots down from any other vehicles and get out with the lilies in hand, my hood raised, my chin tucked close to my chest. In a pair of jeans and nondescript shoes, I could be anyone. There's no way of identifying me on any camera that might pick me up.

One thing I learned when I was a John Doe: act like you know where you're going, and nobody will pay attention to you. That doesn't mean I'm not careful—using the side entrance to the cafeteria to get inside the building rather than going through the front doors, where the security person on duty would definitely ask why I'm here.

It's dead down here, the cafeteria closed, which is another thing that sort of baffles me. What, people don't get hungry or thirsty during the night? What about the doctors and nurses? Don't they deserve to eat?

Whatever. It works for me now as I walk quickly down the hall, my shoes soundless against the linoleum. The elevators further down the hall lead straight up to the various floors, giving me the opportunity to bypass the front desk. I'm glad Colt remembered to tell me where she is. He's known all along I would have to see her. It doesn't matter how much time we spend apart. He knows me too well.

The ICU floor is quiet, with a single nurse currently on duty at the desk and another couple of people in scrubs going from one room to the next. All it takes is waiting for the phone to ring and the girl to turn her back. I dart down the hall, Mom's room number running through my head, not coming to a stop until I'm inside and behind the curtain that gives her at least a little privacy from the people walking by.

There she is. Sleeping, the TV on with the volume turned down low. Some random 24-hour news station is playing—without thinking about it, I find the remote on the table next to her bed and change it to something she'd like better. There's an old movie playing, one of those black-and-white romances she used to watch sometimes. I leave the flowers beside the remote, knowing somebody will probably take them away but hoping she'll see them before they do.

She looks good. Better than I imagined. What did I expect? Tubes coming out of her, a respirator, that sort of thing. But no, she's breathing on her own. There are thin streaks of gray in her hair—she would've hated that, would've colored it the second her roots started showing. I want more than anything to reach out and stroke her hair, but I know better than to wake her up.

As it is, every second ticking by on the clock is one second closer to being discovered.

But she does look good, clean and cared for. Not that I had any doubts about that. Colt would kick the shit out of anybody who dared not treat her like a queen. At least he was here to do that for her if I couldn't be.

"Welcome back," I whisper to her, listening to her slow, soft breathing. Dad couldn't kill her. She's too strong for that. She knew she had something to stick around for: her sons, one of whom is standing at her bedside and doesn't look much like himself anymore.

I wonder what she would think of me if she knew what I've done. Who am I kidding? I don't have to wonder. I know what she would think, and while there aren't many things in this world that can shame me, that's one of them. She would be disappointed. She would probably wonder if she did something wrong. She didn't—I would need her to understand she didn't. She always did her best for us.

And look what we did for her.

"I'll try to do better," I whisper, listening hard for any sounds from the hallway. Things seem quiet out there, but that can change anytime. I swear, these people wait until a patient is deep asleep before going in to take vitals. "I will. All you have to do is rest and get stronger. I'll be back to see you, I promise."

It's surreal, doing something I never thought I'd be able to do again. Speaking to my mom, looking down at her, listening to her breathing. I don't know what to do with this feeling besides hating the man who put her in this condition—but no! He doesn't deserve to be part of this moment. If there is a hell, he's in it, and I hope he's suffering.

If I'm not careful, I'll end up there with him.

It doesn't take much to sneak back out before anybody notices I'm here. If I felt safe responding to Colt's emails, I would warn him about the shitty security around here.

But then again, no, because that shitty security means I can see her. This can't be the last visit. We have so much time to make up for.

7. COLT

It's not like me to be impulsive—at least, not in a positive way. I've done plenty of things off the top of my head, last second, not giving them much thought. But nothing like this.

Watching from the front window, I confirm for myself the delivery has been made according to our agreement. Once I'm satisfied, I make sure to send a tip to the guy who drove the car over and parked it in front of the building like I requested. Leni is in the kitchen, humming to herself while she wipes down the counters after dinner.

There are times, like right now, when I want to pinch myself and ask whether this is really us, living this domestic fantasy. Then again, I don't want to wake up if it is a dream. No pinching.

"Hey, there's something downstairs." Sliding my phone into my pocket, I shrug when she looks at me in confusion. "I don't know. Something down on the street. Maybe we should go take a look."

"What are you talking about?" she asks, laughing in disbelief but following me anyway once she's dried her hands.

"It's just something you need to see for yourself." I feel like a kid on Christmas morning, running down the stairs to the lobby, keeping an eye on the brand-new cherry-red Mustang I bought for Leni.

Will she like it? Who wouldn't? What I'm more worried about is whether she'll see it as the gesture I intended. This is my way of showing her how sorry I am for everything that went on in the past. She deserves something like this, something big and dramatic. The sort of gift anyone would dream of receiving. Because she's a gift to me. I wish I could find the words to tell her, but I can't. So this will have to do instead.

Once we reach the sidewalk, I let out a high-pitched whistle of appreciation. Really, it's a fucking gorgeous car—the kind that turns heads when it passes on the street. Sleek, shiny, fitted with every extra feature the guy at the dealership suggested. I'm sure he's still glad I walked in a couple of days ago and made the purchase. I can only imagine what his commission must have been.

"Wow. That is really beautiful." Of course, Leni hasn't put two and two together, admiring the car the way anyone else would. I do a lap around it, peering inside, making sure everything is where it should be. "But I'm not sure why we had to come downstairs to look at it."

"Hey, look at this." While she watches in wide-eyed surprise, I open the driver's door and take the keys from under the visor.

"What are you doing?" she gasps, looking around with her mouth hanging open. She is so innocent. "You can't just take somebody else's keys! Why would they even leave them there?"

Good question. "Because they left them for you."

"What is this?" She's laughing a little, breathless, standing still by the front bumper. I see the way she's taking in one part at a time, her eyes darting over the car's surface, but the rest of her doesn't move.

"What does it look like?" I ask with a grin.

"It looks like a really beautiful car." Finally, she reaches out and touches her fingertips to the hood before gliding them over the shining ornament mounted to the grille. She's afraid to touch it much more than that.

"It is a really beautiful car." Holding the keys high, I dangle them enticingly. "Your beautiful car. Surprise."

What did I expect? She's not the kind of girl who would jump up and down, squeal and clap her hands. She wouldn't throw her arms around me, bounce up and down and promise me a blowjob in exchange—not that I would turn it down. I'm not out of my mind.

That doesn't mean it wouldn't be nice to see a little excitement or hear a little gratitude. No, in fact, she looks disappointed. Like she's not sure how to react.

"What's the problem?" It's not easy keeping a smile plastered on my face when one uncertain moment goes by after another. "Wrong color?"

Her mouth moves, but nothing comes out at first. Finally, she shakes herself and tries to smile when she looks my way. "What is this for?"

Did I wake up in the fucking *Twilight Zone*? Who asks a question like that? "Usually, people use cars for getting around. You know, so they don't need their boyfriend or their best friend to drive their ass from point A to point B all the time. Not that I'm complaining," I add, because of course there are worry lines now deepening across her forehead. "I thought you could use a little freedom. The chance to go wherever you want, whenever you want."

"Oh," she murmurs before letting out a soft sigh. Her shoulders slump before she adds, "I see."

Yeah, she sees. And she's still... what is it? Disappointed? "Are you all right?"

"Oh, sure," she replies, still studying the car like she's never seen one before. "It's beautiful."

"You already said that. Are you okay? I know you're different from a lot of other girls, but usually when somebody has a Mustang handed to them, they say more about it than *it's beautiful*."

"I guess I'm just a little overwhelmed." She runs her hand through her hair, and I notice the way it trembles. "I mean, it's not every day something like this happens. Especially not to me."

"Get used to it." Rounding the car, I meet her at the front, draping my arms around her waist and pulling her close. Why is she so fucking stiff? What did I do wrong?

"This is the kind of thing I want you to get used to. Knowing you're taken care of, that you have everything you want or need. You can snap your fingers, and it's yours."

It's like I can't say the right thing tonight. Her eyes widen at my choice of words, her head pulling back instead of leaning in like I would expect if she wanted to kiss me. A kiss would be nice right now. Some sign that she's not heartbroken after her boyfriend just handed her a luxury car.

"Are you sure this isn't a little too much?" She looks back at the car, and her frown makes me grind my teeth. We're so close to each other, but in some ways, we are miles apart.

"I think I can decide for myself what is or isn't too much. I wouldn't have bought it for you if I couldn't afford it."

"Oh, I didn't mean it that way. Not exactly."

Don't do this. Don't let it win. I need to keep the anger contained. It's not her I'm mad at, anyway. It's myself, for not being able to do the right thing. It seems like I'm always making mistakes. Pushing too hard, wanting too much. "What do you mean, exactly?"

It's better if I'm not touching her right now. I let her go, taking a step back, putting a little space between us.

And it's obvious that offends her, too, when her brows draw together and her lips pull into a pout. "Don't get angry."

"Who said I'm angry? I just want to know what's going on here. I'm not asking you to drop to your knees or anything like that, but I would think you would at least thank me for buying you a car."

"But why did you do it, really?"

"I told you why. So you can get where you want to go, and you don't have to rely on me or anybody else. Don't you want to have a little freedom?"

"If it was just about me having freedom, you could've bought me a used Mazda or something," she points out, waving a hand like she pulled the name at random. "This is a really expensive car."

"A really expensive car I can afford. That's my problem, not yours."

"I just... It just makes me wonder..." Folding her arms, she bites her lip hard enough that it has to hurt.

"Keep going. What is it you wonder?"

This is all wrong. We were supposed to be happy. How fucking idiotic can I be, imagining she would want to take me for a ride, maybe show off a little? I feel like all I can do is throw darts at a board, and every shot misses the mark.

It's like she has to force every word from her mouth one at a time. "It makes me wonder... if you think you have to... like, buy my affection or my trust."

Why not come out and kick me in the stomach? All the breath rushes out of me the way it would have if she hit me. "Are you serious? Is that how little you think of me?"

Color floods her face until she's as red as her hair before she snaps, "Don't make it about that! Why are you putting words in my mouth?"

"It's really not that hard when you basically just accused me of trying to buy your love."

"That's not how I meant it."

"How the hell could you have meant it?" Folding my arms to mirror her posture, I sneer, "Really, tell me."

She tosses her head. "Not if you're going to be childish like this. You're not interested in listening to anything I have to say."

"I was only trying to do something nice for you."

But was I, really? Maybe I'm pissed off because she saw through me so easily. Because yeah, I do have another reason for going out of my way to buy her this car.

There is so much I have to make up for, so much we did to her, so many ways we hurt her and broke her down. This is the least I can do. This is nothing compared to what she suffered thanks to Nix and me—and Dad, always Dad, the one pulling the strings and calling the shots.

There's a large part of me that feels like I have to repay that debt, and I don't have the first clue how to do it.

What's worse is, she doesn't expect me to. How is that even possible?

"Well, if that's all it really is, thank you, but it's too much. I don't even think I feel comfortable with the idea of driving it, to be honest with you. You didn't have to spend all this money."

"Would you stop worrying about the fucking money?" I snap, and God help me, it feels good to watch her head snap back while fear darkens her eyes. I'm a weak, pathetic shit, taking strength from her fear, feeling gratified because of it. I'm basically a slug crawling on the ground, leaving slime wherever I go.

"You know what? I don't need to be here right now. This is not a conversation we need to have when we're both feeling tense."

Before I know it, she's on her way inside again, and I have no choice but to follow her, my feet pounding on the stairs. "Don't walk away from me."

"I'm not walking away from you," she calls back over her shoulder. "I'm walking away from a fight. That's what grown-ups do."

"Oh, don't start that shit with me."

"Well then, maybe don't be so immature just because I didn't fall all over the place thanking you for something I didn't ask for." She's already in the apartment with me right behind her, grabbing her keys and shoving them in the pocket of her hoodie. "Thank you for the gesture, seriously, but I can't spend our entire relationship trying to convince you I'm with you because I want to be. You don't have to buy my love. There's no score to settle."

I can't even tell her she's wrong, or that I wasn't coming from exactly the place she just described. Because that's exactly why I bought the car. A wild shot at making it up to her. Telling her how sorry I am for hurting her. How grateful I am that she would ever even look at me, much less say she loves me.

I mean, how can I possibly deserve it?

"I'm going for a walk. I need to clear my head." She barely looks at me as she's leaving, her gaze grazing the floor as she makes her way back to the door.

Should I stop her? Would it be selfish if I did?

Who am I kidding? I would only end up saying something stupid again and making things worse. It's easier and better for both of us if I let her go, so I do, standing aside while she walks out with her hands jammed in her pockets.

Once the door is closed, I pick up the closest thing—a throw pillow on the sofa—and hurl it at the wall. Right, like that's going to do anything to make me feel calmer, less... wrong. Less broken and fucked up and completely undeserving of love and understanding.

Standing in the middle of the living room, fists clenched at my sides, I spend a long time breathing heavily, my chest heaving, shoulders rising and falling. There's a ringing in my ears, and the world is red, and I really want to hurt something—or someone.

I want them to feel the way I feel now: helpless, useless, out of control.

But after a minute or two, that surge of rage starts to lessen, and I can breathe without feeling like my lungs are going to explode. Normal people don't solve problems by trashing an apartment or beating the shit out of someone. If I want to be different, I need to act differently, so my mind turns to the only other option I can find.

Dropping to the sofa, I pull out my phone and open my email app. My thumbs fly over the screen as I type out a message to the only person I feel comfortable sharing all of my thoughts with. Whether he reads them or not.

Brother,

How the fuck am I supposed to live anything close to a real, normal life after what Dad did to fuck us up? Do you ever feel that way? Do you ever ask yourself what it would be like if we had a normal father who wasn't such a twisted, sick bastard? He put all these things in our heads, and we accepted them because we didn't feel like we had a choice. But after a while, it all became a habit. Was it that way for you? I wish we could've talked like this before. Maybe I wouldn't feel so out of my mind now.

I can't do anything right for Leni. It's like I have good intentions, but I'm always wrong. I want her to trust me. I want her to know she's safe with me, but I can't find the words to tell her. And it doesn't matter how many times she tells me she understands, she forgives me, whatever. It never feels like enough. I can't imagine how she could be telling the truth. Who could find it in themselves to forgive after what we did?

I just want a life. A real life. A normal life. But I'm worried there's so much darkness in me, it's impossible. How do I care for her like a normal person does when I am anything but normal? Sometimes I wonder if I should let her go so she could have a real chance at happiness someday... Then I remember there's no way I could ever let her go. It's not possible. I can't win.

And that's it, summed up in three words: I can't win. Tossing the phone beside me after sending the message, I lean my head back and cover my face with my hands, groaning in frustration.

8. LENI

I JUST DON'T UNDERSTAND HIM. I DON'T THINK I EVER WILL.

What does he think he's doing, spending all that money on a car for me? Like I'm even the kind of girl who drives a car like that. Sure, it's beautiful, but so what? Does he think he can buy my affection that way? Because that's exactly what this is, whether he wants to admit it or not. He's trying to buy my love because he doesn't believe he deserves it. I'm not stupid, and he's not that hard to see through now that I know him better than I did before. He's not a mystery anymore.

Well, maybe in one way. I still don't understand how he can't accept Nix being dead, but otherwise, I can read him like a book.

Maybe I'm the one with the problem. My feet slap the sidewalk a little harder with every angry step. When I think about it that way, I can't help but feel a little disappointed in myself for my reaction. Maybe I should just learn to accept a gesture and be grateful. He wanted to make me happy, and I basically threw his gesture in his face. It must've hurt.

Is this what it means to be part of a relationship? How would I know? This is my first try. My entire life was about gymnastics before I got hurt; there was nothing else. I didn't have the same experiences as other girls do—boys and dating and all that. And it's not like I ever had an example of a happy, stable relationship to draw from.

The thought makes me chuckle darkly. The night is cool, almost crisp, which makes me hunch my shoulders further up than I already have. Where am I going? I have no idea. I went out because if I didn't, things were only going to get worse, and I didn't want to be the reason for that. I'm heartsick, I'm tired, and all I want to do is go home and throw my arms around Colt and apologize for not being gracious enough to accept his gift. That was his way of reaching out to me, and I basically threw it back in his face and told him it wasn't good enough.

Dammit, how long will it take before we get past this stage? I have to believe the time will come. Things will get easier once we're used to being together. Maybe, with enough time, Colt will actually believe I mean it when I say I love him and that he doesn't owe me anything. I am ready and willing to forgive what happened in the past. I would rather put it behind me and pretend it never happened, even if I know that's impossible. It's always going to be there, like a ghost hovering over my shoulder, reaching out to tap me at the most random times. It doesn't like to be ignored for long.

"Hey, baby! Who let you out all by yourself tonight?"

There's a difference between being catcalled and being taunted, and what's happening right now is the former. Most girls get used to it by the time they've hit puberty, if not earlier—men can really be pigs. It's not hard to ignore them as I walk on, barely catching sight of a trio of men hanging out next to a car like they're working on it.

"What, you can't say hi? You know you should smile more," another of the guys calls out, and I almost stop in my tracks and roll my eyes for all of them to see. Can't they come up with something a little more original?

They might not be a real threat, but they remind me of something I forgot when I was angry and looking for a way out of the situation: I'm all alone, and there is somebody in the world who has made it their mission to threaten me. Maybe being out here alone at night isn't the best idea. Our apartment is in a nice neighborhood, pretty safe, but all it takes is ten or fifteen minutes on foot in any direction, and things get a little sketchier.

Right now, I'm in a sort of business district. Only a lot of the shops are closed for the night—the grates pulled. It's a bleak atmosphere, almost a little sad. I'm sure during the day the street is thriving, bustling, but now it's dark and empty enough to send a chill down my spine. Still, it's not completely abandoned. A few people pass on the sidewalk, and I shift to one side to give them more room, keeping my distance.

Behind me, something breaks, shattering on the ground. The sound makes my head snap around—reflex, that's all—and when I'm not looking where I'm going, I bump into a wall.

No, not a wall. A chest. Just as firm and unforgiving as any wall, though.

"Oh, sorry," I mumble, ready to step aside and keep going.

But he stops me, matching my movement, a barrier of unyielding flesh.

When I get up the courage to look into his face, the ski mask that covers it makes me fall back a step while a gasp lodges in my throat.

Without saying another word, he grabs my arm—rough, unforgiving—and shoves me into a narrow alley between two buildings. It's completely dark, deep in shadow, the brick wall behind me icy cold. He shoves me against it hard enough to rattle my bones.

With one arm on either side of me, he's holding me in place while I pant for air. The only thing I can make out in the darkness is his hard, cruel eyes. They glimmer down at me, and I have to look away, my heart pounding in my chest, my head spinning. I'm going to faint if I don't breathe, but I can't breathe. Not when he's so close to me, close enough that I can barely take a sip of air.

"Please… Please, don't hurt me," I whisper, and the words sound ridiculous even through my panic. How pathetic and unoriginal.

And when he laughs, I know how pointless they were, too. Leaning in closer, his breath heating my skin and making me shudder in revulsion at the sensation.

"Just let me go," I say, as if that would help. I doubt it will. People don't walk around at night wearing ski masks because they're feeling friendly. He wants something from me. "I don't have any money."

His short, sharp breath sounds surprised before he releases a soft laugh.

A scream shoots into my throat and is about to come out before his hand clamps over my mouth, stifling the sound. I wish I could see more of his face, as much as I don't want to look into it. It would be easier if he looked more human, I think, but what do I know? My brain is looking for a way through this.

"Stop," I beg when his other hand slides down my side, but it only comes out as a muffled whine. Now I'm afraid I'm going to throw up. Or maybe my heart will give out and I'll die here and now in this dark, narrow alley where it's so cold and the smell of garbage and urine are almost strong enough to overcome the smell of his breath in my face. Sort of minty, like he just chewed gum. It's the one tiny mercy out of all of this.

He shakes his head, his fingers crawling down my hip,

around to my ass. Tears roll down my cheeks and onto his hand while he laughs softly at my fear and disgust.

Suddenly, his touch is hard, unforgiving, almost brutal as he grabs my throat in one hand. Trying to protect myself, my arms fly up, and I dig my fingers into his arm. I try to push him away with all my strength, but he is too strong. With his free hand he pulls something from his jeans.

My eyes go wide as I stare at the blade in his hand. He lets go of my throat and replaces it with the knife. I suck in a quick breath before holding it, scared to move.

His other hand finds my shoulder, and he starts to push me down.

No. Not this. I go stiff, locked in place by horror, but he's not going to take no for an answer. Soon his fingers are digging into my shoulder painfully, and he's shoving down hard until my knees buckle. Somehow, I'm able to keep myself from slamming against the ground, but only barely, and the cracked concrete is rough through my jeans.

He's breathing harder now, faster, one hand holding the knife against my throat while he unbuckles his belt with the other.

This isn't happening. It can't be happening.

Go away. Pretend you're not here. Oh, my god, I'm going through it all over again, disassociating from my body to escape the horror I'm being put through. How can I go through this again? I thought this was all behind me. I thought I would never have to hide from reality.

But here we are, with him unzipping his fly inches away from my tear-stained face. "No, no," I moan, my voice getting louder until a sharp tug of my hair cuts me off.

He's powerful, strong, and brutal.

And big. Very big. Once he reaches into his pants and pulls himself free, my already racing pulse takes off even faster while panicked revulsion uncoils in my core. He guides himself to my lips and drags the head across them. A sob tears its way out of me, the tears flowing faster, nausea making my head spin.

Clearly, I'm not playing along to his standards. He thrusts his way into my mouth all at once, groaning as he fills me.

Right now, I'm focused on not choking. He hits the back of my throat, and I gag, but somehow, manage to hold on until the urge passes. The salty taste of his precum coats my tongue once he moves back, leaving the ridge of his swollen head against my lips before plunging in again.

What choice do I have? All the old memories come back while I do as I'm told, sucking him the best I can through my sobs. My vision is blurred, but then what does it matter? It's so dark, I can barely see anything. Maybe the less I can see, the better. The less I'll remember.

But there won't be any forgetting his soft grunts, his pleasured groans. The way he swells in my mouth, the way he starts to move his hips. Fucking my face. Using me, humiliating me, my scalp stinging, knees aching, and my heart shattering a little more every time I reach the nest of short hair at his base.

It's like my gagging only excites him more, makes him move faster, holding my head firmly in place now so he can deliver brutal thrusts.

I can't breathe! I slap at his thighs with both hands, whimpering loudly, but it's no use. He doesn't listen.

The world is starting to fade out by the time he slams deep one more time. Breathing loudly, he fills my throat with his cum. I have no choice but to swallow as fast as I can, glad it's over and wishing I was dead. Why did I come out tonight? Why couldn't I have stayed home?

I could cry with relief when he lets go of my hair and slides free. I sink back on my heels, dizzy and panting. God, I feel so dirty, the sort of dirty you can't wash away. The kind that soils a person's soul. Why does the world have to be like this? How can anybody be so cruel? What did I ever do to deserve this?

I'm never going to get any answers.

Without a word, he pulls me to my feet and leaves me leaning against the wall. What I wouldn't give for something to rinse my mouth out with. I run the back of my hand over it, catching the tears on my cheeks at the same time. His hand circles my throat again, pinning me against the bricks.

This is it. This is when he kills me. It was all leading to this. *Colt, I'm sorry. I didn't know this would happen.*

"Do not ever, ever walk alone at night again." It's like the slither of a snake, that voice, the sound wrapping itself around me, tightening like a noose. I'm so out of my mind that it takes me a moment to realize how familiar that menacing voice sounds.

His glittering eyes meet mine, staring deep into them, almost staring into my soul. The world is still spinning, and I could die from shame, but right now, all I can focus on is his eyes.

And the feeling I've seen them before.

It's unbelievable, but I can't ignore what seems so obvious now. His voice, his touch, his eyes... "Nix?" I whisper in disbelief.

And just like that, he lets me go, pulling his hand away like my skin burns him, yet holding my gaze for another heartbeat before ducking out of the alley and disappearing.

It couldn't be. Nix is dead. He died in the explosion.

So why did this guy run away like that? All he had to do was say no, but he didn't. No, that can't be. I'm only telling myself what I need to believe, clinging to a tiny shred of hope that would make all of this a little less horrifying.

For now, the best thing to do is get the hell out of here and get back home on shaking, pained legs. After tonight, I might not ever leave.

9. NIX

Motherfucker.

What was that all about? Why the hell did I do it?

All these months, I've been telling myself to stay away for her sake. Forcing myself to stay away. It's for the best; she doesn't need me in her life. It's time for her to heal, to forget, to move on.

She doesn't need the threat of me hurting her, so what did I do? I hurt her worse than ever. I threatened and degraded her, assaulted and humiliated her. I forced her on her knees in that filthy, disgusting alley. She deserves so much better than that. How could I do it?

That's an easy one. Because I wanted to. Because it felt good, and I knew it would feel good, because there has never been a pleasure deeper and more complete than the pleasure I get from forcing her to submit to my will. To fulfill every dark, ugly fantasy that's ever entered my mind. The temptation was too much to resist. I've spent months fighting it, sweating my way through sleepless nights, gripping the pillow with both hands, jerking off so much I was afraid I would chafe.

And all the time, I was thinking of her. Dreaming of her. There was only so much resistance I could put up.

Even now, cursing myself as I stalk through the dark, quiet streets, I can't help but relish the memory of her whimpers. The way she tried to scream against my hand, the way I silenced her so easily. I can still smell her on me, a sort of sweetness and freshness I haven't smelled in months. I can feel the warmth of her soft skin against my palm where I covered her mouth.

Oh, god, her mouth.

Sick fuck. I can't do this. I was only supposed to be teaching her a lesson, making sure she doesn't take risks like the one she did tonight. What the hell did she think she was doing, walking alone? And around here, of all places? She's supposed to be smart.

Is she trying to hurt herself? Did we push her that far? There are a million questions running through my head as I take the route back to my apartment. I had to stop her when I did, knowing the further she walked, the worse her surroundings would get. If I hadn't stopped her, someone else would have.

And they wouldn't have stopped where I did. Hell, she would've considered a forced blowjob in a dirty alley a gift compared to what some of these other fuckers would've done to her.

Something tells me she wouldn't feel so grateful if I explained things that way.

Did she really think it was me? I'm sure she'll talk herself out of it. I've watched her at my grave, leaving flowers, talking to my headstone. Colt has said more than once in his emails that she doesn't believe him when he says I'm alive. Maybe she was so overwhelmed, she saw what she wanted to see. Maybe her overwhelmed brain wanted to believe she was with me and not some diseased stranger.

It really doesn't make a difference, does it? That will never happen again. I scared her badly enough and gave her a memory she'll never escape from. I don't have to worry about her now.

I have to worry about myself.

"Hey, buddy, you got a few bucks?"

With my hood pulled up and the ski mask still pulled over my face, I have to turn my head to find the source of the voice. A bum in a doorway, covered in newspapers meant to keep out the cool night air. He smells like a backed-up toilet, and his face is red from exposure and maybe illness. In the glow from a nearby streetlamp, I see the desperation in his eyes.

There might've been a time he was like me, living a normal life—or at least one that looked normal on the surface. If there's one thing these months on my own have taught me, it's how quickly and completely life can change. People have stories we can't see on the surface. I never had much sympathy for others in the past. I would've needed to actually think about them in order to feel sorry for them or empathize or whatever.

Reaching into my jeans, I pull out a couple of bills and thrust them his way. "Here. Good luck," I say without bothering to check how much I gave him. Whatever it is, he needs it more than I do.

What a shame an action like that can't erase the harm I just did. I could give away a fortune and it wouldn't make a dent. I couldn't help myself. Once I had her where I wanted her, trembling against my body, getting me hard with every short, terrified breath, there wasn't a chance I'd be able to keep from pushing her further.

The sight of a taco truck up ahead makes my stomach growl. It's as good a choice for dinner as any, and there's no line. Lifting the ski mask up to my forehead and keeping my hood in place, I approach, my head low as I mutter my order. The people on the other side of the window don't seem to care either way if they can see me. My money is green. Really, when you get right down to it, the world is very simple. Everything is an exchange. Everything has a price.

And tonight, Leni paid the price for being stupid and careless with her safety.

Not only her, either.

My fists clench in my pockets when I think of Colt. Colt, who's so damn worried about her, thinking she's hiding something from him, knowing there's something she's keeping from him. Colt, who would let her walk around out here by herself. He should know better than that, shouldn't he? Then why wouldn't he do everything in his power to keep her home, where she's safe? Does he just let her wander around on her own?

Maybe he doesn't deserve her, then.

A sharp whistle from further down the street catches my attention, and I lift my head just far enough to see where it comes from. A car is slowing down as it reaches the corner, where a couple of girls wait. Not just girls. It looks like they're trying to make a little money tonight. One of them leans into the open window and has a short conversation before getting in the car.

We all do what we have to do. I never would've seen this side of life if it wasn't for having to hide from everyone who's ever known me.

And where is Colt right now? Sitting in his apartment, probably, waiting for his girlfriend to come home. His girlfriend, who just sucked my dick in an alley. A smile of grim satisfaction stretches my mouth before I accept my order and keep walking, in a hurry now to get out of the grim, unforgiving night.

He doesn't know how good he has it. He never will. He's been able to go on living the life we both enjoyed, now he can enjoy the girl we've both enjoyed.

I shouldn't do this to myself. I can't. Things are bad enough as it is. I have enough to wrestle with without adding the pressure of feeling like a piece of shit for resenting my brother. There's nothing to resent him for.

Nothing but the way he would let Leni wander around by herself, unprotected, like she's not worth taking care of.

He needs to learn a lesson, too.

My mind is made up by the time I reach the apartment, where the same two guys are sitting on the steps—the way they are morning, noon, and night. I'm pretty sure they're selling drugs out here, but it's none of my business. I jerk my chin at them and go inside, taking the stairs at my usual pace, ignoring a screaming baby on the second floor on my way up to the third. As soon as I'm in the apartment, I pull out the burner phone I bought at a corner store and type out a text to Colt. He'll never be able to trace who it came from. It'll probably drive him nuts, wondering who's reaching out.

Or maybe it won't. Maybe he'll know it's me, just like he somehow knows I'm still alive.

Watch out. You're not taking care of her like you're supposed to.

After that, I sit down on the creaky sofa with my tacos, wishing it was as easy to swallow down my guilt as it is to swallow the food.

And knowing that, even though I finally gave in and satisfied my craving for her, it's only a matter of time before I'll want her again.

10. COLT

WHAT IS TAKING HER SO LONG? I can't stop pacing the apartment, clenching and unclenching my fists, unable to sit still. I'm going to explode. All this anger and frustration is boiling in me, upping the pressure in my head, the tightness in my chest. I'm going to blow, and it's not going to be pretty when I do.

Where the hell would she go for this long? It's been almost an hour, and she still isn't back. God forbid she answers her phone. Why would she want to let the man she's supposed to love know she's at least alive? No, that would be too much to ask, I guess.

"Goddamnit," I snarl, picking up my phone again, ready to make another call. Should I go out and try to find her? Right, then what happens if she comes home and wonders where I am?

I'm maybe a split second from calling her when a text

comes through. My heart jumps into my throat—it's her. It has to be. Finally getting back to me.

It isn't. It came from an unknown number.

Watch out. You're not taking care of her like you're supposed to.

What the fuck is that supposed to mean? It doesn't matter how many times I read it—it never makes more sense. Who would send me something like this?

Who is this? I type back, pounding my thumbs against the screen. I'm still waiting for a response when the front door opens.

I don't know what's stronger: my relief or the anger that's had nowhere to go and has only gotten stronger in the hour I've spent waiting. "Why the hell were you gone for so long?" I snap, making her flinch. Maybe not the best thing I could've said right away, but goddamnit, I'm tired of fucking around.

She closes the door with her head down, not even bothering to look at me before she hurries down the hall into the bathroom. Before she can close the door, though, I shove it open and stay in the doorway.

"I'm talking to you. Where have you been? Since when can't you answer your phone when I call?"

"I took a walk. That's all. This doesn't have to be a huge deal, you know?" As I watch, she almost frantically washes her hands. The water is hot enough that steam starts rising from the basin before she turns off the faucet, only to pull out her toothbrush and turn on the water again to wet it.

"You took a walk. That's all? You've been gone for an hour."

"It was a long walk." She brushes her teeth just as thoroughly as she washed her hands, the brush moving fast.

"Are you trying to knock your teeth out of your mouth?" I may as well not be here. She's in her own world, and something is between us. Something I can't see or touch, which only makes me more determined to get it out of my way.

She's rinsing her mouth when I come up behind her, smelling the fresh night air in her hair, feeling the warmth of her body. "You can't even look at me? Much less kiss me." That's usually the first thing she wants to do when she walks in the door, like she can't wait. "I try to do something for you, something I think you'll like, and you won't even look at me now."

"This isn't about that. I wasn't even thinking about it." She groans softly when I take hold of her hips, but it's not the kind of groan I was going for. More like she's… dismayed? "Please, just give me a minute, okay?"

Just give her a minute. One more thing I'm supposed to understand with no explanation. Maybe I would understand if she would bother telling me something every once in a while instead of acting like I don't deserve to know what's going on in her head. Because I'm not good enough, and I never will be.

"Maybe I don't want to give you a minute." My grip tightens, and my dick starts to get hard, pressing against her plump ass. "Maybe it's time for me to get what I want. What do you think about that?" My mouth touches her neck, and she goes stiff, trembling—but isn't that the way it always is? She'll loosen up. She'll remember why we're together, how much she wants this. She always does in the end.

"Just let me... please..." I can barely hear her whimpering over the rush of blood in my ears, the drumbeat of my heart.

It doesn't take much to pull her jeans down over her ass so my hands can cup her flesh, squeezing and molding it in my hands, getting harder every second. She's wearing a lacy pink thong that I tug gently, playing with her, staring down at her creamy skin.

"Tell me you don't want this." With a hand between us, I cover her mound, pressing against her slit through the lacy fabric, feeling where it's hot and already moist because this is the one thing we can always come back to. The two of us. When I yank down the thong hard enough for the seam to tear, she gasps and trembles, and that's good, too. Yes, it's time to get what I want.

"Let's see how wet you already are." Dragging a thumb through her slit, I find her a little drier than I expected, but it's nothing a little spit can't fix. It dribbles down her crack and into her pussy while I drop my jeans and let them settle at my ankles. I'm rigid, straining, and my spit plus the precum dribbling from my tip lets me slide easily through her folds.

Is there an animal in here? A strangled whimper that reminds me of a wounded puppy makes me stop and look around in surprise. No, the only wounded animal here is the girl I have pinned against the vanity, the girl whose reflection I look at in the mirror for the first time since I started this. Her eyes are squeezed tightly shut, teeth sunk deep into her lip. Tears roll down her flushed cheeks and tendons stand out on her neck like she's fighting to hold something terrible inside.

What am I doing? I love her. What am I doing to her? "Leni…" I whisper, letting go of my dick so I can take her by the shoulders and turn her around to face me. Now I can't imagine touching her with the same force. I'm gentle, cupping her jaw, tipping her head back until her face is angled so I can see it clearly.

She's in pain. Did I hurt her? Maybe not physically, but there are other ways to cause pain.

"I'm sorry," she whispers, hanging her head once I let go of her chin in favor of stroking her hair. "I'm just… I'm all mixed up inside. Don't think I don't want you. It's complicated."

"You know you can tell me about it." Right, and how much proof have I given her of that? I just tried to force my way into her when she was clearly not into it, and I went far enough to make her sob. She's supposed to believe she can open up to me?

"It's not that easy. I wish it was." When she closes her eyes, another pair of tears roll down her cheeks. I can't believe the sight of those two tears is enough to make me ache the way I do inside. All I want is honesty, for her to feel like she can trust me. What could be so serious and shameful she wouldn't want to tell me about it?

"You know..." I'm already half undressed, so I might as well finish the process. Kicking off my trainers, I continue, "Have you thought any more about what we talked about? Seeing a therapist?"

With her arms wrapped around herself, she shrugs. "Yeah, a little bit. Now and then." I'm surprised, since she basically shut me down and ended the conversation when I brought it up.

"And? How do you feel about it?" I take off my jeans and shorts, stripping off my socks. It's almost easier to have this conversation while I'm doing this, giving me something to focus on rather than the anguish she's trying and failing to hide.

"I don't know. Maybe that's what I need to do. It can't hurt, I guess. And there is all the stuff I need to get out."

"I agree. You won't get anywhere holding all of it inside."

"I just feel like it's getting in our way," she whispers. I'm glad she said it, because I agree with that, too. One of us had to finally announce it. "The whole idea is a little scary, though."

"There's nothing to be scared of. You'll only be talking to somebody who knows how to help you get through all the memories." And I just gave her a good one, didn't I? When am I going to learn?

There's sorrow in my heart as I pull my T-shirt over my head. "I'm gonna take a shower. Do you wanna join me?" Reaching out, I cup her cheek, stroking it with my thumb. Her face is still flushed, her skin damp. What she needs more than anything is tenderness and understanding. I need to be the one to give it to her.

Her head bobs so I turn away toward the glass door of the shower stall, reaching to turn on the water so it will run hot by the time we get in. She undresses slowly, wincing almost like she's in pain. Are her knees redder than they should be? Probably from when I pushed her up against the vanity—they must have been pressed against the cabinet doors underneath. Hardly the worst thing I've ever done to her, but that doesn't mean I feel good about it.

There's no need to talk anymore once we are in the shower together, with nothing between us but the water running down our bodies. Instead of getting soaped up right away, I hold out my arms, and she walks willingly into the circle of my embrace.

Something inside me goes still and peaceful once I have her close to me, her head on my shoulder, her heart beating against my chest. The water from the showerhead soaks into her hair, turning it a darker shade of red. I stroke it slowly while she loosens up a little bit at a time and eventually melts against me.

I'm only human. There's only so long I can stand with her like this before I start getting hard again. Soon I'm pressed against her hip, twitching and throbbing every time she makes the slightest movement. When she lifts her head, blinking away the shower spray to look into my eyes, I see the longing there. The need.

Instead of taking her hard and fast the way I wanted to earlier, I cover her mouth with mine, savoring her shivers as electricity flows between us. I claim her again with my tongue slowly stroking hers and my touch changes, becoming more demanding as hunger starts consuming my being.

But she goes with it, letting me back her against the wall, lifting a leg and draping it over my hip so I can enter her all at once. She arches against me as I fill her, her mouth falling open, moving with me. "Oh, yes," she whispers, closing her eyes, letting herself sink deep into the pleasure while I sink deep into her. So deep, joining us, connecting us.

"Fuck..." I groan, taking her hands and linking our fingers before holding them over her head. My forehead rests against hers, our breath mingling. She's so tight, gripping me like a vice, trying to milk me dry. "Fuck, you feel so good..."

"So... do you..." she moans, straining upward for a kiss I deliver gladly. My teeth graze her lip, and she shivers, moaning into my mouth when our tongues mingle. This is what I need, what we both need. To lose ourselves in each other. There's nothing but us now, no outside world, no questions. Only the power of being inside her, moving slowly, feeling every inch of her slick, hot walls against me. Wrapped around me, pulling me deeper, promising escape.

I don't know how long I can take it slow like this. She's starting to get tighter, her breath sharper, when she breaks the kiss to moan against my lips. "Yes, fuck me," she begs. I let go of her hands, and she wraps her arms around my neck, burying her face against my shoulder. That's all I need to hear to unleash hard, sharp thrusts that make her slide up and down the wet tile. Tighter, tighter, her high-pitched cries lost against my skin, pushing me to give her more. Everything I have.

My body is taking over, taking what it needs, and I give her all of me before she gasps and arches against me again, practically squeezing my dick off before her muscles start to flutter and her juices coat my balls. "Oh, god," she moans, and the sound plus the feeling is too much. I can't fight it anymore. The tingle at the base of my spine grows, and my balls lift before I explode. I give her all of me, every drop of my cum filling her cunt in one blissful spurt after another.

That blissful wave carries me through our shower and drying off together, leaving me floating in a haze. I'm calmer now, peaceful, able to treat her with the tenderness she deserves.

The feeling lingers by the time we lie in bed together, with her head on my bare chest and my arms around her, keeping her close. I always sleep the best when we're like this, when I have her next to me.

Not tonight, though. At least not right away. All I can do is stare at the ceiling and think back on that text and wonder who sent it. What the hell it meant.

What she's hiding from me.

11. LENI

"Is it okay if I go? Do you mind being home alone?"

Shit. I never did respond when Colt told me a couple of guys from his psychology class wanted to get together over pizza and beer to work on a project tonight. It was like my mind went blank as soon as he mentioned he would be out. It went straight to where it's been for the past few days: that alley, with that man I was sure was Nix.

I'm not so sure anymore, but that's only because I've had plenty of time to question myself and remember Nix is dead and gone. It's probably not that unusual for somebody to have a crazy thought like I did when they were fresh off being violated the way I was. I needed something to comfort me, some concept to make me feel better, and the idea it was Nix out there was the closest thing to comfort I could think of. The idea that he's still alive, that Colt isn't wrong or deluded. And maybe he could finally be happy—really happy—because he'd feel whole again, like there isn't a part of him missing anymore.

Or I could just be crazy. That's totally possible. Colt is right; I do need to see a therapist. Because between the messages that keep coming through my phone and the DMs I'm getting across social media from random anonymous accounts, I don't know if I can take much more.

You're going to die, bitch.

Count your days. The clock is ticking.

They're going to bury you next to your mother.

The worst part is, I can block the numbers and accounts all I want, but that doesn't stop them. They just create new accounts, new numbers to message me from. It's enough to make me want to disappear. To just fade out completely. There are times when it feels like that's the only solution.

And I guess that's why the second Colt mentions leaving me alone tonight, my thoughts go straight back to the alley and what happened there. It's not like I want to revisit and commemorate the experience or anything. I'm just wondering if I could find him there. Maybe I can draw him out. He did make a big deal about warning me against going out by myself, right? If he's following me, or if he lives down there and sees me, there's a chance he'll make contact again.

I need him to. Either he's Nix, or he isn't. I need to know for sure.

"Go ahead," I chirp as cheerfully as I can, looking up from the laptop where I've been trying like hell to focus on the paper I'm writing. My thoughts are so scattered, I have to fight for each sentence. That's another reason I need to go out tonight. I have to clear my head, get some answers. "I think I'll manage on my own."

He's not convinced, walking slowly toward me, running a hand over my hair. His touch is soothing, a promise of calm and safety. What I wouldn't give to close my eyes and let go of everything on my mind.

"You sure? Maybe you should call Piper, see if she wants to do something."

I love him for that. Smiling up into his blue eyes, I shake my head, then brush my lips against his palm once he's finished caressing my cheek. "I really do have to work on this. She would only distract me. You know how it is; she never has to work that hard for a good grade."

"Hey, if you can get her to write it for you," he suggests with a wink. It's not a bad idea, actually. Though I would never do anything like that. At least he's not studying me so closely as he grabs his keys and wallet. "I won't be too late, but if anything comes up, I'll let you know."

"Have fun," I offer as he opens the door.

"Not too much fun," he reminds me, grimacing. "I would like to get a decent grade on this. I can't believe I actually give a shit."

I could say the same thing. He never exactly cared about grades before—everything has always come so easily to him. I'm not delusional. I won't act like I'm the reason he's changed, but it does seem like a coincidence that my presence in his life came around the same time as him deciding it was time to care about things.

Am I seriously considering this? Staring at my screen, I don't see the words in front of me. All I see are those glittering blue eyes. Eyes that are so familiar. Just like Colt's.

Once enough time has passed that I doubt Colt will come back because he forgot something. I get up from the table and close the laptop, bracing myself for whatever is waiting for me. This time, I'll know to watch my back. It's not quite as late as it was last time, which I hope means there won't be as much of a chance of danger rearing up and biting me in the ass.

Am I crazy for doing this? Catching my reflection in the mirror next to the front door, I can't ignore the look of fear in my eyes. I can't deny I'm more than a little freaked out over the idea of walking into possible danger.

But that's not going to stop me. I'm never giving in to fear again.

It's chilly again tonight, and I zip my hoodie up to my throat before shoving my hands into the pockets and starting off. My heart is pounding like a bass drum, and every step I take makes me wonder whether I should turn around and go the other way. He's probably not even going to be around—Nix or whoever he is. I'm being stupid and taking risks I shouldn't take.

But I need to know. If it takes another ten walks through a sort of dangerous part of town, that's what I'll do if it means knowing for sure whether my attacker was Nix or some random stranger. My keys are threaded between my fingers in a claw, ready to slice or gouge anybody who pulls anything with me. I'm not going to leave myself as vulnerable this time. I tighten my grip, more determined than ever.

It's bad enough I have people sending me death threats. I don't need to also worry whether I'm losing my mind, imagining things that aren't true.

And maybe I need to know for Colt's sake too, since I know how much it means to him, thinking his brother is alive. If he is, I'm going to find out, for both of our sakes.

And then I still might use these keys on Nix, because damn him. For running off, for hiding, for doing what he did to me in the alley.

Crossing the street, my eyes sweep to the right and left. They've been doing a lot of that lately, because it isn't just on walks like the one I'm taking right now where I've been looking for Nix. I've been glancing over my shoulder for three days, sure I'll see him lurking somewhere, watching me. Maybe I want to find him. I don't know. I only know I can't live in this state of limbo much longer. I have to know.

And then somehow, I'll have to break the news to Colt—if any of this is true, of course.

This is the route I took, isn't it? It has to be. I just walked in a straight line the other night, not really paying attention to where I was going, with no destination in mind. All that mattered was getting away.

Little did I know the real danger was ahead of me.

There's less and less traffic the further away from home I go until I start to recognize the businesses I saw before. I wonder how they expect to make any money when they're closed after people get out of work for the day. Slowing my pace, I pay closer attention than ever to my surroundings, jumping a little when a sharp laugh bursts out of one of the upper-floor windows. There must be apartments up there. I need to chill out—I am way too jumpy. It's just that the closer I get to the alley where it all happened, the fresher the memories are.

Soon I pass a car where two vaguely familiar men lean against the front. "Hey, baby! What, you decided to come back and make friends?"

Oh, great. These guys. I wish I had pulled up my hood—maybe then they wouldn't recognize me if they didn't see my hair—but it's too late for that now. All I can do is pretend not to hear them and keep walking with my head down. Is he out here somewhere? He's taking his sweet damn time if he is.

"You're a rude little bitch, you know that?" Oh, no. The voice is closer this time. They're following me.

"For real. Whatever happened to girls being able to take a fucking compliment?" They laugh nastily as they fall in step behind me, muttering to each other about my body, whistling.

Aren't there cops in this town? Why the hell can't one drive by right now? Or just a good Samaritan, for God's sake? But no, it's just me and these two guys. Two guys who decide to take me by my arms and turn me in place.

"What the fuck are you doing? Get off me!" I can't use my keys on them with them holding my arms like this. I do everything I can—kicking my feet, making myself as heavy as I can, going dead weight in hopes they'll stop— but they don't. All they do is laugh, pulling me toward their car.

"We're just gonna have some fun," the shorter of the two tells me, snickering. "Relax, you'll enjoy yourself."

"Let's see if that red hair is natural," the other guy suggests, and sheer animal panic floods my system, making me fight harder than ever.

"Help me!" I scream, pulling and struggling, getting closer to the car with every step.

"Get the fuck off her!"

I know that voice. The sound of it is an arrow piercing my terror. Looking up, I find him standing in front of us, his hood pulled up over his ski mask to hide his face.

But he's not hiding the switchblade in his hand, the streetlights making the metal gleam. "Get off of her," he commands menacingly. "Or I will make you eat the ground before I slice both your dicks off. Got it?"

Cowards. Just like that, they let me go and hurry off, looking over their shoulders as they scurry to the car like a couple of scared rabbits. I would laugh if I wasn't so busy trying to stay upright, swaying on my feet, panting for every breath.

"Are you okay?" That voice again. He's not whispering this time. Maybe he forgot to—or maybe I called him by his real name, and he knows he doesn't have to hide anymore.

At first, I can only nod until I catch my breath. "I'm all right. Thank you."

It's like thanking him flips a switch. Taking a step toward me, he asks, "What did I tell you?"

"I know what you told me." I will not cower. I will not apologize. "But I needed to see you again. I needed to be sure it was you. I want to see your face." I reach for his ski mask, but he takes a step away from me before I can reach him.

"Is that what this is about?" Putting away the switchblade, he shakes his head, his face still hidden. "I'm disappointed."

"Disappointed? Why would you care that I'm out here?" I counter. Every word makes me feel a little stronger because I know I'm right—it's the only thing that makes sense. "Show me your face. Or else I'm never going to stop looking, and you're just going to have to follow me around and threaten people with a switchblade every day."

"Don't be a fucking child." To my surprise, he brushes past me and starts walking fast, like he can get away.

"Coward!" I have to almost jog to keep up with him, my eyes glued to his broad back. "You're going to run away again? Are you only brave when you're carrying the switchblade?"

"Enough." He's as quick as a cat, whirling around and grabbing hold of me, pushing me against the closest wall. Leaning in, his breath hot in my face, he asks, "Do you wanna play games? You think you're brave enough? You're so tough?"

"Who's talking about being brave when you won't even take off that mask?" I whisper. Am I ready to die from fear? Maybe. But I'm getting through to him. I feel it.

"Is that what you want? Is that really what you want, little girl?" He looms over me, blocking out everything around us, but I'm not afraid. I know who he is. I might've been afraid of him in the past, but not anymore. We're past that now.

"Do you want to see? Fine. Don't say I didn't warn you."

Holding my breath, I watch him lower the hood and rip off the ski mask. I'm somehow able to keep from gasping at what I see.

One side of his face is exactly the way I remember it.

The other?

"Oh," I whisper with a sinking heart, staring in horror at the scar tissue covering the other half of his face. "What happened to you? Oh, my god..."

"And you wonder why I didn't want you to see?" In a flash, he puts the hood in place again, snickering. "Aren't you glad you know what happened?"

"But I don't know what happened. What did this to you?"

"Give it a little thought. You'll figure it out." He scoffs before turning away.

I can't believe it. He's going to walk away. He's actually going to leave me standing here. Before I can think about it, I reach out and grab his arm. "Don't go! Come with me. You don't have to hide!"

"I know what I'm doing. Let me go," he warns, looking down at my hand.

"I won't. Don't you understand how it's been driving Colt crazy, with everyone thinking you're dead? Even me! Why would you stay away now?"

"Do you really want to know?"

"Yes!" I almost sob. It's real—he's alive. Colt was right. Who's in his grave? How did he get burned? There are so many questions. I can't possibly let him go.

Leaning down, he whispers, "I'm staying away because if I don't, what happened in that alley is going to happen again and again. It's all I can think about, Leni. Hurting you again the way Dad did."

A wave of nausea washes over me before he scoffs again. "Trust me. This is for the best. So if you know what's good for you, pretend this never happened and go. The fuck. Home."

Yanking his arm away, he adds, "And don't even think about telling Colt. You tell him, I'll disappear for good," he threatens.

It doesn't occur to me to ask him to stop or call after him again. I'm too shocked, horrified. He wants to hurt me like his dad did? Is he really that twisted?

There's nothing I can do but watch him as he disappears into the darkness. When a cab rolls down the street, I throw my arm out, desperate to get home now. Maybe I'll be able to piece it all together when I'm there, where it's safe.

Although that's not going to help once Colt gets home, and I have to pretend once again I'm not hiding any secrets.

I don't think there's ever been a secret as big as this. Or one he might hate me more for keeping.

12. NIX

After the rest of the week passes, I know one thing for sure: She hasn't told him. She couldn't have, or else Colt would burn the city down looking for me. The emails he's been sending haven't changed, either, which is another clue. He would've sent me another message immediately if he thought for sure I was alive and close enough to where he lives that it's within walking distance. A long walk, but what else do I have to fill my time?

I walked tonight, since there's never a guarantee I'll be able to get a parking space close to their apartment. So I hang out across the street in an alley, staring up at their apartment. Sometimes I lose track of time while I do it, standing for hours. I watch their shadows move across the ceiling and imagine what they're doing up there. I don't deserve to be any part of it.

At least one good thing came out of showing her my face: she hasn't been around the neighborhood since. She learned her lesson. For all I know, she's more scared of me than she is of the other dangers out there, but that's fine. It's better if she hates me, if she's scared of me. She should be.

I can't stand the anticipation. Knowing he has to leave at some point. He can't stay home forever, right? Not my brother. It seems like they spend a lot of time together, but he's going to need time on his own. He can't change everything about himself just because of the woman in his life. Even one he's as obsessed with as he is with Leni.

It feels like a lifetime passes while I wait. Cars roll by, people talk on their phones or text while walking. No one notices me, because people don't look into the darkness. They don't want to see what's in the shadows. I have come to rely on that, and it's kept me safe all these months. Anonymous.

They may as well not exist. There is one person I need to see, the person I've been waiting for every time I stand here and watch. He has to leave her alone sometime. He can't be with her always.

The front door to the building swings open, and my chest goes tight at the sight of my brother. I've seen him so many times, always from a distance, but I've never been gladder than I am tonight. He's on his phone, oblivious, climbing behind the wheel of his car and pulling away without looking toward where I'm waiting for him to go. My blood is pumping, my body seized by anticipation. The longer he's kept me waiting, the more time I've had to plan out what comes next.

I have to force myself to wait a minute, making sure he doesn't come back, before crossing the street with my head down and my shoulders hunched. Will she be surprised to see me? She shouldn't be. She should know me well enough by now to know I couldn't possibly leave things the way they were the last time we saw each other.

The security in this building is a joke. No one bothers to stop me as I cross the lobby, probably because people don't pay attention to someone who walks with purpose. Another thing I've learned, living the way I do. It's been a real education.

And tonight, Leni will get an education. She's going to learn she never should have kicked the hornet's nest. She should've left things the way they were instead of coming to look for me. All she did was convince me to do this, because something deep inside her can't stay away from me any more than I can stay away from her.

She's so trusting, she doesn't bother looking through the peephole before opening the door at my knock. How do I know? Because she falls back a step with a gasp when she recognizes me standing in front of her. "Nix! What are you doing here?" Her face goes white as a sheet before she bites her lip, wincing. "I thought you said you didn't want him—"

That's enough out of her. When I lunge, throwing myself into the apartment, her only reaction is to fall back a few stumbling steps. Her mouth opens like she's about to scream, but I'm too quick, slamming the door shut with one hand and grabbing for her with the other. I have an arm around her waist and a hand over her mouth before she knows what's happening.

"I told you, didn't I?" Fuck, I forgot about this. What it's like to have her so close to me, her body moving against mine, so warm and full and firm. I can fantasize all I want, but there's not a fantasy in existence that could come close to the real thing. Her muffled cries, her breath hitting the top of my hand, her tits rubbing against my chest. I'm already rigid, straining against my zipper, and it only gets worse the more she wiggles and struggles.

"This is what I've been dreaming about all these months." She stops whimpering and goes silent, listening to me, her eyes still wide with fear that only excites me more. Like every part of her was created to get me off. "Taking you like this. Waiting for him to leave so I could have you the way I want you."

Now there's not only fear in her eyes. There's anger, a hardness that wasn't there before. Good, let her think she's strong. Let her think she's got any say in what's happening.

Her squeals rise in pitch when I lift her off her feet, which she kicks uselessly in the air. "Where's your bedroom? Let's get reacquainted." She won't stop screaming behind my hand, tiring herself out when there's nothing that's going to stop me. Even if Colt walked in this very minute, it wouldn't be enough to stop me. Not now I've started. I've gotten a taste of the forbidden fruit that's been held back from me all this time. Like whetting my appetite. I only want more, right this minute.

Their bedroom is down the hall, and I'm happy to see the headboard with its iron bars against the wall. It's perfect for what I have in mind. I feel like I'm living out a dream right now, which I guess I am. A dream that's been growing for a long time. Having her like this, totally at my mercy, with no one calling the shots but me. Nobody telling me how to touch her or where, just me following my needs.

Dropping her on the bed, I reach behind me to pull the coiled length of vinyl rope from where I tucked it into the back of my jeans. Her gasp fills the room when she sees it, and right away, she tries to scramble backward. "No! Not like this! Why are you doing this?"

I barely hear her, completely focused on what's about to happen. She manages to back away a little bit, but all it takes is grabbing one of her ankles and pulling hard to make her slide back toward me over the silky striped duvet. "That's right, keep fighting," I urge, my heart pounding in anticipation. This is already so good, and it's only going to get better.

"Please!" she sobs, but she should save her energy. Nothing's going to stop me now.

It takes no time to grab a hold of her wrists, binding them together with the rope, making her wince in pain when I cinch it tight. "That hurts! You don't have to do this! Why are you doing this, Nix?"

"I already told you." Does she think the answer is going to change? I honestly don't care. I'm having too much fun. "I need this, I need you, all of you," I confess, not knowing if she is even listening to me.

She's still kicking and twisting, though, as I move her closer to the head of the bed. She even tries to fight against me, raising her arms so I can't tie the rope to the headboard, and all I can do is laugh. "All you're doing is making this take longer than it has to," I warn, laughing again.

Deeper fear touches her eyes—she might as well be licking my cock. It's so enticing and exciting to see. "I don't want to do this. Please, stop!"

I don't care. It's never mattered what she wants, not when it comes to this. Nothing has changed. I'm in control of her when it comes to sex. I need that from her, the monster inside me hungers for it.

Once she's secured, arms over her head, I take a second to admire what I've missed out on for too long. Her soft, plaid pajama pants and thin tank top hint at what I've already touched, tasted. Her chest is heaving—after all that fighting, her tits have almost worked their way out. Her nipples stand out hard against the cotton, and the sight of them makes my mouth water.

That's what I want first, leaning over her and pulling the shirt up to her armpits. Her pert nipples are begging to be licked, so that's what I do, bending down to drag my tongue around one while squeezing the other tit, rolling the nipple between my fingers while she writhes and squirms.

She tastes so good! I can't help but rub myself through my jeans, aching, dying for the pleasure of being inside her. So hungry for her body, moving down to her navel and back up again with my tongue, nipping and licking, painting her skin.

"You... You shouldn't do this!" She bucks and rolls like a wave, harder the further down I go. "What if Colt comes back? He won't be gone long. You have to stop!"

Who does she think she's kidding? There's not as much fight in her voice anymore. Already, she's weak for me. She knows she wants this as much as I do. She can't help but give in when I make her feel this good.

"If you don't stop," I whisper, lifting my head. "I'm going to have to fill your mouth to shut you up. Is that what you want? Are you hoping I'll give you my cock?"

She closes her mouth, pressing her lips together, shaking her head. Her nostrils flare with every sharp breath, and those breaths only come quicker when I climb between her legs and work my fingers under the waistband of her pants.

"I've missed your pussy," I confess, pulling the pants down along with her thong in one quick motion that makes her gasp louder than ever. A tiny squeal sounds in her throat when I lift her legs and spread them open wide so I can look down at her pink perfection.

It's even better than I remembered. Shaved smooth, glistening, her little clit poking out from under her hood. "Maybe I'll just jerk off, staring at this," I whisper, staring down at the heaven I've missed so much. "I could paint your pussy with my cum, and there's nothing you could do about it."

Looking into her eyes, I snicker. "But I wouldn't want to deprive either of us. I need to feel you wrapped around me."

"Nix..." she moans, eyes welling with tears. I don't know if I like the sight or the sound more. "Not like this. Please."

"Your pussy doesn't feel that way. You should see how wet it is." I can't help but reach down to drag a thumb over her bald lips, picking up her essence and bringing it to my tongue. The taste explodes there, turning my mind into a blazing inferno of need. Nothing will satisfy it but the grip of her muscles around me. She's right—Colt could be back anytime, so this is dangerous. As much as I would love to take hours making her scream, I need to finish what I started.

That means unbuckling my belt and dropping my jeans to my knees. "Remember this?" I ask, laughing at the way she groans with her chin quivering. "Relax. You're already dripping wet. Don't pretend you don't like it."

When her cheeks flush and her eyes dart away, I know I'm right. Her body loves this, even if her brain tells her she shouldn't.

She tries to push herself away from me, heels on the bed, when I touch my tip to her core. "That's right, keep fighting," I urge with a dark laugh. I barely recognize my own voice. It sounds more like Dad's than mine, something that should bring all of this to an end. I can't be like him, yet here I am. Maybe I need to embrace it. "It just makes me want you more."

"You're better than this!"

"That's where you're wrong," I whisper before pushing forward, making her cry out in surprise, in pain, I don't know which. I only know the sound is music to my ears that makes me drive myself deep and hard, grunting in pleasure once I'm buried to the hilt, and she's gripping me tight with her hot, tight cunt.

It only gets hotter and tighter when I pull back and go deep again, hard enough to make the headboard hit the wall in a quick rhythm. Her teeth are gritted, eyes closed, but she loves it. "Stop fighting it," I say breathlessly, taking her legs and spreading them wider, grinding my base against her clit.

Her face is red, tight with strain, but she can't lie to me. Not to the man who's balls deep inside her heat.

"Too… hard…" she grunts, but I ignore her. This is the way I need it, the way I've dreamed of it. I am not going to miss out on this.

In fact, I'm tired of hearing her talk. Her eyes fly open wide when I pull out, only to go even wider when I flip her over. She's face down on the pillow, arms still above her head, simply twisted now, and I like this better. Her smooth ass up in the air once I pull back on her hips, her pale skin going pink when my hand strikes hard enough for her to scream into her pillow.

Maybe Colt will see that handprint. I told myself I couldn't mark her, but that was before I got started. I can't help myself now.

I can take her deeper this way, faster, holding her by the hips and pulling her back to match my strokes. Her ass jiggles in time with our bodies slapping together. Faster, I feel the tension growing, and no matter how she wants to deny it, I feel her getting tighter around me. Her juices are flowing, running down my sack, she's moaning, and soon I realize she's pushing back against me. Fucking me the way I'm fucking her.

The way I knew she would.

"This is what you wanted," I grunt, watching my dick disappear inside her again and again. There is nothing like this feeling of owning her. "This is how you need it." She's lucky I don't have time to do more than this. She wouldn't walk right for a week.

"Nix!" she screams into the pillow, clenching around me, squealing, driving me insane. "Oh, my god!"

And when she comes, drawing me deep, I barely have time to pull out and take myself in one hand. The sight of my pearly cum splashing her skin is better than any work of art. By the time I'm finished, she's dripping with me, sloppy and used. This is what she was made for, whether she knows it or not. Made to be used like this.

She falls to one side, sobbing through her gasps for air. "Oh, god," she moans, quivering, and even that is satisfying. I did that to her. I made her sound that way. Her body sags, wrists still bound tight, and she wiggles her fingers weakly before moaning again.

"Clean yourself off," I sneer, releasing the rope, unwinding it and shoving it into my waistband again once I've picked my pants up. "And next time, don't fight so much. We might have more time to enjoy ourselves."

Her eyes are closed. She doesn't want to look at me. I can't blame her—I can barely face my own reflection most days.

"There can't be a next time. This can't go on." Her voice is small, almost far away. Probably all that screaming she just did. "He needs to know. You can't expect me to lie to him forever."

"Let me worry about that," I tell her as she rubs life back into her wrists. "Just keep your mouth shut about it. Don't say a word."

Because I'll be damned if I'm going to quit her now that I've experienced the exquisite pleasure of her body again. My brother has never been somebody who likes to share —neither have I, but this isn't like sharing a toy when we were kids or childish shit like that. I'm not about to give this up, which I know he'd make me do now that he thinks she's his.

Let him keep thinking that. The longer he does, the longer I'll be able to live out every sick, twisted desire she brings to life in me.

She's still in bed when I try to leave her, trembling, curled in a ball.

Guilt creeps up my spine like a snake. I don't like seeing her like this after sex. It reminds me of how much of a monster I truly am.

I know she enjoyed at least part of this, but she is confused because it was with me and not Colt. At least, that's my conclusion.

"Do you need something?" I ask like an idiot.

"I need you to leave and not come back," she tells me in a stern voice.

"I know you came around my cock, so don't pretend this was so bad."

"You are delusional," she responds, curling into herself even more.

I grind my teeth together before going into the attached bathroom to get a wet rag. When I come back into the bedroom, she has gotten up from bed and is quickly putting her tank top back on.

"Let me at least clean you up before you put your bottoms back on."

"What a gentleman," she quips sarcastically, but when I come closer, she sits back down on the bed and spreads her legs for me so I can clean her up.

As soon as I'm done, she shoves me away so she can grab

her pajama pants from the floor. She puts them on quickly while looking anywhere except at me.

"Don't be mad at yourself."

"I'm mad at you, not at myself," she tells me, fresh tears in her eyes.

"I'm sorry," I say honestly, making her laugh humorlessly.

She crosses her arms over her chest. "No, you're not. You don't care about my feelings or you wouldn't constantly hurt me."

"I am sorry I'm hurting you, but I can't control myself when it comes to you. I want you more than I want anything else. I know I'm a monster. I know I'm fucked up inside and out. But I also know part of you wants me too." And that's the part I have to hold onto.

13. COLT

Something is wrong.

There's a weird charge in the air when I get home after another study session. I feel it throughout my body, can almost taste it as I step into the kitchen. Like the feeling before a thunderstorm.

"Leni?" I ask, my voice echoing in the otherwise silent space. "Where are you?"

"Be right out!" There's a strange sound to her voice. It's too loud, too bright.

"I brought you something," I call out, holding up a bag where two pints of ice cream wait to be devoured. "I wasn't sure what flavor you'd want, so I figured I'd eat what you don't want. But if you don't come out from wherever you're hiding, I'm taking both."

Finally, she answers from the bedroom. "Be right there!"

Rather than take the ice cream to her, I put it in the freezer for later, wondering why she sounds so off. Maybe I'm misunderstanding. Maybe she is planning something naughty. What does she have in mind? I can't wait to find out. My cock is twitching as I follow her voice to the bedroom, wondering what she'll be wearing when I find her.

She's not in a sexy outfit, waiting in bed. If anything, she looks annoyed when I come in, frowning and everything. "I said I'd be right out."

Yeah, something's wrong, and instead of my brain being full of hot, tempting images, there's nothing but ugliness now. "What's going on?" I ask, noticing the balled-up sheets in one corner of the room. She's stripping the bed. Why would she need to do that?

"Stop what you're doing," I demand while she pulls the case off a pillow. "Now. Fucking stop."

She flinches, but does go still instead of continuing with the bed. The pillow she was stripping is now in front of her, with her arms wrapped around it. "What's wrong?" she asks, still staring at the bed. Her damp hair hangs along the sides of her face. Fuck, she even took a shower.

There are only so many ways I can interpret this.

Everything is starting to go fuzzy. There's a thumping in my head, loud enough to drown out everything else going on around me—the traffic on the street, the gentle hum of the HVAC system. My pounding heart overpowers it, getting louder with every second that passes without her being able to look at me. She can't even face me.

Somehow, I'm able to keep my voice soft, asking, "What did you do when I was gone?" Her mouth works, opening and closing, but finally, all she does is chew her lip the way she does when she's afraid to tell the truth.

"Answer me," I command. There's a storm brewing, and it's not going to be pretty when it explodes. I can barely contain it, but I'm trying. I'm fucking trying, for her sake, to be a better man. And for what? For her to cheat on me?

"I took a shower, and now I'm cleaning a little. Is that all right?" she whispers.

I know I'm not imagining the defiance in her question. Almost like she's pissed off. At me? What did I do? Another reason I'm sure she's hiding something from me —she's never like this.

Swinging the bedroom door shut, I lean against it with my arms folded. "Tell me the truth. We're not leaving this room until you tell me the truth."

"Who says I'm not?"

"Why don't you try looking at me? Why don't we start there, Leni? Because right now, what I see in front of me is somebody who's lying to cover their ass. Why are you lying to me?"

"I'm not."

Fuck, she doesn't even sound like she believes it. She sounds tired and weak, if anything. But why?

And then I see it. When she goes back to putting the pillowcase on the pillow, the sleeves of the oversized cardigan she's wearing slide back a little so I can see her wrists.

And the marks around them.

The sight launches me across the room, where I take hold of her arm to pull the sleeve further back. "How did this happen?" I demand. Fuck trying to be understanding, so she's not scared. I'm tired of tiptoeing around and not getting anywhere.

She doesn't answer quickly enough, and I shake her a little. "Tell me! Where did these come from? What did you do to yourself?"

"I didn't do anything!" She almost bares her teeth, yanking her arm away. Her breath hitches as she turns, her face hidden by hair again. "Please, don't do this. I'm begging you not to."

"Begging me?" Nothing she's saying makes a damn bit of sense. "Tell me the fucking truth, Leni. What happened when I was gone?"

Throwing her hair back to glare at me, she raises her voice. "Could you just listen to me for once? Please!"

"Why should I listen to you when I know you're lying? You don't think I know you by now? I'm looking in your fucking eyes, and I know you're lying!"

There's even more than that. There's pain in her eyes. Maybe fear, too. Fear of me? The way I'm feeling, she should be afraid. I don't know if that makes me like Dad or what. I only know my head is going to explode if I don't get answers.

A soft, almost silent sob bursts out of her when I grab her arm tighter this time. "The truth. What did you do when I was gone? Who was here? And don't tell me nobody was," I warn when her mouth falls open. "I know someone was here. I feel it. What, do you think I'm stupid? You don't know me better than that by now?"

"Please," she whispers, closing her eyes. "It's not what you're thinking. Trust me, it's not."

"Until I get an explanation, I'm not going to trust a fucking thing you say. Why are you lying to me? Why?"

Only when she cringes and closes her eyes do I realize I'm screaming. But fuck it. I've been trying the whole kind, gentle boyfriend thing, and it's not fucking working.

Shoving her away from me makes her land on the bed hard. I stand over her, glaring down at her wide eyes, noticing the tears there. There's something powerful in it, something I haven't let myself feel in a long time. I've missed it. I've missed this sense of control. It heats my blood in the most satisfying way. I'm even getting hard, thanks to the way she whimpers and cowers.

It's her fault. It's all her fucking fault.

"I didn't want to tell you!" she cries. When she closes her eyes, tears roll down her cheeks. "I promised myself I wouldn't!"

"What did you promise yourself for? Why are you hiding shit from me?"

I'm going to lose her. She's slipping through my fingers while I stand here, staring down at her. The one good thing that has ever been a part of my life, and she might as well be gone.

"Because..." she whispers, so softly I almost don't hear it. "Because he made me promise."

"He?" I snarl. I'm losing it, I feel it. I'm going to do something terrible—something I'll probably hate myself for later. "Who is he?"

Her eyes open, and she looks at me, her chin quivering. "Nix."

One word shouldn't have the power to blow a person's life apart. One single word, that's all. But that one word is a bomb landing on my ears, tearing me apart inside.

I rock back on my heels, forgetting my anger, staring at her, waiting for the punchline that never comes. "Nix was here?"

"I'm so sorry," she whispers. "It's been tearing me apart inside, wanting to tell you. I didn't believe it at first—that he's still alive—but he is. He came here tonight. I told him it leave..." She keeps babbling, almost hysterical. "But he wouldn't go. He... he tied me up," she admits, and now the tear that falls from her eye stirs absolute fury in me.

He made her cry. He was here; he hurt her, and he made her cry.

He's been alive all this time and never fucking bothered to tell me. I don't know what's worse.

"I wanted to tell you!" she weeps. Her trembling hands cover her face, and her shoulders heave. "I did! But he made me promise not to. I don't know why he's hiding—he wouldn't tell me."

It seems pretty obvious to me, but that's not what makes my fists clench. She's mine, just mine, and now he wants her for himself.

"What did he do to you?" I can't believe I'm able to whisper. I almost sound rational. "Tell me. I need to know."

She pulls her sleeves down over her fists, sniffling. "I didn't want him to, I swear. I begged him not to. I tried to fight him, but…" Her head hangs before she shakes it. "It was no use. He tied me up. Please, I don't want to talk about it. Don't make me, please."

Fine. I won't. The way I'm feeling, it's probably better. Just one more thing making me want to hurt somebody.

He's alive, and I should be happy about it, but goddamnit. Why does it have to be like this? "Did you know he was alive before tonight?" I whisper, fighting for every breath.

"Why are you asking me that?"

"Because you didn't mention being surprised when you said he showed up here," I mutter, teeth clenched. It's the only way I can describe how strange this all seems. When I put that together with how she's been acting lately—so secretive and distant—it all makes sense.

She releases a ragged breath. "The night you bought me the car. I went for a walk. And... he found me. He..."

When she came in that night, refusing to look at me, crying when I tried to fuck her. How did I not see it? "Tell me everything."

"He cornered me in an alley and forced me to suck him off. I didn't know who he was at first, but when it was over, I realized it was him." I'm still processing this when she adds, "When I said his name, he ran off. But I knew."

"And you didn't tell me?"

"He—"

I cut her off with a wave of my hand, slashing it through the air. "I don't care what he wanted from you," I snarl, making her eyes go wide with fear before she tries to creep backward on the bed. Away from me. "You lied to me. What do you owe him that you don't owe me? We're supposed to be together, right? A couple? But you kept his secret. He used you, and you let him get away with it because... why?"

My fists tighten a little more with every word, the anger and betrayal growing. "How could you do that? How could you fucking lie to me that way?"

"I wasn't trying to hurt you! I was... I don't know what I was thinking."

"That's pretty fucking obvious," I growl, ignoring the sob she lets out, ignoring everything. How could she?

How could he?

I can't even be glad he's alive—that I was right all along. I hate him for that. He's taken away my ability to feel any satisfaction in being right, in knowing that he didn't die, that I still have a brother out there in the world.

He took what's mine. He hurt her.

"I was only trying to give him time or whatever he needs," she says weakly.

"Why the fuck does he need time?" I snap.

"He... he was injured," she murmurs. "He didn't explain exactly what happened, and I don't know if he would even if I asked, but the side of his face..." She covers her cheek with her hand. "It's all scarred up. That's why I didn't know for sure it was him in that alley until he spoke—until I saw his eyes. He hides his face. I think that might be part of the reason why. He was there that day, with the explosion and everything. That's what he's been hiding, I think. That might be why he didn't want you or anybody else to know. He's probably afraid."

Funny how I don't care all that much right now. He still didn't trust me enough to reply to a fucking email. Does he think I would turn him over to the police because of some scars on his face? Doesn't he know me better than that?

My head feels like it's in a vise, my skull ready to crack open. My brother is alive, and he fucked my girlfriend. Not that he hasn't before, but that was different. We were forced to do it back then.

Weren't we? Am I just telling myself that?

Now I know one thing for sure, at least. That text came from him, telling me to take better care of her. Like he knows anything about it. I'm the one who loves her.

"What are you doing?" Her tearful question doesn't stop me as I throw the bedroom door open and grab the phone I left on the kitchen counter.

So this is how he wants it? He wants to play games? He wants to hide from me, like there's anything we couldn't get through together? He'd rather sneak around and take what's mine than be a man about it.

Pulling up the anonymous text he sent the night he forced Leni to suck him off in an alley—the thought alone is enough to make my stomach turn—I type out a response.

You fucking coward. You can't tell me where you are, but you can sneak in here while I'm gone? Why don't you show yourself?

That's not even half of what's on my mind, and by the time I send the message, I already know there's more to say. Thinking of the way Leni described him, I add:

You hurt Leni. You made her cry, but I'm still open to hearing you out. Whatever happened, whatever you did, we'll figure out what to do next. Together. But I need you to tell me where you are.

And then I wait, staring down at the phone, willing him to respond. He has to. He can't ignore me. I'm his fucking brother. I'm the only person who will understand. He has to know that. We've been through too much for him to forget it.

But either he has forgotten, or he doesn't care. Whatever the reason, he leaves me hanging—one minute passing after another with no response.

I'm going to explode. I'm going to hurt somebody. He can't do this. Not to me.

But he is, and the feeling of helplessness that comes with it makes my hand curl into a fist, which I slam against the closest wall hard enough to leave a dent. The pain in my knuckles is almost welcome. It gives me something else to focus on instead of imagining all the ways I want to make my brother pay for keeping this secret.

And for touching what isn't his to touch. For seven months, she's been mine alone.

Knowing I've shared her with him puts everything in a different light. An uncomfortable and ugly light that shines on things I would rather leave in the dark.

14. LENI

"You know, we've spent the better part of the past hour together, and all you've done so far is talk about your boyfriend and his brother." Dr. Miller removes her glasses and pinches the bridge of her nose, sighing softly. She doesn't usually reveal her feelings about what I'm saying —I guess that's the way it's supposed to be. She's meant to be a blank page, a surface for me to imprint my thoughts on so she can help me figure them out. This is only our third session, but I'm already getting the sense of how things are supposed to go.

Obviously, if she's already calling me out, it's a problem.

"I care so much about them." The words feel empty, but there's no way I could possibly express the depth of my feelings. Or the depth of my confusion—how conflicted I feel whenever I think about Nix, how he treated me, how frightening he is now. It's been four days since he tied me up, and I'm no closer to understanding how I feel about it than I was when I heard the front door slam shut while I trembled in bed, aching and quivering and hating myself.

I don't know what to think about how I reacted. How easy it was to come with him inside me. I fought against it—or at least I tried my hardest—but it was like my body took over. I might as well have told myself to stop breathing.

He brought up all the old thoughts, questions, fears. Maybe there's something broken in me. The sort of broken that can't be fixed by spending a couple of hours a week with a therapist.

"I'm sure you do, and it's commendable—how much you love and how worried you are for them." She shifts in her chair, frowning while looking down at her notes.

When I was competing, I always hated the feeling that I'd disappointed my coach, something I always worked hard to avoid when I was practicing and competing. There were times I worked as hard as I did not for me, but for them, for Mom, for anybody who was counting on me. And I'm getting that feeling now.

"Is there anything you're trying to avoid addressing? Because, you know, it's very convenient for us to focus our attention on the people around us instead of working on ourselves." She lifts her gaze, staring hard, challenging me. "That's what you're supposed to be doing now, during these sessions."

"I know." I can't help but look down at my lap, where my hands are folded, my fingers twisting together while I fight the discomfort of being called out like that. She's gentle about it, always professional, but her insight stings.

"What does all of this represent to you? You tell me your boyfriend and his brother were very close, and something has gotten between them. Why is it that this is taking up so much space in your mind and your heart?"

That's the tough part about this whole therapy thing. There's so much I can't tell her. What's the point if I can't be completely honest? Then again, what do I do? Tell her I'm pretty sure Nix set the fire that ended up killing my mom?

I know there's such a thing as confidentiality, but how far does that extend if I'm talking about a crime?

I don't know how I feel about Nix right now—it's all too confusing. I'm conflicted, a battle waging between resenting him for using me and wishing he and Colt would come together again as brothers so they can figure things out. Because I know it would make Colt happy in the end, once the smoke is clear and everybody understands each other. Without Nix, he's half of himself.

I want him to have everything he needs. That's what it means to love him.

Even if, right now, it doesn't seem like he wants my love.

"I feel like Colt resents me," I whisper, and some of the tightness in my chest eases now that I've said it out loud.

Tucking a strand of honey blonde hair behind her ear, she peers at me from over the frames of her glasses. "Why would he resent you? What reason would he have for that?"

"Because his brother reached out to me and not to him. I can't tell if he thinks there's something deeper going on, or if he's just hurt or what. But it's affected life at home, for sure. There's this feeling in the air," I confess, shivering when I think about it.

"What kind of feeling?"

"He's angry, but he doesn't know who to be angrier with: himself, his brother, or me. So he's just angry in general, all the time."

"How does that make you feel?"

What does she expect me to say? Why do I feel like there's a right and a wrong answer? I have to remind myself this is not a test. I won't be graded. "Like I don't want to breathe too hard sometimes. I feel uneasy."

"Your home is where you should feel safest."

"I know," I whisper. "It's not that I feel unsafe. I just feel… uncomfortable."

"Have you tried talking to Colton about this?"

I avoid answering directly. "I mean, what is there to say?"

"You could start by telling him what you just told me—that you feel uneasy. You said before this is essentially the first relationship for both of you, right?" When my head bobs, she shrugs. "First relationships require a lot of patience and compromise. There are always going to be growing pains involved. But I encourage you to work through them," she insists.

In response to my uncomfortable silence, she continues, "When you first came to me, you talked about wanting to claim your power. We agreed that was something we could work on together. Finding ways for you to stand up for yourself, speak up for yourself, make sure your voice is heard. There's no time like the present."

She makes it sound so easy, like all I have to do is snap my fingers and become a better, stronger person.

What else is she supposed to think? I've only ever given her fragments of the full story.

Maybe this was going to be a waste of time in the end.

I can't tell her that, of course. All I can do is thank her when the hour is up and leave, feeling no better than I did when I arrived at the office. I should tell Colt to stop wasting his money—he's been so generous, so determined that I go to therapy and learn to get through the dark, ugly memories. I want to. I just wish it were that simple.

Instead, I'm stuck looking over my shoulder all the time, wondering if Nix is watching as I leave the building situated in the middle of a row of shops and offices downtown. It's a lot safer here than where I walked when I first found Nix, but I can't escape my nerves. How am I supposed to live the rest of my life if I'm always nervous when I'm out alone?

But I made a big deal of telling Colt I'd be fine, that he didn't have to pick me up after my session. Sometimes it's better for me to walk so I can process what I talked about with Dr. Miller before getting home. I need to be alone with my thoughts for a little while.

I know she's right about a lot of things. I can tell myself all I want, that she doesn't know the full story, but that doesn't change anything. There are all kinds of reasons I can give for devoting so much of my energy to Colt and Nix and everything surrounding them, but I need to figure out how I feel about everything instead of worrying so much about the way Colt feels, or about how isolated Nix must feel. I didn't set any of this in motion—none of it is my fault. So why am I constantly biting my tongue to keep from begging Colt to forgive Nix? Why do I keep hoping Nix will finally reach out and the two of them can settle the questions into accusations?

Why do I keep wishing so hard for Nix to come back when really all he's ever done is hurt me? It's got to be unhealthy, sacrificing myself like that, no matter how much I love Colt. Maybe that's something I can talk to Dr. Miller about during our next session. I just have to find a way to explain it that won't make her ask a bunch of questions I can't answer. This is all so messed up. It's enough to make me wonder if I'll ever work my way through the trauma James inflicted on me. How am I ever supposed to get past it when Nix still seems stuck in the past? At least Colt has moved on—a little, anyway. The cruelty is gone. He wants to make it up to me, all those terrible things. All Nix wants to do is hurt me the way he did before.

Maybe it would be better if he did stay away, even though I know how it hurts Colt. He might not want to admit it out loud, but I know it does. The doctor is right. I need to stop worrying so much about them and think a little more about me, about what would be best for me.

"I knew you were a fucking head case."

The nasty laughter that follows that charming observation makes my skin crawl. Why? Why can't Deborah leave me alone?

She's leaning against the car parked up ahead, her arms folded, a nasty grin stretching her mouth. She doesn't know it, but she has picked the wrong day. I have too much on my mind to worry about treading carefully around her when all she seems to care about is following me around town.

"Deborah, you really need to get a life," I mutter, scoffing, determined to keep walking without moving aside. She wants me to be afraid. She wants me shaken up. I'll be damned if I give her the satisfaction.

"Did you tell your shrink all about the vandalism you've been up to lately?" she asks with a nasty laugh.

"You're deluded, too." I'm ready to keep walking, to leave her behind me, but she's got other ideas. Pushing away from the car, she steps in front of me, feet planted at shoulder width. For one wild second, I can see myself shoving her hard, knocking her on her ass. She wouldn't expect it, meaning I could probably make it happen—

catching her off guard, having the pleasure of laughing at her surprise.

Then again, all I need is for her to accuse me of assault, which she would definitely do. As it is, she's trying to accuse me of vandalism when I don't have the first clue what she's talking about. Just another thing she's made up, I guess. An excuse to hate me.

"Deluded? No, honey," she whispers, her lip curling, eyes narrowing. "You're deluded for thinking you could slash my tires outside the movies, and I wouldn't know it was you."

Slashing her tires? "I never did that."

"Yeah, right," she snaps. "I guess it was a coincidence."

"Or maybe you pissed off the wrong person," I suggest with a shrug. "I can't be the only one." Was it Nix? Was he following me around even then? Would he take a risk like that?

"Listen, bitch." Baring her teeth, she snarls, "I'm sick of you strutting around like your shit doesn't stink, acting like a goddamn queen bee when we both know you're not. We both know how worthless you are. You're trash. Pretend all you want, but that's all you'll ever be."

Pausing, she adds, "You're a liar, too, and probably a murderer."

"Wow," I muse. "I must be pretty busy. Maybe you better get out of my way—I have all kinds of murders and other crimes to plan. You're wasting my time."

"You're not going anywhere." She shoulder-checks me when I try to walk around her, making me stumble. There are a few passing cars now and then, and a woman across the street pauses in the middle of getting into her car, eyeing us with curiosity. She must decide to mind her business because she wastes no time getting behind the wheel and closing the door.

"Just let me pass, please." I sigh. "I didn't do anything to you, and I would rather pretend you don't exist, if you don't mind."

"See, that's your big mistake, even bigger than thinking you belong with Colt."

Because in the end, that's what this is all about. "I think Colt knows what's best for him. If that's your problem, maybe you need to get in his face instead of mine. But I'm sure you're afraid to do that," I conclude.

"Why would I be afraid of him?" She lifts her chin defiantly, her eyes cold. "Especially when I know what he's done."

"You've lost me again. You really need to stop being so deluded. It's sad," I whisper. It's the truth, too. I'm sad for her. "I'm sorry, there are no answers. I really am, but I'm not the person who can give them to you."

"Bullshit."

"Whatever you say."

"We're going to find out what happened to Bradley."

"We?" I ask, and for the first time, real fear slithers down my spine like a snake. I didn't think about Bradley. The way he disappeared around the time of the explosion. The body, the grave. Why didn't I think about that until now? How could I have missed it?

When Deborah's mouth twitches into a knowing smile and a look of satisfaction comes over her face, I know this is it. She has seen through me. I've just gotten to the heart of why Nix won't come back. It must be Bradley in his grave. And now she'll know all of her accusations were correct because I've never been very good at hiding my thoughts.

It's only when I hear someone step up behind me that I realize I was worried about the wrong thing. Hot breath fans out across the back of my neck, making me flinch, but I don't have time to run. It's already too late.

That same hot breath hits my ear in time with a cloth covering my nose and mouth, a cloth cupped inside a large hand that clamps down hard. "This is for my brother," a man whispers, and I know it must be Dennis holding me in place.

I'm forced to breathe in whatever is on the cloth.

Dennis holds me up as my body begins to slump, and Deborah opens her car's back door in the moments before the world goes dark.

They're going to hurt me, and there's nothing I can do to stop them.

15. NIX

Now I know what real torture feels like. Before today, I only thought I understood. Keeping myself away from the world, living in the shadows, holding myself back. It's been hell, and I thought it couldn't get any worse.

Now I know better.

My pulse is pounding and sweat rolls down the back of my neck as I follow the car Leni is in. I don't know how I managed to sit there silent and still when my instincts screamed at me to stop them. I could've hit the horn, so they knew someone was watching. I even saw myself hitting the gas, aiming directly for the car they stood next to once I spotted Dennis approaching Leni from behind. Why didn't I stop them?

Because they, of all people, can't know I'm still alive. It's bad enough Colt knows—it was stupid to think Leni would be able to keep my visit a secret. I told myself she could because it meant getting what I wanted, and now I have to be more careful than ever.

But showing myself to Dennis would've been the biggest mistake of all. Especially out in public, on the street.

Meaning all I can do now is follow them. The sun is setting, and traffic is getting thinner the further we drive away from the center of town. I have to hang back half a block, sometimes more, to make sure they don't get suspicious. Deborah might be a dumb bitch, but she's sneaky. She'll be keeping watch, making sure nobody noticed what they did.

I only hope Leni is unconscious, the way she looked when they shoved her into the back of the car. I don't want her to know this is happening. If she's ever going to be afraid, I want her to be afraid of me, of what I can do to her, not of these pathetic assholes. What do they think they're doing? What's the point of this? Fuck, if I could only ask. Not that it would make a difference even if I could.

Farther and farther, Dennis drives until the landscape changes around us. The buildings thin out, changing shape from homes and shops, turning into factories and warehouses. There are a few other cars on the road to give me cover, mostly trucks and vans, but at least I don't stick out too much.

By the time the car in front of me slows down and the right turn signal blinks, my palms are sweaty enough to make steering a challenge. I go around them, slowing down, watching in the rearview mirror as Dennis turns into the gravel lot of an old, darkened building whose windows are either broken or boarded up. After driving another block to make sure I don't raise suspicion, I make a U-turn and park across the street.

My feet don't make a sound as I run, or maybe that's the pounding of my heart drowning out everything else. What the fuck do they think they're doing? And what can I do to help her? How can I do anything when I can't let them see me? But I can't stand back and watch without doing everything possible to help her, either.

By the time I reach the building, they're inside, bickering. Dennis must be desperate if he is willing to put up with Deborah's shrill voice. "Tie her the fuck up," she demands. "I can't wait to have a little fun with her."

"Remember what we talked about," Dennis warns. Peering through one of the broken windows, I find the space barely lit by a handful of lanterns surrounding a folding metal chair where Leni is now slumped, with her head hanging forward and her eyes closed. The only thing keeping her up is the way they've tied her hands behind the chair. She's going to be in pain when she wakes up.

They are going to make her hurt.

Everything around me goes red while my heart pounds harder than ever, and I imagine the satisfaction of snapping Dennis's neck. Deborah's, too.

But I can't do it alone. Fuck me, I need help.

There are only three people in the entire world I care enough about to do what I'm going to do now: Mom, Leni, and Colt.

Backing away from the window, I take my phone from my pocket and dial up one of those three people. All I can do is hope he won't waste any fucking time on things that aren't important now.

Shouldn't I know him better? "Oh, so you're finally going to sack up?" Colt asks as soon as he's answered the phone.

"There's no time," I whisper, cutting off anything else he was about to say. "They took her. Deborah and Dennis."

"What?" he barks. "Where?"

"A warehouse on Lake Street between Pine and Poplar," I tell him. "I need you to get down here now. We've got to go in and get her out of there."

My brother isn't perfect, but he has his good points. Right now, that means taking my word for it without asking a bunch of questions. "I'm on my way. Don't do anything until I get there." The thing is, I can't make that promise when I can't predict what they're going to do next. All I can do is grunt in response before ending the call and hoping he gets here soon.

Creeping back up to the window, I see Deborah leaning down, lifting Leni's chin. "Wake up," she croons, giggling nastily. "It's time to have some fun. But we can't if you're still sleeping."

"I soaked the hell out of that rag," Dennis explains. "She's going to be out of it for a little while."

"We'll see." Deborah pulls back her hand, and I bite my tongue, watching her slap Leni hard enough to make her head snap to the side before her chin drops to her chest again.

"Wake up, you stupid bitch," she almost sings, giggling before taking Leni's jaw and squeezing. "Time to answer some questions, just the three of us."

I am going to enjoy the fuck out of bringing her pathetic life to an end. Grim satisfaction spreads through me at the thought and even makes my dick twitch before finally, there's a buzz in my pocket. A text from Colt. **Almost there.**

He needs to hurry. Deborah is getting frustrated, like a kid who can't wait to play with a new toy. "How is she supposed to give us any answers if she's unconscious?" she whines, wiping her hand on her thigh like Leni's skin soiled her. Like it isn't the other way around.

"She'll come around soon," Dennis mutters. I recognize the tone in his voice. He's tired of her, probably wishing he hadn't gotten involved in the first place. "Be patient."

Patience isn't something I have a lot of, either. Looking over my shoulder, I catch sight of a car pulling into the lot with its lights turned off. Smart move. He pulls to a stop close to the chain-link fence at the sidewalk, then jogs my way.

My brother. Not the way I saw us reuniting, but then I never really planned on reuniting with him. I was ready to stay away forever.

"She's in there?" he whispers once he reaches me, because there's no time to talk things over now. He knows it and so do I, both of us creeping closer to the window so we can see what's happening. She's starting to stir, groaning softly while Deborah taunts her.

"That fucking bitch," Colt whispers. "What are you thinking?"

"I'll go around to the rear—there's a door on the other side of the building. Can you see it from here?" I whisper. He nods, and I point to the entrance Dennis and Deborah used. "You distract them by going in through this door and I'll take advantage."

"Have you seen any weapons?" he asks, watching them.

"No, but I doubt they brought her here without one."

"Okay. Wait, though." His words bring me up short before I can sneak away. My mouth is opening, ready to ask why he wants to wait, when the sight of his right fist cocking back answers my question. Pain bursts to life in my jaw when he makes contact hard enough to send me stumbling backward.

But I keep my balance, remaining on my feet while touching a hand to my throbbing face. "I deserve that, I guess."

"Damn right, you do." He surprises me again, this time by taking hold of me and throwing his arms around me in a brief but fierce hug that fills a hole I didn't know existed in what's left of my heart. "Asshole."

I deserve that, too. Before he can ask any questions or hit me again, I jog around the building, barely avoiding tripping over weeds growing up from the cracks in the pavement. From the looks of it, people have been using this place as shelter—there are bottles, fast food wrappers, even an old blood-stained mattress sticking out from under a tarp. It doesn't seem like there's anyone else here tonight, thankfully. We don't want any witnesses.

"What do you think you're doing with her?" Colt's voice rings out inside a second before I reach the partly open door opposite where he's standing. From the looks of it, Dennis and Deborah are shocked, frozen stiff, staring at him while Leni's head moves from side to side, and her soft groans get a little louder.

"What, do you have a fucking tracking device planted on her?" Deborah demands.

"I told you this was a bad idea," Dennis mutters before stepping up behind Leni. From where I'm standing, I can see him reach into his back pocket. The lantern light is enough to make out the metal gleam when he withdraws it. A knife. They're going to cut her.

Leni gasps when he steps up behind her, wrapping an arm around her shoulders to hold her still with the blade against her throat. "Get away from her," Colt warns in a voice that trembles with rage.

"What are you gonna do about it?" Deborah demands with a high-pitched laugh. "Tonight we're getting answers, once and for all."

"Take a step, and I will open an artery," Dennis promises. With his attention on Colt, I'm able to creep up slowly, silently, while Colt pretends I'm not here.

"She has nothing to do with any of this," he insists. "You have a problem with me? Talk to me about it. Not her. She's innocent."

"And you're not innocent?" Dennis asks. I'm only a few feet away now, and I see what needs to happen next. It's all in front of me, crystal clear. My heartbeat slows, my breathing goes even. I've never been more prepared for anything.

He doesn't realize what's happening until I have a handful of his hair in my fist. There's not even time for him to gasp in surprise or pain by the time I take his wrist in my other hand, the one holding the knife.

"What—?" That's it. That's all he has the chance to say before he buries the blade in his own neck, with my help.

Deborah spins around at the sound of his strangled gurgling. "Oh, my god!" she screams while I pull Dennis away from Leni, still holding onto him while he thrashes weakly.

"Don't worry. You'll get your turn," I promise her before forcing Dennis to remove the knife from his flesh. Blood pours from the hole we created, splashing across Deborah's dark hoodie, spraying her face.

From the corner of my eye, I see Colt rushing to Leni, untying her, helping her out of the chair. Right now, I'm more interested in the blood-soaked girl staring in horror as Dennis drops to the floor. She's too shocked to move and too stupid to realize she's looking at her own immediate future.

The blade is still coated with hot, sticky blood when I take the knife from Dennis's hand. He presses that hand to his neck, but it's no use. Every beat of his heart makes his life force pour from between his fingers, looking more like oil in the lantern's light.

"You said you want answers?" With my other hand, I pull back my hood. Colt's soft grunt is nothing compared to Deborah's gasp of horror as she realizes who she's looking at.

Her eyes go round, her mouth falling open. "How?" she whispers, backing up, stumbling over the empty chair and landing on her ass.

"You just couldn't leave it alone, could you?" I whisper, savoring her horror as I advance one step at a time. "This didn't have to happen."

"But... you're dead!" Her terrified gaze bounces from my scarred face to the knife and back again. "Please!"

"Oh, no," I reply, reaching down and taking a hold of her platinum hair when she tries to scramble away. Her pained gasp is music to my ears. I yank her head back until her tear-filled eyes meet mine. "It's too late for that."

The satisfaction of sinking the knife into her chest is indescribable. I don't think I've ever enjoyed penetration this much. The parting of her lips in a gasp, the look of surprise, the way she claws weakly at me—I don't even feel it. I only drive the blade into the hilt, then turn it before pulling it free.

"Say hi to Bradley," I whisper, watching the life drain from her eyes while blood drains from her wound, pouring out to soak her sweatshirt, bubbling from her lips with every wet breath she tries to take.

To her, it probably lasts forever, but to me, it's over in an instant. I'm almost disappointed by how short her suffering lasts. Dennis, too—he's dead now, his eyes wide and unseeing, blood pooled under his head.

Now what?

Colt is already thinking along those lines. "We have to get her out of here," he decides, his arms around Leni. She sags in them, still dazed from whatever they drugged her with.

"What do we do with them?" I ask, wiping my fingerprints off the handle before dropping the knife on the floor.

"We have to leave them here, at least for now," he replies.

"We can come back for them once we figure out what we want to do. Nobody's going to find them here tonight."

He's right. The most important thing is getting Leni out of here and home, safe. "And you're coming with us," he adds, lifting her in his arms, cradling her close to his chest. "Now, come on. I need you to open the door for me so I can get her into the car."

Home with them? I'm against the idea, coming up with reasons why it won't work as I follow him out of the warehouse and across the lot. "That wasn't the idea," I argue as we reach the car, opening the passenger side door for him to place Leni inside. She falls back against the seat, her eyes half closed, a pathetic little groan stirring in her throat. What would they have done if I wasn't watching her today? The thought is enough to make me wish I could kill her kidnappers again.

"I don't care what the idea was." Once he has her safely belted into her seat, he closes the door and faces me. "You're coming home with us so we can figure out what to do next," he insists. "Got it?"

"All right," I agree, because at the end of the day, it feels damn good to be back with him. With both of them. Like the part of me that's been missing these past seven months is finally back.

And we do need to discuss what happens now. What to do with the bodies, and how to keep Leni out of this.

"No, ride with us," he insists when I start off for my car.

"We can come back and pick your car up. No offense, but I don't trust you to follow me."

He has a point. I don't bother arguing before climbing into the back seat, feeling more alive than I have in a long time. Whatever happens next, I won't be alone. For the first time in months, I don't have to be alone.

16. COLT

This is bizarre. The one thing I wanted more than almost anything in my life, and I have it here, now. My brother is in the shower—he went first, being bloody and everything—and I've stayed with Leni while we wait.

"They're really both dead?" She's barely aware of what was happening back there—whatever that bastard used to knock her out, he used a lot of it.

She wraps both hands around a mug of tea, which probably tastes like shit because I brewed it for her. I know tea isn't exactly a challenge, but I'm not used to taking care of her like this. "Yeah, they're definitely dead. You don't have to worry about it."

"How can you say that?" There's something small and sad in her voice. Defeated. "How am I not supposed to worry about what happens next? I mean, they're dead, and people are going to want to know how it happened."

Down the hall, the bathroom door opens, and Nix strolls out in a pair of my sweatpants that I left out for him. I still can't believe it. He's actually here. I never believed he was dead, but there were times I wondered if we would ever breathe the same air again, since he was so determined to stay away.

He walks on silent feet, like a ghost, and I notice how slowly he approaches Leni, rounding her end of the sofa like he's afraid of getting too close. Sure, now that I'm around, watching him, he wants to be all protective and gentle. Where was that when he decided to tie her up and use her? "We'll take care of the bodies. Don't worry," he insists. "We'll go back in the morning, first thing."

She's not convinced, wrapping her arms around herself once she's drained her mug. "It is really weird, having you here like this," she admits. I'm glad she said it, so I didn't have to.

"Yeah, you're usually busting in and doing whatever you want when you show up around here, right?" I ask, and I'm glad when he flinches. He deserves a hell of a lot worse than that.

"It's weird being here," he admits. "I didn't expect this, whatever happened. If I wasn't watching you earlier..."

Leni shivers, and he winces at the sight. "But some things matter more than staying away. I couldn't sacrifice you to keep myself safe."

"Okay, okay." I've had enough of this. "Let's not throw a

parade for you or anything, you know? What the hell is with you letting me think you were dead all this time?"

"You didn't believe I was."

"That doesn't matter—you get my point. Why did you stay away all this time? And how…"

He waits with a smirk twisting his lips until I finally have to look away. "Come on, brother," he invites. "What were you going to say?"

Asshole. "How did your face end up the way it is?"

He runs a hand over the scar tissue, covering almost half of a face that used to be as familiar to me as my own. With a soft sigh, he lets himself drop into an armchair across from us. "I'm not proud of what I did, but in the moment, it felt like the right thing to do. Really, it was Bradley's idea—and I know he can't defend himself now, but it's the truth. If it was all me, I would tell you. And it's not like I didn't go along with him," he adds with a bitter laugh.

"What are you talking about?" Leni whispers, though I think I know. It's the only thing that makes sense, the only reason he would have for letting me think he was dead.

And he knows that, too. His eyes meet mine before he confesses, speaking slowly, like every word takes effort. "We set the fire in the house. Bradley and me."

Leni flinches, and I take her hand while he keeps going. "I never gave him any specifics of the shit he made us do, but he knew I hated Dad. And that day, I'd had enough. I was ready to explode. There was all this shit inside me, all this rage, and I wanted to make him hurt. I thought burning down the house that meant so much to him, burning up all his things, he might finally feel a little pain. And... I don't know." He can't look at Leni anymore, can't watch her crumble in pain. He looks away before muttering, "It got out of hand. I don't know what the hell we were thinking, but it all got out of hand."

"Did you know they were home?" she whispers. The pain in her voice—I wish somebody would hit me and get it over with, because I could stand that. I can't stand the sound of her pain.

"I didn't know your mom was there. I swear. I wouldn't have done it if I knew she was there. She wasn't home when I got there with Bradley, and we went down to the basement for a little while hanging out—that must've been when she got home. It was so stupid. We were drinking; I wasn't thinking straight. I am so sorry, really. She didn't deserve that."

Leni releases a shuddering breath and looks at the floor, breathing slowly like she's fighting to control herself.

And he knows it, and I see the pain it brings him, but maybe he deserves it.

"Finally, it was all too much, and we started to run for the back door. I thought we would have more time. I really did, but it spread fast. Bradley pushed me in front of him—he was screaming at me to get out. And I did. I made it out maybe a handful of seconds before the explosion. But he was still inside."

"It's Bradley in your grave?" Leni whispers. "I was visiting Bradley all these months?"

His head bobs slowly. "Yeah. I was a John Doe at the hospital. Somebody picked me up after I stumbled through the woods and finally found the road. I was so out of it, and all bandaged up after they treated me at the hospital, and I didn't have my ID on me. I heard reports on the news from my bed, and I knew I couldn't tell anybody who I really was."

"And what you really did," Leni whispers with an edge to her voice, like she's spitting the words out. "Because they would know from the burns that you were there when it happened. But you could've pretended it was an accident. You could've told them you were dazed and didn't know what you were doing. Right?" She looks at me for backup, her eyes wild and wide.

"Yeah, that's true," I agree. "There were so many things you could've done that wouldn't involve, you know, basically gaslighting me for seven months into thinking my brother was dead when he's really alive. And do you know what that did to her, too?" I demand, jerking a thumb toward Leni because it's not easy for me to admit what it did to me. It's easier to bring her into it and make it more about her. Less embarrassing, too. "And Mom! I guess you saw the message about her being here, being awake now, right? You know about all of that."

"I do, and I went to see her one night when she was asleep. Thank you for keeping me updated."

He's being sincere, and I get where he's coming from, but something about it makes me burst out laughing. "Listen to you. Acting like I was, like, watering your plants for you while you were on vacation or some shit. You could have told me. You should have told me."

"I didn't know what the hell you were going to think or how you would react," he argues. "For all I knew, you'd be pissed over what I did."

"Fuck off," I growl. "That is such bullshit. After everything we've been through? You think I would betray you over something like this? You think I wouldn't help you? I would've done everything in my power to keep you—"

"I didn't want you to do that!" he snaps before I can finish. "Maybe I didn't want you to have to, like, harbor a fugitive or whatever you want to call it. Maybe I don't even want to be here now," he adds with a growl. "I'm putting you both in danger by being here. I shouldn't have come."

"It's too late for that now," Leni tells him, but there's no anger in her voice. Nobody in the world would blame her for being furious, for never forgiving him. I wouldn't even blame her if she refused to be in the same room or the same apartment. Even if he did save her tonight.

"It's not too late to get out of here before the two of you have to pay for what I did. I'm not going to stay."

When he stands, I stand too, shaking my head, laughing at him. "Oh, right? Because it's that easy? You come here, get cleaned up, and then you go? What if I go to the authorities tomorrow, tell them you're alive and in town somewhere?"

"What if I leave before you can do that? I could go somewhere else, anywhere else, and you would never know where."

"If you were going to do that," I point out, folding my arms, "then why haven't you done it yet? Why are you still here? I know why." All it takes is the slightest shift of my gaze, glancing to the side where Leni sits. The way he lowers his gaze tells me I'm right.

His fists hang at his sides, flexing rhythmically. "I'll do what I have to do. But I will not let you two get caught up. I haven't spent seven fucking months living like a goddamn hermit to sacrifice you now. I could only ever hurt you." When he says that, it's Leni he's talking to, Leni who he watches like a hawk. He can't stay away from her. It makes me wonder how deep his feelings are—I didn't know he had feelings for her in the first place, at least not the kind I have.

"And it would hurt if you ran away now," she whispers. "Not only me. It would hurt Colt, too, even if he won't say it out loud."

"I don't know," I mutter, talking to her but glaring at him. "Maybe I wouldn't give a shit. He didn't give a shit about what it did to me all these months, did he? Reading my messages, not bothering to say a word back." I can hardly believe the way it makes me feel when I say the words and remember all the time I spent typing those emails, keeping him updated, hoping like hell something I said would get through to him. Believing, being the only one who did believe, wondering how we were ever going to tell Mom he was gone, since even telling him she was still alive wasn't enough to get a response.

Now, I'm the one whose fists are clenched. One punch wasn't enough. I could knock him flat on his back and it wouldn't be enough. "Yeah, maybe he should go. It was a mistake to have him here."

At least he looks sorry now, but it doesn't change anything. I can't get back all the time I spent hoping and wondering and wishing the rest of the world could understand what I understood.

"I'm asking you to believe me," he mutters. "Just try to understand. I thought I was doing the right thing. For all of us."

"I'm not going to thank you."

"I didn't ask you to."

"Then why bother telling us any of this?"

"I only want you to understand why I did what I did. And how sorry I am—really, really sorry," he whispers to Leni, who only sniffles in response. "I wish I could take it back. I know that sounds empty and stupid, but I do. And maybe that's why it was important for me to stay away," he adds with a shrug. "I'm no good. I cause pain. That's all I've ever given you, right?" he asks her.

"Maybe you were just too much of a coward to face up to what you did," I murmur, because I have never been so pissed off at anyone in my life. And not just pissed off, either—it goes much deeper than that. He betrayed me by not trusting me with the truth. He made a fucking fool out of me. He made my girlfriend think I'm crazy for believing what was true all along. And I'm supposed to understand him?

"Maybe I was," he snaps, scrubbing a hand over his head. "Maybe I've been living in a fucking pit ever since as punishment for that—and so many other things, things I don't deserve to be forgiven for."

"Do you really want forgiveness?" she asks while I fight to make sense of the storm raging inside me.

I watch, silent, as he thinks this over. "I never imagined getting it. But now that I'm here… I mean, now that I'm with you, both of you… is it possible? Can you forgive me for what I did?"

I hear the agony in his voice. I see it on his face. I know it's the right thing to do, forgiving him, and there is definitely a part of me that wants to. It doesn't matter how I feel about what he did or how long he stayed away. At my core, in the deepest, truest part of me, I'm too happy he's back to want to keep fighting. At least not tonight. We've already been through enough.

And deep down, I'm afraid if I push too hard, he'll leave for good. I don't want that. And it would haunt Leni, just like everything that happened tonight is going to haunt her, probably for a while.

It's too much for her, the way I knew it would be. "I need to go to sleep," she whispers, shivering, rubbing her arms. "My head is going to explode. I can't think about this anymore tonight."

I know what she means, since I feel the same way. The adrenaline rush passed a long time ago, and now I feel empty. I should be overjoyed at having my brother back, but right now I'm numb. "That's a good idea. Things will look better after we sleep for a little bit."

When Nix frowns, I add, "You're staying here. With us. You know how much room we have in the bed." A quick flash of pain in his eyes makes me feel good. I want him to regret what he did. He deserves much worse than that for using her.

But still, I want him to stay. He's my brother, and I know who he really is inside. I know how Dad twisted him, but I know he doesn't need to stay that way.

And if I push him out of my life now, what hope does he have?

"Okay," he says with a sigh, like he had a choice. Leni leads the way to the bedroom, where she doesn't bother to flip on the light before stripping down to her underwear and crawling into bed, curling up in a ball in the center. I strip down to my boxer briefs and get in behind her, drawing her close, watching him over her head.

He only hesitates a second before sliding under the duvet, lying on his back rather than facing us, bending an arm under his head and staring up at the ceiling. "Please, don't leave," Leni whispers in the dark.

Something tells me even if he was planning to, he won't now. All because she asked him to stay.

For a long time, we were the ones who had power over her. Somewhere along the way, that shifted, and now she's the one holding the cards.

The thought stays with me as she starts snoring softly, and after my brother closes his eyes. I'm the only one still awake, caught between wondering what happens next and feeling complete for the first time in forever.

17. LENI

No!

A hand clamps over my mouth and my nose. A hand holding a rag that smells funny, and it makes me twist my head from side to side to get away from the smell, but I can't do it. He's too strong, the hand is too strong. I can't hold my breath long enough.

I need to breathe!

But I can't, because I can't breathe in whatever is on the rag, only it's already too late. I'm already inhaling; that's what my burning lungs demand. I need to inhale. I need to...

My eyes snap open all at once. There's no slow wake up. I'm wide awake, fully aware, and about to throw up.

I can't move—my body is frozen in fear, muscles locked, my lungs unable to pull in enough oxygen after a nightmare that was really a memory playing itself out in my overwrought subconscious. The memory of being taken off the street while Deborah laughed coldly, and Dennis drugged me.

I'm glad she's dead. It's a horrible thought, but it's true. She can't hurt me anymore, neither of them can. I'm safe here, sandwiched between two warm, solid bodies. They rescued me together; they brought me back here. Nobody is going to hurt me.

If anyone had tried to tell me a year ago that Colt and Nix Alistair would be my salvation, I would've told them to have their head examined.

That's the truth of my life now. They've gone from my worst nightmare to my protectors. I'm pretty sure I would be dead now if it wasn't for them.

But Mom is dead because of Nix.

No. I don't want to think about that. Not when I'm warm and uncomfortable. All I want is to curl up between them and sleep. To let go of everything for a little while, to trust that they'll take care of whatever comes up.

But is that childish? Probably. After everything I've been through, who could blame me for wanting to finally put down my burdens or at least hand them to somebody else to take care of for a while?

I'm facing Nix, who is still on his back, with my back to Colt. I can only see the left side of Nix's face, his perfect, unmarked profile, reminding me of the cold, haughty boy I first met. He's a different person now in so many ways, but like this, I can pretend he was untouched by the fire.

Colt stirs behind me, and the pressure against my ass tells me he's sporting the same morning wood that's tenting the comforter over Nix's crotch. "You okay?" The whisper in my ear is soft and loving and protective. It goes nicely with the arm he drapes around me, holding me tight against his bare chest.

"Better now," I whisper. "Just had a nightmare."

"You're safe." With his lips against my ear, he whispers, "Here with us. Nothing's going to hurt you."

Life changes so fast. I can't believe I actually crave Colt's nearness now. I can't help but wiggle against him a little, tucking myself closer to his body.

"Careful," he warns, and there's a growl running under his words. "Don't make any moves you can't back up with action." Like he's trying to prove a point, he moves his hips, thrusting his erect dick against me, and heat bursts to life in my core. My nipples tighten when his hand brushes over my chest. I close my eyes, hungry for escape. He can give that to me.

But Nix is right here, too, and I guess the movement wakes him up because his eyes open, and he turns his head, blinking hard like he's confused.

The confusion doesn't last long. He doesn't have to say a word—I can see it in his eyes, in the needy light that fills them. That hungry gaze travels over my body, watching as Colt fondles my boobs.

We've been here before, haven't we? Except we haven't. It's different now. It's just the three of us in this bed. Nobody else watching, nobody calling the shots.

Closing my eyes again doesn't take me any further away from the ugly memories that are never far from my mind. I don't want to go back to that place. I can't. This is my life. James isn't in control anymore.

"Are you enjoying that?" Nix asks before I open my eyes again, ready to fully experience what's about to happen without fear, without the past holding me back. The two of them exchange a look—neither says a word, and I don't think they have to. They understand each other.

Which is probably why Colt doesn't stop Nix from taking my hand and guiding it under the blanket, where his erection awaits. I could stop him if I wanted to.

I don't want to. For some reason, closing my fingers around his thick shaft takes the heat that was already building and turns it into an inferno.

His helpless groans when I start to pump my fist up and down his length are nothing compared to Colt's grunts in my ear while he humps me from behind. "What do you think?" he whispers while his hands grope and caress. His hot breath fans across my skin when he asks, "You think you can take us both?"

Do I? Throbbing and aching and already so wet, I want to try. Maybe one day I'll figure out what it is about them that unlocks this deep, dark need in my soul.

Right now, all I want to do is give into it.

"Why don't you use your mouth instead of your hand?" Colt suggests, wedging a hand between my legs, toying with my swollen lips until I spread my thighs so he can touch more of me. "Let me watch you suck him off while I fuck you. Does that sound good?"

Anything would sound good while he dips deeper, making my body sing with the way he plays with my wet, swollen flesh. "Oh, yes…" I moan, stroking Nix faster, working my hips to rub my ass against Colt's rigid member. I'm already so close, sinking deeper and deeper into the pleasure the three of us are creating together.

"Put it in your mouth," Nix grunts, settling back with his hands behind his head, watching me position myself so the dripping slit at the tip of his head is close to my tongue. He thrusts upward with his hips, and I part my lips to take him inside.

"Oh, fuck, that's it." His deep, satisfied groans mix with Colt's heavy breathing while he positions himself behind me. Without saying a word, Colt takes me by the hips and lifts them, then presses a hand to my lower back so my ass is on display for him to toy with. Cool air touches my slick, bald lips, making me shiver before something thick and wide slides through my folds.

I moan around Nix, who moans in response. "Make her do that again," he tells his brother, who rubs his head in circles over my clit until I start to lift my head to let Nix fall from my lips.

He stops me, clamping a hand on my head, holding me in place. "I didn't tell you to stop," he grunts, moving again, feeding me his cock while Colt drives me crazy. I'm aching, needy, ready to beg for it when all at once Colt shoves himself inside me, rocking me forward before he pulls me back by the hips.

It's all so good. I don't know what to focus on—the way Colt fills me up, the taste of Nix's salty pre-cum on my tongue, or the deep satisfaction, knowing I can pleasure them at the same time. It takes the sensations running through my body and amps them up, making me suck harder while I push back against Colt's strokes.

"You like this, don't you?" Nix asks, pushing my hair aside so he can watch me bob up and down his length. "That's right, nice and slow. Just like he's fucking you. Fuck me with your mouth just like that."

With a soft moan, I do as I'm told, matching my pace with Colt's, and soon the three of us are moving together. I know it's wrong, and maybe that's what makes it feel so right.

This time, it's different. This time, nobody's forcing me. They're not using me like I'm an item, a thing, a sex toy for their amusement. "So fucking tight," Colt says under his breath, his fingers gripping my hips, digging in, and even that is so good, better than anything I could imagine.

And when pleasure races through me like fire in a dry forest, I don't have to feel guilty for the way my body reacts. I can go with it. I can enjoy it. I can own it.

I feel the tension build, and my moans get louder. "Fuck, I wanna watch you come," Nix groans, lifting my head away from his dick to fuck his fist.

Now all I have to focus on is the way I feel, losing myself a little at a time with every stroke, every time Colt crashes against me. And when he adds a finger to my clit, I howl, throwing my head back, almost sobbing as the tension breaks and nothing is left but sweet bliss radiating through my limbs, making me melt.

"That's my girl." There's pride in Colt's voice once I can hear it, when the heavy drumming of my heart softens a little. "You think you can take more?"

Do I think I can? No, I know I can. I know I want to.

I'm still limp with satisfaction and offer no resistance when Colt lays me on my side, facing him, my back to Nix. Nix runs a hand down my side, letting it slide around my hip, cupping my sensitive mound. "Are you still pulsing down there?" he asks. Instead of waiting for an answer, he invades me from behind, stretching me with every inch of him. "Oh, fuck, yeah," he moans, only stopping once he's as deep as he can go, and we are locked together. "Fuck, I feel it."

Colt turns my face toward his and runs his tongue over my lips before parting them and plunging inside. He cups my boobs, massaging them, playing with my nipples while Nix takes me from behind in deep, slow strokes. The sounds of his pleasure make mine grow.

"Yes, yes," I gasp when Colt lets me up for air so he can kiss and lick his way down my neck, over my chest. He finds my clit again, treating it gently, and somehow that drives me even wilder than it would if he was rough. My nerves are sizzling and my soul cries out for more.

"Our little slut," Nix whispers, then grunts as he drives himself deep and hard.

"My turn," Colt decides, and Nix slides out so Colt can take his place. While Colt fucks me, Nix touches me, grinds against my ass, kisses and nips at my neck with his teeth.

I don't know who's touching me anymore, who is inside me, I only know it feels right. Somehow, it feels right, because now it's what I want. I don't have to follow anybody else's orders anymore. No one is going to tell me how to do this or where or with whom. I make the choices.

And even if I submit to them, it's my choice to submit.

My soul is singing, soaring high, by the time Nix speeds up, not just fucking anymore but rutting like an animal, and his animal grunts push me over the edge again. I'm still coming when he pulls out and rolls me onto my back.

Then he and Colt fuck their fists for those last breathless, furious seconds before spilling cum across my pussy and inner thighs, painting my skin until I'm a coated, dripping mess.

"Fuck, yeah," Nix whispers, his head falling back as he pants. Colt gets up and goes to the bathroom, bringing back a warm washcloth, which he uses to gently clean me up while I lie back and catch my breath.

The only word that comes to mind is fulfilled. I can't believe how ridiculously fulfilling that was. It reached a part of me I didn't know existed, and I can't help wondering when we'll be able to do it again. There was more to it than my body reacting to a little friction. It felt... freeing.

At least until my head clears and reality leaks in.

"As much as I'd love to lie around and recover, we have to get moving soon." Colt scrubs a hand over his head, heading for the bathroom again. "I'm gonna take a shower. I won't be long."

Right. The bodies. I can't forget what happened last night. I can't ignore it. I can only try to make sense of it as I sit up and swing my legs over the bed, avoiding Nix's gaze as I cross the room on shaky legs and grab my bathrobe from the back of my closet door.

This is too awkward. The man was just inside me, and I can't bring myself to look at him before I go to the kitchen. When he joins me, he's wearing a pair of Colt's sweatpants. Now that I'm in here, I can't remember why. My head is all mixed up.

"You know, you can look at me. You don't have to be embarrassed."

"I'm not embarrassed," I insist. Okay, I am a little bit. But there's so much more than that. I can't find the words.

"Hey. It's understandable if you have a lot of shit you need to process." When he approaches me, I take a backward step without thinking about it. Pain touches his eyes, stopping him in his tracks.

"There's something I need you to understand." Honestly, I'm not sure if I'm saying this for me or for him. All I know is that it needs to be said. "Don't get this twisted. What happened just now doesn't erase everything else. Neither does you rescuing me. I'm grateful," I add, because I'm not completely heartless.

The old Nix would've laughed that off, I think. He at least would have pretended to think it was funny for me to act like I have any say in my own life. But he's changed, and not just physically. Nodding, he replies, "I'm not asking for your gratitude. I did it for you, but I did it for me, too. And for Colt."

"Anyway, there's still too much unresolved." Wow, I'm really doing well with this, aren't I? I can't find the words to express what's swirling around in my head and heart. "I can't just forgive you out of nowhere. The good things you've done... they don't outweigh the other things."

Every part of me wants to shut down, to run away from what I've just started. Every word, every heartbeat that accompanies them, brings up another ugly memory of being powerless, used by James and his sons like I wasn't even human.

And no matter how good things were back in the bedroom, no matter what Nix did to save me last night, I can't forget the glee that was on his face more than once. How happy he was to use me, whether he was forced to or not. He might have felt like he had no choice, but he didn't have to like it as much as he did.

And then there's what he did to me in the alley. Nobody was forcing him then. "You hurt me—here, I wave my hand indicating the apartment, and in that alley. I'm not just going to let that go. You don't get off that easy."

At least he's decent enough not to argue. He doesn't make a big deal about blaming himself, either. If anything, it would be worse to have him beat himself up just to play on my sympathy. He's done a lot of things I can't agree with, things I've hated him for, but he's not manipulative like that.

Not that it makes him a good person or even someone I should be sharing this apartment with. At the same time, I can't deny how good it felt to be with him and Colt together. Feeling pleasure without hating myself for it.

I've never stood a chance against these two. There is something about them that will always mix me up inside and make me question who I really am. What is this power they have over me?

"I understand. I'll keep my distance if you need it," he offers. "But Colt is probably going to have other opinions about that. He wants me to stay."

This is all so overwhelming and much too confusing. "I think it would be for the best if you did stay here," I admit, because it's the truth, even if it makes things complicated. "It'll make him a lot happier, and it will be a relief to know you're safe. But that's as far as it goes," I remind him. It's not easy to stand up for myself like this, but it's something I want to get better at. "It's going to take time to trust you after everything."

His shoulders rise and fall in a deep breath before he nods again. "I get it, and I respect it. Thanks for being honest with me—I never could stand a passive-aggressive girl."

Taking one last look at his scarred face, I wrap my arms around myself, suddenly feeling chilly. "I'm going to get in the shower now." Because I don't know how much more of this I can take at once. How am I supposed to look into the face of the person who killed my mom and tell him I want him to be part of my life?

At the same time, how am I supposed to feel otherwise? Because he is part of my life—a messed-up, twisted, complicated part—but I can't deny our connection, just like I can't deny wanting Colt to be happy. That means being with his brother.

And for me, being happy means being with Colt.

Will I ever win?

18. NIX

One thing is obvious: she is not the girl she used to be. She found her voice, finally. I won't flatter myself by thinking I had anything to do with that, like I toughened her up or anything. There was always toughness inside her, and it used to piss me off when I couldn't make her bend to my will.

That strength isn't just on the inside anymore. She's letting it out, finding her voice. Between that and the way she expertly handled both of us in the bedroom, I have to say I like what I'm seeing.

So, it's a shame she has mixed feelings about me. But what did I expect? What, was she supposed to forget everything all at once? I just confirmed I killed her mom. That's the kind of thing I don't know if I'll ever be able to make up to her.

But I understand now, knowing there's a wedge between us, that I would do whatever it takes to earn her trust.

How can I make her understand I wasn't thinking about her when I did it? Do I even want to try? Because that's kind of shitty, too. Why don't I just come right out and admit I've made huge, deadly decisions without considering the consequences? I don't think that's going to earn me any points.

There's one thing I can do while standing around, feeling like an asshole. It's been a long time since I've had a really good cup of coffee—it doesn't look like the coffee maker gets a lot of use around here, but the coffee itself isn't some cheap-ass brand, so I'm glad to brew some. By the time Colt joins me in the kitchen, the aroma fills the air.

"That smells good. Leni's in the shower, but you can go wash up as soon as she's finished," he offers, raking his fingers through his wet hair.

Is it wrong that I don't want to? I like having her scent on me even more than I like smelling the familiar aroma of freshly brewed coffee. Of course, I doubt her boyfriend would like hearing something like that, so I keep my thoughts to myself. "Sounds good. Are we... okay, after what just happened?"

At first, it looks like he doesn't want to answer, and that can't be a good sign. I can see him being into it in the moment. When most of your blood is in your cock, you can't do a lot of thinking. But he probably feels differently now.

He glances down the hall toward the bathroom where Leni is showering, then shakes his head. "Later."

So, it's going to be a complicated conversation. Now I wish I hadn't asked.

It's easier—and probably safer—to pour some coffee and sit down at the table. I need the caffeine; sleep wasn't easy to come by last night. Not like I was wracked with guilt or anything like that, but the whole situation was strange. I've gotten used to being alone. Going from learning how to sleep through fights next door and a baby crying upstairs to trying to sleep in a silent apartment was awkward.

Colt turns the chair across from mine backward and straddles it, setting his cup on the table. "I have to admit, I never saw us doing this again."

Looking across the table at my brother brings hundreds of mornings to mind. Having breakfast together the way we did so many things together. Most of the time, we ate without saying a word. We didn't need to talk. We understood each other.

Besides, what the hell is there for kids to talk about? Retirement accounts? The weather? The thought makes me snicker before taking a gulp of my coffee. "Neither did I," I admit.

"I mean, I knew you were alive."

"I can't tell whether you're gloating or what when you keep saying that."

"I'm not gloating." When I narrow my eyes, he rolls his. "Okay, I might be gloating a little bit. But I think I deserve it. I'm the only one who believed you were alive when no one else did."

"The whole point was for nobody to know."

"They don't know you like I do. I knew you would make it out of there in time."

"I almost didn't," I remind him in a quiet voice.

"Well, there was Bradley's disappearance, too," he admits, looking down into his mug. "It seemed like too big a coincidence to really be a coincidence, if you know what I mean. I knew there had to be something else going on."

"Maybe you just didn't want to believe it," I point out. "That would be okay, too."

"Anyway, it's a waste of time to talk about it because here you are."

"Yeah, and I just made both your lives a lot more complicated. No, let me say this," I insist when it's obvious he wants to cut me off. "I've done a lot of awful shit in my life, but dragging you two into the mess I made would be the worst. You know I'm right."

"Don't tell me what I know."

"And stop being so fucking stubborn," I mutter. "Nothing pisses me off more than when you act like you don't see what's in front of you. This is reality. I killed two people, and a third one is in my grave. I killed another two people last night," I continue. That one, he can't help but wince at. That one, he witnessed. "You don't need this. Leni sure as hell doesn't. She's been through enough."

"So, what? You're going to be the big hero now? Sacrificing yourself for everybody?"

"I didn't say that. Walking into the police station isn't in my plans." Looking down at the mug, I spin it in place on the table. "I'm not turning myself in, so don't worry about that. But they could track me somehow—you know they could."

"Not if you're careful."

"So, what do you think I'm going to do? Stay locked in this apartment day in, day out, for the rest of my life? Because that's the only way I could stay here and not risk getting discovered and traced back to you."

"Last night, you said you live in a pit." Dammit, now he decides he's going to listen to me and remember the shit I say. "Why would you decide to go back there if you don't have to?"

There's no chance for me to tell him to mind his own damn business before Leni's soft footsteps ring out down the hall. It's actually kind of funny, the way he quickly smooths out his expression, like he doesn't want her to see him so stressed. She's not a child—she knows what's going on. He wants to protect her from that. I guess I can relate. There's a lot I would like to protect her from, too.

Starting with myself.

Her gaze darts away as soon as it lands on me, and the color in her cheeks tells me she's either embarrassed or pissed off. Maybe both. Her reaction has an interesting effect on me: on the one hand, I can understand it. If anything, the way she can't let it go and pretend nothing is wrong makes me respect her more. She's not a pushover; she's not weak. I always knew she had strength in her, but now I see it.

On the other hand, I've killed for her. I put myself in danger for her, exposed myself to outsiders who thought I was dead. That was a huge risk—something could've gone wrong. I didn't even stop to think about what it might mean for me. I went after her. I called Colt for her sake, and I took a punch to the jaw for it. I think that earns me at least a little forgiveness.

"Are you guys going back there?" She asks with her back turned while she pours herself coffee, but there's tension in every line of her body. Her shoulders are up close to her ears, her jaw clenched until she practically has to force the words out.

"We have to," I reply while looking at my brother for confirmation. "We can't leave the bodies where they are."

"Do me a favor and don't talk about it in front of me, okay?" Dipping a spoon into the mug, she stirs like the coffee did something to offend her. "The less I know, the better."

"You don't have to worry about that." When Colt gets up and wraps his arms around her from behind, the strangest feeling washes over me. No, it doesn't wash over—it hits me like a truck. There's no way to describe it more gently than that. It's one thing to watch him fuck her when we're taking turns, and my cock is in her mouth. It's another thing to witness this intimacy. Like they're a real couple, which I guess they are from the way he's described it.

What is this feeling? It's not anger. I don't hold it against him.

The uncomfortable pressure in my head only gets worse when she lets her head fall back against his chest. Her eyes close, and a smile touches the corners of her mouth. I would swear I'm about to explode. Heat blazes in me, racing through me like I'm nothing but dry tinder.

It can't be jealousy. I'm not a jealous person. Whatever I want, I can have.

At least, that used to be true. In my old life, with my old face. When I didn't have to hide from the world.

That's not my life anymore. It never will be again. Why does he get to have the life I used to have? And he expects me to want to stay here with them? What, so I can be reminded every day of what's never going to be mine?

I have to force myself to swallow that burning feeling, since there's other shit we have to do. "We better get moving," I announce, finishing my coffee and getting up to leave the mug in the sink. "I'll shower when we get back. We've already hung around too long."

I have to pretend I don't notice the way Leni flinches when I come close. How could she fuck me the way she did, then act this way now? I don't get her. Colt has had seven months to get to know her better. I wonder if I'll ever get the chance to catch up, if she'll even let me try.

Colt waits until we're in the car to murmur, "Give her a little time. She'll loosen up."

"Who said I was worried about that?"

"Did we meet yesterday for the first time? I saw the way you were looking at her upstairs." He won't look at me, and there's nothing in his voice that gives me a hint of what he's thinking.

"She told me not to expect her to forgive me right away," I confess, peering out at the world from under my hood.

"Wow. I wish I knew some advice I could give you on that."

"That's my problem to deal with, not yours. You're not the one who fucked up the way I did."

"Listen. If there's one thing I know about her, it's how forgiving she is. If she wasn't, why would we be together?" he points out. "Give her time. I'm sure she already understands you didn't mean to get her mom involved."

"That's not all she's mad about."

From under my hood, I can just barely make out the way his jaw tightens. "Yeah, well, that's not going to happen again. Right?"

"What about what just happened this morning?"

"Not the same thing, and you know it. There's a difference between letting her participate in something she wants and tying her to the bed when I'm not there."

What he doesn't understand—and I can't find the words to say—is this morning was hot... but tying her up was better. Forcing her, feeling the way her body tried to resist but couldn't help giving in, giving me what I wanted. There's nothing in this world that could match the satisfaction I got from that. And now that I've had it, how am I supposed to live without it?

"I didn't want to say this last night," I mutter as we roll down the street, passing only a few cars this early in the morning. "But a lot of the reason I stayed away was for her sake, too. Because what I did to her that night at the apartment is something I fantasized about the whole time I was away from her. I know that's probably weird for you to hear, but it's true."

He is quiet, gripping the wheel tighter but keeping his thoughts to himself. I wish he wouldn't. He can call me an asshole or threaten to kick me out of his life forever, and it would be better than sitting here wondering what's going through his head.

Finally, he clears his throat when we're a few blocks from the warehouse. "You'll just have to figure out how to get over that. I'm not going to let you hurt her. I love her. And we might have learned a pretty fucked-up version of love when we were growing up, but that shit stops now."

We're both quiet for the rest of the drive, which doesn't take all that long. My car is where I left it, and there are no other cars parked either on the street or in the lot besides Dennis's vehicle. The place looks even worse in the early morning, rays of sun highlighting what darkness hides. There's something depressing about it.

"So what's the plan?" Colt asks, since we never talked about it on the way here.

"Burning them is the first thing that comes to mind," I confess. "But I saw a bunch of stuff next to the building last night, like tarps and shit. We could wrap them up, put them in my trunk, take them down to the river, and dump them. Fire might draw attention."

Scrubbing his hand over his head, he groans. "Now I wish we had just gotten it over with last night."

"But you had to think of Leni, too." I look around to make sure there's no one nearby—no random homeless people or whatever—before getting out and lowering my hood. Colt's trying his best to pretend it doesn't freak him out, seeing me like this, but he sucks at acting. He can't hide his pained expression when he first looks at me. I wonder how long it will be before he gets used to it and if I'll be around long enough for that to happen, since I still don't think it would be a good idea for me to stay.

As it turns out, there's a bigger problem to deal with, and we find out what it is once we enter the old warehouse we left just hours ago.

"What the hell?" Colt says, walking more slowly, taking one careful step after another as he looks around in confusion, while I stare at the place where I watched Deborah bleed to death.

There's still a dark stain on the floor where her blood poured out onto the concrete. The memory is clear—the way her life force bubbled out of her mouth when she took her final breaths.

But she's not there. Neither is Dennis. The car they used is still outside, but they're both gone.

Somebody has been here.

And they know what I did.

19. COLT

"Hey! How was your weekend?"

I have to consciously put on a happy face for one of the guys from my calculus class as we pass on the quad on Monday morning. "You know, nothing big. Kept it quiet. You?"

I shouldn't have bothered asking since Leni's anxious, choked noise next to me steals my focus. She's remembering Friday night. How things were the opposite of quiet.

After telling him I'll see him later, we keep moving, hand in hand, down the wide path. It's a gorgeous day, with the sun's rays dancing through the tree branches and painting shadows on the ground. Who am I turning into, noticing things like that?

"Are you honestly in such a good mood, or are you pretending?" Leni's tight whisper reminds me not everybody shares my opinion about the way life is right now.

Looking down at her is like looking at a ghost. The makeup she put on today isn't enough to cover the dark circles under her eyes—eyes that are wide and full of fear as they shift back and forth while we walk.

"I know it's easy for me to say," I murmur through a smile, "but you really need to calm down. Everything is fine."

"How can you say that?" she whispers, gripping my hand tighter. Her palm is damp with sweat. "How can anything be fine?"

It was probably a bad idea to bring her to school today. It's not like she couldn't make up any missed work, and I wouldn't be leaving her alone. Nix is there at the apartment, keeping an eye on the news in case there's any mention of a pair of dead bodies or missing people who happen to be named Deborah and Dennis.

Because there hasn't been anything about them anywhere. Considering Leni spent all of Saturday and Sunday scouring the internet like she's Sherlock Holmes trying to solve the case but found nothing, I think we're in the clear. I don't know what happened to the bodies—and I'm not going to pretend it didn't freak me the fuck out to get there and find them gone—but there is nothing connecting us to them.

"What if I left evidence in the back of that car?" she asks now, and her chin trembles.

Obviously, I need to pull her aside, so I stop before we get to the library and sit on a bench under a massive oak tree whose branches give us a little shade and privacy. "I already told you. That's why we broke the window on the driver's side—so if anybody wanted to use the car for shelter, they could. By now, there's plenty of DNA all over the inside of that car, I bet."

"Do you think that's enough, though? If anything happened to you…" Her face crumples before she stares at the ground. "What would I have? I can't lose you. I've already lost everything else. I can't lose you, too."

Fuck. "I didn't think about it that way. I shouldn't have brushed off your worries. But I'm telling you, everything's going to be fine."

I'm not worried, but that doesn't mean we can be careless. I want to show our faces around here, to keep things normal, just in case rumors do start going around about those two assholes going missing.

I don't think it's wrong to think of them as assholes now that they're dead—I never did get that whole don't-talk-ill-of-the-dead thing. Especially for people who went out of their way to make others miserable when they were alive. Like my dad. He fits that description, too.

So even though I know Leni won't pay any attention in class, and I'm going to spend all my time wondering and worrying about her, we go through the motions like any other Monday. I keep my eyes and ears open for anybody talking about Deborah and Dennis disappearing, but it never happens. There hasn't been enough time for rumors to blow up. Right now, they could be on a long weekend somewhere together.

Only we—and whoever moved the bodies—know the truth.

I don't want to think about that now. There are too many good things in my life to focus on the shit. I'm looking forward to taking Nix to see Mom when she's feeling a little stronger—his face is a lot to get used to. I'm still working on it, and I didn't spend years in a coma.

No matter how determined I am to focus on the good things, I'm still tired and a little irritable by the time we approach the apartment door. Spending the day trying to be normal was more draining than I would've imagined.

Leni is feeling the same way. "This was one of the longest days of my life. Which is saying something."

"But like I told you, everything was fine." It's going to take a little time, but eventually, she has to figure out that we are in the clear. There is not a damn thing to worry about.

Not until we get inside the apartment, at least.

"Thank fuck. I've been going out of my mind."

Nix turns on his heel and walks the length of the living room in long, quick strides. "I can't fucking stand this. I can't stay here. This is a mistake."

Leni makes a move like she wants to go to him—I don't know if it's reflex, like she feels sorry and wants to do something, or if she actually thinks she'll make a difference. It doesn't matter. I have to put an arm out across her chest to keep her still. She looks up at me, eyes filled with confusion.

"Don't," I mutter, teeth clenched.

I don't think he'd hurt her, not physically. But if he pushed her away, which he probably would, he'd hurt her more deeply than a bruise.

How do I know? Because I have felt that way. There aren't many things either of us has felt that the other hasn't also experienced.

"Don't tell me there haven't been times you've had to stay indoors," I remind him. "At least during the day."

"That was different. And if I wanted to, I could still go out. I didn't have to sit around here, waiting to see something on the news."

He couldn't have picked a worse thing to say.

"Did you?" Leni asks him. I'm surprised she doesn't jump on him—she's so desperate to know.

"No. I would've told you already if I did."

He looks at me, and my face must give an idea of how much I want to smack the shit out of him for talking to her like that.

"No, I didn't hear anything."

"We need to take a breath. All of us."

That's easy for me to say. The longer I spend with this energy in the air, the more tense I feel. There's only one thing that ever really clears my head when something like this is happening—when I feel the darkness pulling me under and almost wish it would, because the brush of it is so damn sweet.

When inspiration strikes, I lean down to whisper in Leni's ear. "Would you do something for me? It'll be fun."

She pulls her head back, looking up at me with even more confusion than before.

"Like what?"

"Just trust me. Do you trust me?"

"Yes."

It's the way she says it without hesitating that reminds me why I love her like I do.

Turning to Nix, I ask, "It's not the same as going out and having freedom, but we could enjoy ourselves here too."

When I take her hand, he tips his head to the side. "What do you have in mind?"

He's wary, but at least he doesn't sound like he wants to punch something anymore.

"Come with us."

My cock is already twitching by the time I make it to the bedroom, with Leni following close behind me. If we do this right, all three of us will feel a lot better by the time the night is over.

By the time I pull the blindfold from the nightstand, Nix has joined us, arms folded over his chest. His eyes widen when he sees what I'm holding. A slow smile starts to form.

"We're going to play a game," I explain, one eye on Leni to catch her reaction. "How about we blindfold you, Leni, and you get to guess who's doing what to you?"

Her cheeks go dark, but there's a different truth in her eyes. She might be shocked at first, but the idea does something to her. Probably the same thing it does to me.

And to my brother, who growls softly in the back of his throat. "Yeah. I like that idea. But what happens if she gets it wrong?" he asks, playful and sinister at the same time.

Leni questions me silently, her brows lifted. "She gets punished," I decide.

"Do I get to know what that will be?" she asks.

"What do you think? Now take off your clothes." Nix and I do the same until the three of us are standing naked by the bed. It's not so much the sight of her—which is always exciting—but the anticipation of what's going to happen next that makes my cock harden until it's twitching by the time Leni turns around so I can tie the blindfold over her eyes. Nix watches closely, wearing a half smile. He's hard, too, and takes a few strokes of his cock while Leni gets on all fours on the bed at my instruction.

There is something so beautiful about her now. Not only her body: her ass up in the air, her lean legs spread a little like she wants to show off her pretty pussy, her tits swaying gently as she settles into place, but the way she does exactly as I say without asking questions. She's mine.

I hold a finger in my lips to signal Nix to stay quiet before walking around to the foot of the bed, where he stands next to me. "You have to guess which one of us is doing whatever it is we're doing. We're not going to talk, so you won't have any way of knowing until you feel it."

"Okay." There's soft laughter in her voice. Anticipation. I motion for Nix to join me on the side of the bed facing her, then take her by the back of the head with one hand while I motion for Nix to drag his cock over her mouth. I want to see if we can confuse her.

With my fingers massaging her scalp, he works his head beyond her lips and sinks his teeth into his own to hold back his reaction. Right. I didn't think about that, having to be quiet so she doesn't have a clue. If anything, it adds to the game.

She lets him fall from her mouth. "I'm not sure." Nix surges forward, cutting her off, and she gags before turning her head. "Nix! That's Nix."

"Too easy," I mutter, giving him a shove.

"No fair." She giggles. "Don't try to trick me."

Without a word, I walk to the other side of the bed, then waste no time shoving two digits inside her glistening pussy. With a startled cry, she rocks forward from the force. "Oh... oh, that's good..."

It is good, especially when she pushes back against me and envelops my fingers in her wet heat. I pound her hard until my knuckles slam against her taint, and she lets out a high-pitched howl. "Nix!"

"No such luck," he murmurs from in front of her. She lets out a disappointed sound.

My fingers are glistening with her juices when I withdraw them. "Wrong guess." I sigh before slapping her ass hard enough to rock her forward again. This time, she cries out in surprise and pain. "Maybe you'll get it right next time," I tell her while a red mark in the shape of my hand appears on her fair skin.

I then motion for Nix to join me before flipping her over onto her back. She parts her legs eagerly when I start to spread them, then blow across her bald lips until she squirms. But it's Nix who gets on his knees in front of her and plunges in, holding her thighs wide open so he can flick his tongue over the tip of her clit.

"That's Nix," she moans.

Obviously, we're making this too easy. I pull him away, then take her hand and wrap it around my shaft. "Oh, I don't know," she whispers. "I don't know if I can tell the difference."

Nix pulls her up until she's sitting, then uses her other hand on his cock. "What are you going to do to me if I get this wrong?" she asks, stroking us both. I take a handful of her hair in response and yank her head back before wrapping my hand around her throat, tightening until she groans. Precum oozes from my tip and coats me, and I bite back a groan when she starts moving faster.

My hand tightens further, and she gasps, then whispers, "Nix?"

I don't say a word. I settle for giving her a sharp slap against her cheek that makes her head snap partway around before she sucks a pained breath through her teeth.

Still, she takes it without complaining. It shouldn't make me want to do worse to her. I shouldn't want to break her down.

"This is Colt," she murmurs, giving me a slight squeeze before stroking again. "This is Nix," she adds, working him faster. He closes his eyes, his head falling back, and I know the feeling. It's one thing to have her alone, but there's something special about being together.

I push her onto her back with her feet on the floor for Nix to crawl over her, then trace slow circles around her nipple with his tongue. "Oh, god," she moans, spreading her thighs wider so I can watch her pink flesh pulse. "Oh, that's good. That feels so nice."

If I didn't know better, I would think she's dragging it out, refusing to guess because she doesn't want it to end.

"That has to be Colt," she decides before purring like a kitten.

Nix lifts his head, chuckling. "You got it wrong."

He pulls back his hand, and I know what's going to happen before he brings it across her face hard enough that the sound rings out like the crack of a starter pistol.

But it's Leni's high-pitched cry that makes the hair on the back of my neck stand up. That sound. It's like music. A symphony I could never get tired of hearing.

Nix's satisfied grunt tells me he's thinking the same thing.

And that our fun has just begun.

20. LENI

THAT HURT. THAT HURT A LOT.

"Ow," I mumble while my face throbs. Neither of them says anything—I know it must have been Nix who did it, and that doesn't surprise me. But Colt didn't respond. He should've told Nix to take it easy. Why didn't he?

"Let's put that mouth to good use instead." That's Nix again, still hovering over me on the bed. He gets up on his knees—I feel the way his thighs cage me in. He guides himself to my mouth, his precum coating my lips before I part them so he can shove himself inside. When it's awkward for me, he cups the back of my head and holds it in place, thrusting deeper.

"That's right. Give it to her." Colt is standing by my feet. All at once, something invades me. A finger, two fingers. "Fuck her face. She won't get it wrong next time."

This doesn't feel like a game anymore, though. It feels like the opposite. The energy in the air has changed. There's no playfulness.

If anything, Colt sounds almost angry.

"She takes it so nice," Nix grunts like it's a compliment. "Like she needs to swallow my cum. Is that what you want? Is that what you're hungry for?" His heavy breathing matches the pace he sets with his hips, hitting the back of my throat while I groan in discomfort. He has to stop soon, right?

"That's right. Give it to her. Give her what she wants," Colt grunts, pounding me with his fingers, tightening my core, making my pussy throb.

Give it to her... give me a show...

No. I'm not going to think about that. I will not remember it. I have to focus on the present, not the past. I want to concentrate on what my body's feeling. No matter how confused I am, I feel good. In the end, I like it. I want more.

"Get up," Colt tells him. *Thank God.* Nix slips free so I can breathe, and when I do, I gag a little, choking, gasping for air.

Only he's not thinking about taking pity on me, being merciful. Colt rolls me onto my stomach, lifting my hips into the air so he can line his head up with my entrance and push forward, filling me in one deep, brutal stroke that reminds me of the way things used to be. When I was just a thing, an item for their enjoyment. He hasn't been that way for so long. He was trying so hard.

I can't do this. I can't go through this again.

"Push yourself up," Nix grunts, holding a handful of my hair and pulling my head up until I have no choice but to push myself up on my hands so he can fill my mouth again.

"That's good," he groans, sinking deep. "How does that feel? Filled at both ends."

"I think there's another hole we're not using yet." I barely realize what Colt is saying before there's pressure against my asshole. His spit hits it, dribbles down my crack and mixes with my juices as he slams himself into me again, again, while pressing against my tight knot with his thumb.

"That's right." Nix laughs, gripping my hair tighter, making my scalp sing in pain. "Got her nice and relaxed for me. I wanna feel her gripping me tight. Maybe you can take her from underneath," he suggests.

To my horror, Colt laughs.

They have to stop this. I have to stop it. I don't know if I can. My groans around Nix's dick only make them laugh. Like they're feeding off each other, like they're giving each other permission to be their worst selves, the versions of themselves that find it so easy to use, to hurt, to control.

"That's not enough." Colt slides out of me, and I'm relieved before I realize he's only using my juices to lube his thumb before pressing against my asshole again, this time breaching the tight ring of muscle.

Hot, blazing sensation races through me in all directions, starting at that entry point. There's an uncomfortably full sensation that only gets worse when he slides his dick inside my pussy again. Even now, there's pleasure in it. I feel good.

At least my body feels good. It's the rest of me that's a problem.

"Take that ass," Nix grunts. He matches his pace with the pace Colt sets with his thumb and his dick. "That's right. There's our little slut. Taking us so well. So good."

Take it... Take them both... No, this isn't James, James isn't here. He's dead now. He can't hurt me anymore.

But his sons can.

"I want to switch." I almost sob with relief when Nix pulls back, and I fall onto my elbows, gasping for breath.

"Don't get comfortable," Colt warns. I hear him rounding the bed. His dark laughter sets panic flaring in me.

"I don't think I can do this," I whisper, barely choking back a sob. It's like he doesn't even hear me—or he doesn't care. He only pulls me up the way Nix did, takes me by the back of my head, running his head over my mouth. With a soft sob, I take him inside, bracing myself when I feel Nix behind me.

But instead of taking Colt's place inside my pussy, it's my ass he presses against. "Still so tight." He sighs, fingers digging into my ass cheeks, spreading them apart. "Need to loosen you up more."

No. No, I don't want this. I try to shake my head, try to grunt my refusal, but Colt only pushes forward, rocking me backward against his brother's fingers as he begins to probe my ass deeper than Colt did. Blinding hot sensation makes me moan in a mix of pleasure and pain. Their laughter drowns it out.

"I think she wants another finger," Colt tells him, burying himself deep, my nose pressed against his base. *I can't breathe.* Panic takes the place of pleasure, my heart pounding sickeningly, bile rising in my throat.

Give me a good show... Be a good girl and suck those cocks, and maybe I won't have to fuck your face...

No! I'm not in the basement. I'm in my bedroom, my apartment, I'm not back there, the house burned down, James is dead, *I'm not there!*

"Work her slow," he tells Nix, but it isn't Colt, it's James, it's James telling them what to do to me. The pressure from Nix's fingers is unbearable by the time Colt buries himself again against the back of my throat. "That's right. You take me so well," he moans.

It might as well be James saying it, James sounding so happy and satisfied.

I can't make it stop. I need to make it stop, but I can't. The bile rises again, but this time there's a scream coming with it, a scream I can't hold back. I let it loose, even though most of the sound is lost.

"Jesus, fuck!" Colt pulls out all at once, and I suck in a lung full of air before screaming again in the darkness behind the blindfold.

"Leni!" Nix shouts. His hands touch my hips, and I kick out blindly, screaming again.

"Don't touch me!" I rip the blindfold off, tearing some hair from my scalp when I do, but though I hear the sound, I don't feel a thing. "Leave me alone! Stop, stop!"

"Leni! We're stopping!" When Colt reaches for me, I swing my arm, making him jump back. "Fuck! You're all right!"

All right? I would laugh if I could stop crying, but I can't. I can't hold back the sobs and the screams. No words. Just sounds, all the pain, all the rage, all the helplessness, it all pours out of me because I can't, I can't do this, I can't go back to the basement.

"You're safe!" Nix shouts. "You're okay, everything's okay!"

Nothing is okay. "Just don't touch me," I warn, crawling up the bed until I'm huddled against the headboard, my body aching, my ass throbbing, my throat raw. "Don't... touch... me..."

Colt holds his hands up like he's surrendering. "Nobody is going to touch you. Nobody is going to hurt you."

It's too late. It's way too late for that. "I won't let you," I whisper, shaking my head, my arms wrapped around my knees.

"Just tell us what to do." Nix stands at the foot of the bed. I hate the sight of him now. He wants to hurt me. He likes it.

I think they both do. Because he told them too.

"Just leave me alone!" I wail. My body heaves with sobs while I cover my face with my hands. I can't look at them. I can't let them look at me. "Leave me alone, God, please. Don't talk to me!"

"But... but, Leni—"

I feel Colt getting closer, so I drop my hands and scramble away before he can reach me. I can't stand the thought of him touching me. He's too much like James—they both are. I thought it was all over. "No! No, don't!"

"Leave her alone," Nix tells him, pulling him back. "We'll get dressed, and we'll leave," he tells me. "You're safe. We'll go."

"Please," I beg, escaping under the comforter and pulling it up to my neck.

"You just rest," Colt murmurs. I don't say a word. I can't. All I can do is tuck myself into a ball and cover my face again. I can't look at him. Not now, not after what he just did.

Not when the past is so fresh in my memory. I can almost smell the basement. I can hear James's voice. I can feel the couch and the floor, just as fresh as if I came up from there a minute ago.

And the shame. And the pain. I feel them, too. I feel them so hard that when exhaustion gets a hold of me; I go with it, letting myself sink into oblivion because consciousness is just too much to take.

21. NIX

It's like walking on eggshells until Leni falls asleep, curled up in the middle of the bed. Even now, she doesn't seem peaceful—frowning, clenching her fists, and tucking them under her chin like she needs to defend herself even in her sleep. Like she's afraid monsters will haunt her. Monsters with our faces, maybe.

We went too far. That's clear. We lost control, pushed her too far and she paid the price for it.

Colt seems satisfied to leave her alone now that she's settled in, and I follow him out of the bedroom, leaving the door open a crack just in case she needs something.

"You hungry?" he asks, detouring into the kitchen. Right—we did sort of skip dinner. My stomach growls at the idea of food.

"Yeah, I could eat," I reply, sitting down at the counter and watching him go through the freezer. He pulls out a pair of frozen containers of macaroni and cheese, and I know what's coming as he slaps them onto the spinning glass plate in the microwave. His body language isn't just speaking for him. It's screaming.

He turns around, arms folded, and leans against the stove while staring at the gleaming wood floor. It's not like I didn't know he'd be concerned after what we just witnessed, but there's something about the way his jaw ticks that tells me it goes beyond concern. I can almost hear his teeth grinding.

"She'll be okay," I offer. I mean, what else can I say? And I know it's the truth—I'm not making shit up to help him feel better or anything like that. She will be okay. It might take a little time, but time heals everything... or so they say.

Though it won't heal my face. But that's something I need to get over. I touch a hand to my cheek without thinking, remembering when the skin was smooth. It's amazing how much we take for granted every day. I'm a philosopher, all of a sudden.

"Will she? Because I don't know." He glances at me briefly before looking back at the floor. "Sometimes I wonder if we didn't break her for good."

"She's strong. And we're here to help her."

I already know it was the wrong thing to say before he snorts. "Oh, yeah. We really helped her back there. You could tell by the way she was screaming. She's processing things in a healthy way."

"Okay, we didn't know it was going to set her off like that."

"That's the thing." He takes a slow, shaky breath. "I should have known."

"What, are you a mind reader now? You're being too hard on yourself."

"You don't get it." He shakes his head, looking angry. "You haven't been here all this time. We spent these months getting to know each other better, learning to live together, building something. Or I thought we were, anyway."

I don't know anything about that. I don't know how he feels. I don't know what it's like to build a relationship, to learn to trust each other—all that happy horseshit. "I know from all the things you emailed me that you've been trying really hard to learn how to give her what she needs. That's worth something. Don't forget how hard you've tried."

"It's not enough. Obviously. I don't know if it ever will be."

I'm starting to understand what he's hinting at. "What are you saying? Do you want to break up with her?"

When he lifts a shoulder and looks away from me, something snaps in my head. It shouldn't, but it does, and it takes patience I didn't know I had to keep from climbing over the counter and shaking him until his neck snaps. "You fucking coward."

"Very nice." Smirking, he gives me a thumbs up. "Way to make me feel better."

"You're not the one who has to feel better right now. She is. This is supposed to be about her, right? But all you can do is stand there and feel sorry for yourself."

"I really don't need a lecture from you."

"Did I ask? No, just hear me out," I mutter when his mouth opens like he's ready to argue. "You can tell yourself all you want that you're trying to do the right thing by her, but we didn't meet yesterday. You're scared. You don't think you have what it takes to make her happy, to make her feel safe and secure and all that. So you figure you should leave her alone, like that's the best way to help her."

"You're wrong." His eyes narrow, and a flush creeps up his neck as he lifts his lip in a snarl. "What the fuck would you know about it? You sail in here after hiding for months, and now you have all the answers? You give me shit about running away when that's all you keep talking about. Running away."

"It's not the same thing, so don't even try it."

"Oh, please. It's exactly the same thing." If he raises his voice any louder, she'll wake up.

I hold a finger in front of my mouth. "You know I had my own reasons for staying away."

"Yeah. You ran away because you were scared, just like you're accusing me of being."

You'd think he would be more careful around somebody he watched commit murder a few days ago. "There's a big difference between you being a pussy who's afraid to try to help your girlfriend and staying away so you don't attract attention and pull people you care about into your bullshit. Totally different."

"I'm no good for her!" How can a whisper sound like a scream? It does, and I hear the agony in it, just like I see it on his face. I think I'm finally starting to understand. This is someplace neither of us has ever been before. Like landing on an alien planet without the first clue how to survive.

"Why is she still with you?" I ask. "Don't you think she knows who's good for her and who isn't?"

"Right now? No, I don't think she knows," he admits. His hands flex—a sort of desperate gesture. "Because something happened in there that I don't know what to think about."

When he keeps me waiting, I have to ask, "Are you going to tell me what it was, or do I have to guess? There's still another five minutes on the food, so I guess we have time."

"You think this is a joke? Do you really?" I can't remember the last time he looked at me with so much disgust. Maybe he never has before—not even after he watched me kill two people in that warehouse. "I'm trying to tell you something I don't know how to say, and all you can do is bust my balls?"

"Okay." Folding my hands, I nod. "What is it? What do you want to say?"

"I liked it." With his head hung and his eyes on the floor, he mutters, "I liked watching you hit her the way you did. When everything changed, you know? I liked it too much."

"I hear you. If I didn't like it, I wouldn't have done it."

"And you don't think that's wrong?" When he lifts his gaze, the agony in his eyes knocks the breath out of my lungs. He really means it, and now I'm wondering if I should feel the way he does. Is there something wrong with me that I don't?

But it's not like I ever have. I can't pretend. "Do you want to know why I stayed away as long as I did? That's one of the reasons, and I'm not just saying it now to defend myself. I like it too much when I'm using her. When I'm hurting her. That's why I came here and tied her up that night—I waited for days to get the chance to be alone up here with her. Because more than anything, I craved the feeling I used to get when we were using her and dominating her."

Now I can't look at him. Instead, I stare down at my folded hands, clenched on the countertop. "It's like being an addict. It's always there, no matter what I'm doing, no matter what's happening around me. I want to have her under my control again. I never feel as alive as I do when she's at my mercy. I don't know if it's something I was born with or something I was taught, but I can't get it out of my head."

Glancing up at him, I add, "Which is a big reason why I stayed away all this time. Believe me, don't believe me, it doesn't matter. It's the truth. Staying away from her was the only way I could think to protect her from me. Because look what happens when I'm with her."

I point down the hall, grinding my teeth when I remember the way she shrieked and sobbed. "That's all I can give her. And you want me to stay? Really, think about it. You love her? Then you should keep me away from her."

I'm almost surprised when he goes quiet, like he's thinking about it. I would expect him to talk over me, to tell me how I'm feeling instead of listening and trying to understand. Being understanding isn't exactly something either of us has a lot of practiced with.

"I feel that way too sometimes. I've told you that. In my emails?" Yes, he did, and I nod slowly. "I ask myself how I'm supposed to learn how to be good to her when our whole past was made up of how much we could hurt her. And I've doubted myself so many times, today included—maybe most of all," he adds, frowning and clenching his fists again. For a second, I'm sure he's going to hit something, but he swallows back the urge. "Because I love her. I should be trying to protect her from anything that would make her fall apart the way she did. But there I was, almost ready to blow my load when things got serious."

Am I an asshole for feeling better about myself now that he said that? "What are you going to do about it? Do you think we could learn to be different?"

He doesn't hesitate for a second. "Fuck, yeah, I do. I'm not some powerless loser, and neither are you. Unless that's who you want to be."

"You know I don't."

He squares his shoulders and tightens his jaw. I know that look. He's making up his mind about something. "Okay. So what do you do? You take control of yourself. Both of us. That's all we can do. It'll be one day at a time, but we can both handle it, because otherwise, the only answer is leaving her, and I won't do that. I'm not living without her."

I know he means it, just like I know he's right about taking control. I don't know where to start. That's the problem. One of many problems.

"Don't forget, she was already stressed out about those bodies going missing." He rubs his jaw, groaning. "I mean, no wonder she freaked out. She has so much on her mind, and I can't convince her to relax."

"Yeah, I guess we didn't help things. You know her better than I do now. What should we do?"

"We have to be gentle with her." I don't mean to frown when he says it, but at least he chuckles. "I know. I'm not good at being gentle, either. But it's what she needs."

"But what about later, in the future? She's seeing a therapist, right?"

"Yeah, that's where she was leaving when those assholes took her." The growl in his voice is nothing compared to the heat that explodes in my chest when I remember watching from across the street, feeling helpless and useless. "But there's gotta be stuff we can do for her here, at home. Just so she'll feel more secure."

I have to say it. "You really do love her, don't you?"

"What, did you think I was lying?"

"No, I'm just saying you're obviously out for whatever is best for her. That's good to see."

"What about you?"

The microwave couldn't beep at a better time. Talk about a loaded question. Where do I even start trying to answer? I have to search my feelings, not something I usually like to do. But I know him—if I try to shrug off the question, he'll only double down until I have to answer him or kill him.

"I care about her," I decide by the time he slides a plastic container of steaming mac and cheese in front of me. At least stirring it around to cool it off gives me something to do while I try not to choke on my words. "I mean, obviously. Why else would I stay away to protect her if I didn't care?"

"Then you'll help me try to get her through this?"

Shit. Dropping the fork, I hit him with a stare that makes him snicker. "So that's how it is? You're going to use her to get me to stay? When I just got done telling you, she's a big part of the reason I was hiding?"

"You can handle it. You're Nix fucking Alistair. And look what you already did. You escaped the fire, you snuck out of the hospital before anybody could figure out who you were, you found a way to make yourself untraceable. So what, you can't learn how to be a better person? I don't believe that."

But all he did was take me back to the question—the fear—at the center of everything. "What if there's no way to control this? Would you ask a cancer patient to control their tumor with like, positive thinking?"

"I think you're taking it too far."

"I don't think I am." Since I can't stab him, I stab some of the noodles with my fork, not that it helps. "Look at where we came from. He was obviously seriously fucked in the head. What if there's no way to change? What if this is who we are, and that's it?"

"What if it's not? What if we can decide who we are? Besides," he continues before I can say a word, "we didn't only come from Dad, did we? There was somebody else. We came from Mom, too, and she's a good person."

It's funny. I want to be annoyed with him for being right, but I can't when his words actually make me feel a little better. "I didn't think about it that way."

"I didn't think you would. That's why I'm here to do the thinking for you."

That, I would always expect from him. "Okay, since you

have all the answers, what comes next? Where do we go from here?"

"Keep going like everything's normal," he decides, eating slowly, thoughtfully. "Give her space, be gentle with her."

"Me, gentle?" I know we've been talking about learning how to be different, but that seems like a lot to ask.

"You'll get the hang of it." He smirks. "I'm here if you need help getting your shit together. Sort of like one of those sponsors in AA. You're feeling weak, come to me."

I'm about to laugh at him when he pulls out the big guns. "And if that doesn't work, just ask yourself what Mom would think."

Well, shit. "Better than a cold shower, I bet," I murmur.

"I bet it is." Sounds like he's joking, but there's intensity in his eyes, boring holes through me. "You can do it. We both can."

I know he's right... even if it doesn't quite feel that way. Even if I doubt myself.

22. COLT

Here goes nothing.

After tapping on the bedroom door with my foot, I swing it open, smiling like I didn't watch the girl I love break down sobbing last night. "Good morning."

"What is this?" Leni sits up in bed, blinking hard and covering her mouth with one hand before she yawns. "God, what time is it?" she asks, rubbing her eyes.

"Past nine," I tell her, setting a tray of food on her lap once she's settled in against the pillows behind her.

"How are you feeling?" I ask carefully.

"Okay," she answers after a moment. "I'm sorry about last night."

"Please don't do this, don't blame yourself for our fuck up. We're the assholes who went too far. You have nothing to be sorry about."

"We took things too far. We should be more aware of what triggers you," Nix chimes in. "We're sorry."

Leni nods, but doesn't say anything else for a while. Nix and I simply stand in front of the bed, waiting for her directions.

When she finally speaks again, her voice still sounds tired. "I don't want to talk about this right now. I want to forget it and move on."

"Okay," I agree with her, though I know this is not healthy. She should talk about it, if not with us, then with someone else. She needs to heal, and I need to figure out a way to help her without making it worse.

She runs her hands through her hair, then yawns again. "I shouldn't be tired after sleeping as much as I did. I can't believe it's already after nine. I should be getting ready for class." Though she looks pretty interested in the food Nix and I made for her. "This smells amazing."

"I was thinking maybe we could skip class today." Glancing at Nix, standing in the doorway, I take a seat on the edge of the bed. "Let's just hang out today. What do you think? We can do whatever you want."

"Really?" I can tell she's interested by the way her eyes light up. "You think that's safe? I thought we were supposed to pretend everything's normal."

"What's not normal about skipping class?" Nix asks, chuckling. "I probably skipped more classes than I attended." She smirks and shakes her head at him before picking up the utensils and cutting into the French toast.

I have my own opinions about whether it's a good idea for her to go out and pretend to be normal today. After what happened last night, it's probably safer to keep her here, at home. Who knows what could set her off? She'd hate it if she knew I was thinking about her like this—like she's fragile, like she needs to be sheltered—but she's too unstable right now, and I don't want her breaking down again in public.

"I could use a personal day," she decides before sinking her teeth into a thick piece of bread. Her eyes slowly close and her face goes slack. "Oh, my god," she groans.

"I hope that's a good sign?" I ask.

"It's orgasmic."

I don't think I've ever heard anybody say something like that without laughing, but she means it, cutting another bite and practically jamming it into her mouth this time. Syrup drips on her chin—it's amazing how even something as simple as that can make me hungry for something other than food. If I want to be careful with her, that means taking it easy with the physical stuff until she's feeling better. So instead of leaning over to lick it off her skin, I hand her a napkin and point to the drip.

"So, what do you want to do on your personal day?" Nix asks.

With a shrug, she mumbles, "I don't know. Maybe watch movies? Could we order food?"

"You're still eating, and you want to order food?"

"You know what I'm saying," she says, and I almost can't believe how good it feels when she rolls her eyes. Like she's already feeling more like herself. I spent all night on one sofa while Nix camped out on the other, staring at the ceiling and wondering what we could do to make up for what happened yesterday. It looks like this is a good start.

"Yeah, we can order food later on. Whatever you want. You don't even have to get dressed," I offer. "You can bring the blankets and pillows and kind of camp out on the couch all day."

"Yeah, I would like that."

And then she smiles, and it's almost unfair. How am I supposed to remember to breathe when she looks happy for the first time in days? That's all I want. How could it be that simple? All my life, I assumed what other people called love was just made-up shit for movies, to sell candy and diamond rings on Valentine's Day. If anybody told me happiness could come from something as simple as loving somebody and seeing them smile, I would've laughed my ass off at them.

But here I am, almost hanging on her every word and action like my whole life depends on it. In a way, that's how it feels. That's who she's turned me into. I don't hate it, even if I don't know what to do with the feeling.

When she's finished eating, she looks down at herself and wrinkles her nose. "I need a shower." Her smile slips, and pain touches the corners of her eyes. Maybe she thinks I don't notice, but it's too obvious—and when I shoot a quick look at Nix, it's clear he sees it, too. She's remembering yesterday.

"Yeah, do that," I tell her. Am I being over the top? Trying too hard? I honestly don't know. "Or take a bath, even. Light a candle, act like you're at the spa. We can get the living room set up for you."

The sight of tears in her eyes is like a kick in the chest. So much for that idea. The whole point was to keep her from crying today.

But there's a smile, too, even if it's shaky. "Thank you. Both of you. This is just what I needed." She actually seems excited when she gets out of bed and heads for the bathroom.

Once the water is running, Nix leans against the wall and lets out a sigh. "That was a close one. I thought we lost her there."

"I know. But she's strong." That doesn't mean we can't be careful with her, though, since there's still that fragility underneath. I would kill to protect this woman. I would stop at nothing for her happiness. All I want or need is for her to believe that... and maybe forget the past, though I know that's not easy. It might be asking for too much.

By late afternoon, the three of us are sacked out, and nobody really needs to say anything. It's enough to be here, hanging out, pretending the rest of the world has gone away for a while. Leni watches TV with her head on my shoulder, twirling a strand of hair around her finger. How can something so simple fill me with so much relief? Knowing she feels like she can be normal around us after the way we broke her down—it's like a gift I don't deserve. I don't deserve her at all.

Between episodes of the baking show she chose, I pause the TV and get up, stretching after sitting in the same spot for so long. "I think we have some popcorn. Anybody want some?"

"Oh, definitely." She gives me a grateful smile, drawing her legs up under the blanket before pulling her phone from the pocket of her hoodie. "I should check in with Piper. She's probably wondering where I am."

"Try not to burn it," Nix adds, lying on his back with his ankles crossed over the arm of the sofa. I've seen him like that so many times—there's something so familiar about all of this, and it's almost enough to make me wonder if I needed this as much as Leni did.

"Why don't you come in here and pop it yourself if you don't think I can handle it?" I ask him. "Maybe get off your ass and help out a little bit."

"Boys, boys." Leni clicks her tongue and shakes her head with a giggle. "You better be careful, or I'll have to separate you."

I can see us doing this for a long time. It's a surprising thought. Planning on forever with Leni is one thing, but bringing Nix into it? When I search myself, waiting for the microwave, it feels right.

I just don't have the first fucking clue how we would make it work. I don't share—passing her back and forth in bed is one thing, but in real life? I don't know how I could handle that. But I see the way he looks at her. He wants her.

Maybe as more than somebody to control and humiliate.

"Oh, my god!" I spin around in time to see Leni drop her phone and cover her face with her hands. "Why? Why are they doing this?"

Nix is next to her in a heartbeat, putting an arm around her shoulders. "What is it?" Meanwhile, I pick up her phone to look at whatever freaked her out.

You're going to die, bitch. Count the minutes before it's all over.

"What the fuck?" I hold it out for Nix to read and watch rage settle over his features.

"But they're dead!" Leni sobs behind her hands, rocking back and forth. "How? How are they doing this?"

"They're just assholes behind a keyboard," Nix murmurs, though the look he gives me from over the top of her head isn't nearly as comforting as he's trying to be. "Nobody's going to hurt you."

"I don't understand! What did I ever do?" When I sit on her other side, she looks at me through tear-filled eyes.

Her face is flushed, her cheeks shining from what's already flowed down them. "Why are they doing this? I thought it was Deborah. Was I wrong?"

I wish I knew. I thought this part was over, too. I thought for sure she wouldn't have to deal with this anymore.

"Maybe they had other people helping them," Nix suggests. "I mean, whoever they are needs to get a fucking life, but that could be it."

"I bet he's right." I use my thumbs to wipe her cheeks, but fresh tears keep coming. "They're pathetic pieces of shit with nothing better to do than hurt a good person like you." And I would pay for the opportunity to have them in front of me here and now so they could learn what happens to people who can't leave well enough alone. I won't say that to her—she's upset enough—but the desire burns inside me.

Looking at my brother, I don't have to guess what's going through his head. His jaw ticks, and his eyes narrow. It's amazing there isn't smoke coming out of his ears. "Who do I have to kill this time?"

"Don't say that." Her voice shakes when she turns to him, but there's a flat firmness to it, too. "Please, don't ever say that. I know you feel that way, but it's too risky. I don't want you doing it because of me."

She doesn't get it. I don't expect her to. There is never going to come a time when either of us will be able to stand back and watch her hurt without doing something about it. It's just not possible. That's not how we're built.

"Nix is right." The arm I put on her trembling body doesn't seem to help too much, but her breathing does slow down from the way it was before, when it sounded like she might hyperventilate. "They're assholes behind a keyboard. Cowards. Block and move on. Hell, I'll do it for you."

She shakes her head and takes her phone before releasing a deep breath. "No. I'll do it. You're right—they're nothing." I wish I knew for sure she meant it, that she's not saying it just to convince us she's feeling better.

Something tells me microwave popcorn is not going to pull her out of this. There has to be something else we can do to pick up her spirits. "What else would you like to do tonight?" I ask while shooting Nix a look that's close to panic. There has to be a way we can get her through this.

"Actually, can I ask a favor?" He looks straight at her without acknowledging me. "Would you mind if we went to see Mom? I was only there one time, and she was asleep. I've been wanting to ask, but I didn't want to be needy or anything."

Damn it, it was the perfect thing to say. Instead of focusing on herself, Leni can think about somebody else and what they need. I should've thought of that. I'm supposed to know her so much better than he does.

She perks right up, running a hand under her eyes and nodding. "Sure. That would be great. I guess I should put some regular clothes on," she adds, looking down at the pajamas I encouraged her to wear.

"Go ahead—we won't leave without you." He even gets her to smile before she hurries off to the bedroom.

Blowing out a sigh, I murmur, "That was the right thing to say."

"Yeah, I thought it would be. Besides, I want to see Mom," he adds. "I'm dying to see her."

"We should stop and get her some lilies on the way." There's already a plan forming in my head by the time I get up to put some shoes on. Maybe we can pick up food on the way home—hopefully, she'll be in a better mood by then.

Who the hell is behind these messages? And Leni's right: what did she ever do to deserve something like this? She's innocent. She's never hurt anybody. Maybe once it's obvious Deborah's not coming back from wherever she disappeared to, whoever has been getting off on helping her harass Leni will lose interest.

That's what I need to hold onto as we leave the apartment. We have to be careful—Nix walks with his hood pulled up and his head down while I try to look casual as I scan the area to make sure nobody's paying attention to us. Will it always be this way? Is there ever going to be a time when we can go back to living life the way we used to?

I know the answer to that question. Life is never going to be the same. All we can do now is make the best of what we have. For me, that means taking care of the girl who is so eager to put herself aside if it means making somebody else happy for a little while.

Nix sits in the back while Leni takes the passenger seat. "She's going to be so happy to see you," she tells Nix, and the warmth and excitement in her voice would make me cry if I had it in me. She's so pure. How could I ever have wanted to hurt her like I did? How could I ever hate her?

"I hope it's not too much for her," he murmurs, still with his hood raised. "Seeing me like this. I guess I'll have to explain it."

"Keeping it vague will probably be better," I decide as we leave the parking garage attached to the building. "I mean, I don't think she could ever handle the whole truth. We can say you had an accident, but you're okay now."

"Sure, we'll back you up," Leni agrees. "It'll be fine."

Traffic's not too heavy, though I wish everyone would get the hell out of my way. It's corny, but true: I'm looking forward to watching Mom's reaction to having us both together like this. It might shock her to see his face, but she'll get used to it once she sees he's the same person he always was. We'll keep it light for her sake.

"Shit." Thoughts of Mom dissolve into the background when I switch from the gas pedal to the brake as we come up to a yellow light... and the car barely slows down. We end up rolling through the intersection, where a truck's horn blares as the driver slams to a stop so we don't collide.

"What's happening?" Leni's panicked question rings out in my head as I push the pedal to the floor, and we only pick up speed, rolling downhill toward a small lake at the center of a large business park.

"Colt!" Nix shouts, like that's going to help. Like I'm doing any of this on purpose.

There's only one thing I can do. "Hold on!" I bark, steering us off the road while Leni screams beside me and crosses her arms over her face.

Before we run head-on into a tree that brings us to a sudden, shattering stop and makes my head hit the wheel.

23. LENI

This has to be a nightmare. But I don't think I've ever had a nightmare this vivid. One second, we were rolling down the street like normal, and the next, we were careening down the hill before Colt steered us into a tree. For a second, before the impact, when it was clear we were going to crash, I thought it was the end.

Then the airbag hit me, or I hit it. We hit each other.

I can't keep up with what's happening. Clawing the airbag away from my face, the first thing I see is crumpled metal and broken glass. Colt's airbag deployed, too, and I'm surprised not to hear him cursing and groaning.

In fact, I don't hear anything from him.

"Colt!" I turn to him, then gasp when I see him slumped over the wheel with the deflated airbag around him. "Oh, my god! Colt? Colt! Wake up!" I want to touch him, but I'm afraid to. What if he hurt his neck? Somewhere in the back of my mind, I remember hearing you're not supposed to move someone with a neck injury.

"Oh, fuck." Nix groans behind me, his voice deep and raspy, sort of thick, like he's a little dazed. "Is he okay? Are you?"

Looking back at him, I gasp again at the blood running down the side of his face that isn't scarred. "You're cut!"

"I'll live." He leans over the seat to look at Colt, nudging him, but it's no use. He touches his fingers to the side of Colt's neck, and I hold my breath, frozen in fear.

"He should be fine," Nix announces. "Just out cold. Probably hit his head. He might have a concussion."

"Oh my god, he has to go to a hospital. We have to get to a hospital!" I'm panicking. I know I am. Some part of me that's still capable of thinking knows that. Like I'm standing outside myself, witnessing all of this from a distance.

"And I need to get out of here," Nix says, already opening his door.

"What? No! You need help, too!"

"I can't go to the hospital for help. Remember?" Right. I'm not thinking clearly. He's not even supposed to be alive.

"But what if you're hurt worse than you know?"

"I'm not. I have a cut on the side of my head. I'm fine. I'm going back to my apartment to get cleaned up."

We both go silent and still when a car pulls up on the other side of the road and comes to a stop. "Shit. I have to go, now," he whispers. Before I know it, he's out of the car and is making his way through the woods further ahead from where we crashed, out of sight by the time the driver of the other car reaches us.

"I called for an ambulance," the guy says. "They're on the way. We should get you out of the car—a fire could start."

What if Colt can't be moved, though? "My boyfriend. He's unconscious. He might be hurt badly."

"No, I don't think so."

A broken sob bursts out of me when I hear Colt's voice.

"Oh my god," I whimper, running a hand over the side of his face as he lifts his head from the steering wheel. "I was so scared. Be careful, Colt," I tell him as he starts unbuckling his seatbelt. There's smoke coming from under the hood, and the sight chills my blood.

"Nix?" Colt tries to turn his head to look into the back seat.

"Come on, pal. We've got to get you out of there." The Good Samaritan opens the driver's side door while I open mine and step out on legs that feel like they're made of rubber. Where did Nix go? Peering into the dark woods, I can't see him—he's good at hiding, too.

Colt groans as he climbs out of the car. I force myself to stop looking for Nix in the shadows and round the car to wrap an arm around his waist, wedging my shoulder under his armpit. Can I bear his weight? Probably not, but I need to feel like I'm helping him somehow.

"He went to his apartment on foot," I whisper, knowing Colt has to be worried. "He had a cut, but otherwise he seemed fine. He couldn't come with us."

Sirens wail in the distance, approaching fast. It's unnerving knowing they're for us.

"What about you?"

We stop on the other side of the street from where we crashed, and I have to bite back a whimper when I see the damage from this angle. The whole front is caved in—I'm surprised I could open my door so easily.

"What about me? I'll probably be pretty sore later," I admit, "but right now, I'm all right. I'll probably feel better once you're checked out, though."

We sit together on the curb to wait for the ambulance, his head in my lap, and I stare at the wreck as the sirens get louder. "What happened?" I whisper, still shocked.

"The brakes went out. It was either hit that tree or end up in the lake." He covers my hand with his, stopping me from stroking his hair. Increasing the pressure, he says, "Don't say anything about the message you got today."

At first, I don't understand why he would say that. But then my brain catches up, and I get it. I hadn't even thought about the message until just now, and my body goes cold. "Do you think…"

"Just don't say anything about it," he tells me again as the lights from the ambulance and police car paint his face red and blue.

Because if I mention it, they'll want to know more, and it will lead them straight to Dennis and Deborah.

∽

"They said I'm fine." No matter how many times I remind Colt that I'm only a little banged up, he won't stop worrying about me. "You're the one who needs to take it easy."

He's about as far from taking it easy as can be, sitting up in bed with a tube in his arm, feeding him saline. "Why do they always do this?" he mutters, flicking the tube with one finger. "I don't need to be hydrated. I just need to go home."

"They think it's better for you to stay here for the night, to keep an eye on you. You hit your head hard enough to knock you out." And there's a bruise on his forehead as a result. It's starting to swell, too. "You got lucky."

"Oh, yeah," he mutters. "I feel very lucky. Trapped in bed."

"It will make me feel better to know you're all right. Unless you would rather me sit up all night watching you sleep at home."

Some of the frustration etched across his face softens, and he sighs. "Like you won't sit up here, anyway. Though I wish you wouldn't."

"Yeah, too bad." I try to laugh, I do, but I know it comes out sounding weird and hollow. When he gives me a concerned look, I try to shrug it off. "I guess I'm kind of shaken up still."

That's only a tiny part of the story. It's been hours since the crash. Where is Nix? What happened to him?

It's like I'm being pulled in half. One part of me wants to stay with Colt to make sure he's okay and support him through this. The other half wants to get out of here so I can look for Nix. What if he was actually hurt out there? He could've had injuries he didn't feel yet—adrenaline will do that. I didn't feel anything at first, but now that time has passed, my neck is a little sore, and my shoulders ache. Nothing serious, nothing that would land me in a bed like Colt, but enough to make me wonder how much worse it could have been for Nix.

"He can take care of himself." Colt's voice is a whisper, barely audible as he voices the concern I couldn't say. He settles back against a pillow with a sigh that tells me he might not be feeling as well as he wants me to believe. "He made it after the fire, right? He'll be okay now, too."

"But what if he isn't?" I perch on the side of the bed, keeping my voice low like he does. We don't need anybody accidentally overhearing us. "He could be wandering around with a head wound that's getting worse without him knowing about it."

"That sounds pretty dramatic."

"I'm not kidding." I know why he's trying to make a joke about it. He wants to make me feel better. It's not that he doesn't care.

A funny look comes over his face as his eyes search mine. "You're really worried about him, aren't you?"

"Why shouldn't I be?"

There's a knock at the door before a cheerful young nurse walks in. "Just coming to check on vitals. How are you feeling, Mr. Alistair?"

"You can call me Colt," he murmurs. "And I guess I'm all right."

"You got lucky, from what I've heard."

"I don't feel so lucky right now. Are you sure I need to stay?"

"I don't make the rules, but I'm pretty sure it's for the best that you do." He grumbles quietly while she takes his blood pressure, and I go to the window to look out into the darkness. Well, we were on our way to the hospital, weren't we? We ended up here eventually.

Where are you? I hate the idea of Nix being alone out there somewhere. Sure, he took care of himself all these months on his own, hiding, but that doesn't mean I want him to have to do it again. I don't want him to be alone.

Is there something wrong with me? Why should I care the way I do? He killed Mom. He hurt me. I should hate him.

But what I really want to do now that I know Colt will be okay is leave this hospital and find his brother. It's torture, not knowing, having to imagine. He did seem strong, though, didn't he? He wasn't dazed or anything. He knew exactly what he was doing. I need to cling to the hope that he didn't somehow deteriorate once the adrenaline wore off.

"Okay, you're all set." I turn when the nurse finishes her work. She gives me an appraising look. "Are you planning on staying the night?" she asks with sympathy in her voice.

"Can I? I didn't know if that was possible. I would like to."

"You don't have to do that," Colt tells me, but the nurse just smiles and shakes her head a little.

"Men are so stubborn, aren't they?" she asks me, and we share a soft laugh. Pointing to a vinyl-covered sofa under the window, she explains, "That opens into a bed, and there are sheets and pillows in the closet. Just in case you want to get comfortable."

"Thank you so much." It's good to know I have the option. Right now, I can't imagine going home alone, where I can sit and worry for Nix, for Colt, for me. Why did the brakes fail? Who did this? Deborah and Dennis are dead.

Now that we're alone again, I sit down with Colt and take his hand. "I was so scared when you were just sitting there, unconscious," I whisper. The memory is an icy fist that closes around my heart and squeezes tight enough to take my breath away.

"That's all over now. I'm okay. A concussion. It's nothing."

Funny, but it doesn't make me feel any better. "It could've been a lot worse."

"Don't start spiraling. It's not going to make you feel any better."

Too late. "Come on. Like I'm supposed to think this is all a big coincidence? We both know it's not. Since when do brakes fail out of nowhere?"

His nostrils flare when he takes a deep breath, which he releases slowly. It is killing me to see him like this—there's plenty of strength in his voice and anger in his eyes, but he's lying in bed wearing a hospital gown. That sort of takes the edge off. Not that I would ever call him weak, but he's about as close to it as I've ever seen him. "We will get to the bottom of it one way or another. If somebody is responsible for this, they're going to pay."

The machine next to him that's been monitoring his heart rate starts beeping faster. "Okay, let's not talk about it right now," I decide, glancing up at the display. "All we need is somebody running in here thinking you're having a cardiac incident, or whatever it's called."

"Then you definitely shouldn't kiss me, because that will make my heart race too fast."

"I don't know. Maybe we could take our chances." With a careful lean over in his direction, our mouths touch, and I know it's exactly what I needed. I was terrified back there for that one horrifying moment when I didn't know if he was dead or alive. This feels like a gift.

It's such a shame there's still something inside me holding me back from being fully present. And he knows it. There's disappointment in his eyes when I pull back. "You're still thinking about him," he says in a soft voice.

For one second, I consider pretending I don't know who he's talking about. That would get me nowhere. So instead, I lift a shoulder, fighting for the right thing to say. "I mean, it would be nice if he would reach out to let us know he's all right. I'd feel a lot better if he did that."

But when will he? Maybe he never will. It's a good thing there aren't any sensors on my chest, because they'd be going crazy by now. I feel like my heart is going to burst.

"You better be careful," he says, his eyes narrowing as they search my face. "I might wonder whether you love him."

It's like I just dropped over the edge of the first hill on a roller coaster, and my stomach plummeted along with me. "No. I don't. Is that what you think?"

"Relax. I'm not accusing you of anything."

No, but it's pretty obvious the comment didn't come out of nowhere. "Is this something you've been thinking about? Have I done something to make you doubt me?"

"You're getting me all wrong. I'm not accusing you of anything. It's all right if you love him. I would understand."

"But I don't!" And I don't like the direction this conversation has gone. It makes me feel antsy and uncomfortable, like I can't sit still. "I'm concerned. He's your brother. Of course, I care."

He only snorts softly, then lets out a deep sigh. "Fine, have it your way. I'm exhausted. We can argue about this later."

I don't want to argue. I want him to believe me, dammit. It's obvious he doesn't—and it's obvious I'm all messed up about it. Where is this coming from?

While Colt closes his eyes, I return to the window like staring into a dark night will help anything. Maybe I'll make up the couch later. Right now, I want to sit up and keep an eye on him. Besides, I doubt I'd get a minute of sleep with a war going on in my head. Do I love Nix? I mean, I guess there wouldn't be anything wrong with that.

But am I *in love* with him? Big difference. I can't be—not only because I'm already in love with Colt. I can't be in love with both of them at the same time. It's like when they're together, they unlock something inside each other that always exists, but they somehow manage to suppress on their own—at least most of the time.

When they're together, there's no hope of fighting what's inside them. And they always end up taking it out on me. That is the last thing I should want to be around, right? I should protect myself from them.

So why do I still want to see Nix walk through that door right this very minute? Why am I a little twisted up inside, imagining him in pain, maybe even in danger?

Instead of setting up the pull-out like the nurse suggested, I pull a blanket from the closet and curl up in the chair next to the bed. I would rather keep watch over Colt, anyway.

And it's not like I have any chance of falling asleep with Nix out there somewhere, all alone.

24. NIX

I's not like I don't have any experience sneaking around, avoiding notice. It's like I've been preparing for this night all along.

By the time I reach my shitty neighborhood, the blood along the side of my face has dried. I must look like something out of a horror movie—one side scarred, the other looking like I just paid a visit to a butcher shop. My hood hides it all anyway, and I make sure to pull the sides over my face whenever I come too close to people. Not that they would go out of their way to stare for long. It's only a Tuesday night, but it seems like most of the people I pass are either on their way to do something fun or coming back from it, half-drunk and distracted by their own shit.

Besides, nobody likes to stare too long at the weird, secretive guy with his hands in his pockets. He could be trouble.

Right now, I *am* trouble. I almost wish somebody would try to fuck with me just so I could have an excuse to kick their face in.

Who did it? Who tampered with Colt's car? It's obvious the same person is responsible for the message Leni got today—I mean, I'm not a genius, but I can put two and two together. But who did it? How will we ever find out? Those questions, added to the soreness that gets a little worse with every block I trudge, have me in the mood for violence.

As it turns out, there's no excuse to lash out by the time I reach the apartment building. If the guys on the front stoop have missed me, they don't show it, sticking to the usual chin-jerk greeting before they go back to their softly muttered conversation. It's funny how I've told Colt so many times I want to come back here rather than live with him and Leni and put them in danger because, as I walk up the narrow stairs and smell the familiar piss and cooking odors from other apartments, it hits me—I never saw myself doing this again. Not really. Deep down inside, I didn't think I'd ever come back.

It's a good thing I'm still paid up on the rent and my key still works in the locks. It's not like I could go back to Colt's apartment with blood on my face. I managed to sneak past the front desk before, but I don't want to risk somebody deciding to pay attention tonight.

The apartment seems smaller than it did before. Already, spending time with Colt and Leni has made the life I lived for all those months seem pitiful and empty. Not like I saw it any other way before, but now it's like everything's much more obvious. There are times I wonder if this is where I belong, really—someplace cramped and worn down and bleak, without hope. How much better do I deserve?

At least the water is hot when I step into the shower after shedding my clothes. Once I've rinsed the blood off my face, I touch gentle fingers to where it hurts the worst, wincing when I make contact with the place where the side of my head hit the window.

If living through the destruction of my childhood home taught me anything, it's that pain never lasts. I've almost forgotten all about it by the time I finish washing off and step out to dry. Hell, even the towels are better at Colt's. Who am I kidding, telling myself I can go back to living like this when I now remember what it's like to live better?

How am I supposed to go back to living like this when there's still somebody out there determined to hurt Leni —even to kill her?

The snarl I wear when I meet my gaze in the mirror barely scratches the surface of how I'm feeling about whoever is after her. How am I supposed to find them? I can't sit back and wait for them to try again. They might be successful next time. Tonight, we got lucky.

Though right now, I'm still sore as hell, and I wonder how lucky we actually are. I don't feel that way when I lift my arms overhead to stretch out my aching muscles. How much worse does Leni feel? And what about Colt? Shit, I don't even know if he woke up yet or not. I can't sit around and wait. That's not what I do.

By the time I'm dressed, I know what needs to happen next. I'm not going to hang around this shithole and hope my brother is okay. I'm going to go see for myself. First, I call Colt's phone and hope he'll answer. I probably should've done that sooner, but I'm not thinking clearly. It's hard to keep things straight when all I want to do is hurt somebody.

It isn't Colt who answers, but the sound of Leni's voice is like a balm smoothed over my troubled soul. "It's me," I murmur, and her choked sob tells me how worried she had to be. Closing my eyes, I absorb the sound, and I know I don't deserve it.

"Where have you been? I was so worried!"

"I went back to my place. Where are you? Is he okay?"

"They're keeping him overnight at the hospital. He has a concussion, but I think he'll be fine."

"And you're staying?"

"Yes, I have to be here," she explains. "I would worry myself to death at home."

"What room are you in?"

A soft gasp tells me she wasn't expecting the question, and I don't know how that's possible. Like I wouldn't want to be there. "It's too risky."

"Are you going to tell me where to find you, or am I going to walk around the hospital all night looking? There's a lot less chance of me being spotted and questioned if I know exactly where to go, right?"

She keeps me waiting longer than I like but finally gives in the way I knew she would. "It's 836. But there's no way you'll be able to get through without somebody asking who you are."

"Let me worry about that. I'm pretty good at sneaking around in hospitals."

When she makes a worried noise, I have to add, "You need to stop worrying so much about whether I can handle my shit. I'll be there soon."

Really, I should just be glad she cares. Yet another reason why I don't deserve for her to care, because it annoys the hell out of me to have somebody hovering and asking questions. I take it personally, even though I know I probably shouldn't. Maybe it's all those years I spent without a mom—maybe I would be used to it if I had her in my life instead of a dad who wasn't an example of good parenting in any way.

He's the last thing I need to think about when I'm in a mood like this. He's the last thing to think about ever, but his fingerprints are all over my life. He's in everything I do—everything I think. He's even in my scar tissue, since I wouldn't have it if I didn't want to punish him somehow for everything he did. I need to find a way to let go, but now is not the time. I have other shit on my mind.

Like locating my car, which I left around halfway between my apartment and Colt's. It would've been a risk to park in his garage, where you're supposed to have a pass if you're staying for longer than a short visit. I couldn't leave it down by the warehouse, of course, so this was the next best thing: finding a spot on the street with no meter, which wasn't so hard to do early in the morning, after we discovered the bodies were missing.

Is it crazy to think whoever moved them might be the one who sent that message to Leni? It only makes sense. Just like it makes sense that they were the ones who fucked with the car. Even if Leni hadn't been in it, she would've suffered over what happened to Colt. I'm sure they had that in mind, whoever they are.

At least I know there's next to no chance anybody tampered with my brakes once I'm behind the wheel. I'm pretty much moving on autopilot as I make the drive Colt was trying to make earlier, taking me to the hospital where now he and Mom both have a bed. As I drive, I'm always looking around, wondering if random people on the street are responsible for the cut on the side of my head. They're out here somewhere, whoever they are, and they had better hope they never meet me because I'll be the last person they ever meet.

It takes no time for me to reach Colt's room once I've parked and entered through the cafeteria door. All it takes is moving with purpose. Still, Leni manages to look surprised when I duck into the room as soon as the hallway is clear, and no one is watching.

I hold a finger to my lips when her mouth falls open. It snaps shut in response, but she still scrambles out of the chair she was in and throws her arms around me.

Don't do it. Don't feel it. I can't help it. I know I shouldn't. She's too good for me, and she isn't mine. She's Colt's. She loves him. But I can't pretend there isn't a part of me that craves more than her submission and humiliation. Now that she's in my arms, trusting me, happy to see me, I know there's a part of me that wants this, too.

"How is he?" I whisper, since that seems a lot safer than admitting she brings me peace in the middle of so much chaos.

"I think he'll be all right. But you probably can't stay for long," she whispers, clutching my hoodie in her fists. "They come in every hour to make sure he's all right with the concussion and everything."

"Did they give him a scan or anything like that?"

"Yes, and they said everything seemed fine."

"Except for that egg on his forehead," I mutter, wincing at the sight of the swollen bruise. I mean, compared to what I've got going on with my face, it's nothing. But it's a symbol of what might've happened if he had hit the wheel a little harder.

I need to do something about this. That bruise is a symbol of what's at stake, a reminder of what could've been lost tonight. "Can I see your phone?" I ask Leni.

Her head snaps back, confusion touching her features and drawing them together in a frown. "What for?"

"I just want to see the messages, that's all. There has to be a way we can find out who's behind this."

"Sure, maybe you can think of something I haven't." She takes it from her bag and hands it over after unlocking it and opening her messages. "Pretty much every app you can send a direct message on, somebody has sent them to me. I don't have anything to hide. Look around."

She's not kidding. "Why don't you delete them?" I have to ask, scrolling through one evil, threatening message after another. I wouldn't want these reminders sitting around for me to see anytime I opened an app.

"Most of the time, I do. That's just from the end of last week." So, before our meetup at the warehouse, in other words. "I didn't think to go back in and delete them. I thought…"

She doesn't need to tell me what she thought, because we all thought it was over.

Of course, when I tap on the accounts sending the messages through social media, they are all nameless, faceless accounts created for the sake of bullying. There's not much I'm going to get out of sending a message to one of them. "Have you ever tried calling one of the numbers that sends the texts?"

I knew the answer before I asked. "No way. I figured nobody would answer if I tried." And that's not how she thinks, either. She wouldn't call to bitch somebody out. That's not Leni.

However, it's me.

"Hey, it can't hurt," I mutter, placing a call to the number the last text message was sent from earlier tonight. I doubt anyone will answer, but they might. Either way, they'll see we're not afraid to tell them to fuck off.

It rings once. Again.

Then, someone answers.

Leni watches, eyes wide, hands folded under her chin. At first, all I hear is breathing on the other end—heavy, raspy. "Who is this?" I ask, watching her, listening hard.

Again, they keep me waiting until finally, they speak. "Someone who's gonna make you pay for what you did."

Three beeps sound when they end the call.

One thing I know for sure. "That wasn't somebody our age," I mutter, calling back, my blood boiling now.

"How can you tell?"

"Just the sound of their voice. It was a man, older."

This time the phone rings and rings with no answer until finally, I'm sent to voicemail. It's that automated recording, telling me the number I reached without giving me any other information.

"You think you know what I did?" I growl, staring at my brother while Leni chews her lip like she's trying to bite it off. "That's fine. And I know what you did. Why don't you show yourself, you piece of shit? Come out of hiding. Let's talk about this face-to-face."

With a glance at Leni, I add, "And you'll find out what happens to people who threaten what's important to me."

It's not anywhere near what I'm thinking or feeling, but something tells me that's not the last time I'll have the chance to tell whoever this is exactly what I'm thinking.

Though next time, I won't use my words.

25. COLT

"How's that head treating you?" my psychology professor asks as I pass his desk on Friday afternoon after class. Most of the others have already left, with me bringing up the rear. I'm still moving a little slowly, even three days after the crash—the pain in my back and shoulders isn't as bad, but my knees hit the steering column, and there's still a little soreness.

"Getting better all the time. I'll have to take a little time off from modeling," I joke, and he laughs.

"You just take care of it. Any dizziness or sudden pain, get yourself straight to the hospital." Because being a psychology professor apparently makes him an expert.

Really, I know I should be grateful someone cares, and I am. That's why I give him a quick salute before heading out of the lecture hall, my mind on finding Leni. We've both been a little slower than usual since coming back to school yesterday—there was no way I was hanging around, cooped up in the apartment all because of a swollen bruise on my forehead and a few aches and pains elsewhere.

"Oh, you can't handle being locked up, but I'm supposed to be okay with it?" Nix's complaints echo in my memory as I step outside, glad for the sunshine. I reminded him I'm not the one who recently committed murder, even if it was for a good reason.

Leni is waiting for me on the bench in the quad, the halfway point between our two classes. What have I ever done in my life to deserve the happy little smile she wears when she sees me approaching? It feels unfair. There are times when I'm sure she's going to wake up one morning and realize this has all been a mistake, that she can do so much better. That she can love someone who won't put her life in danger. It's only because of my association with Deborah that she was ever in that bitch's crosshairs in the first place.

"How was class?" She reaches up to kiss my cheek, lingering there an extra beat. She's been like that since the crash. Everything feels a little more significant than before. That will ease up with time, once she feels a little more secure again.

"The usual. No big deal. Though I did get a few looks from people who were trying not to stare at this." I touch a finger to the egg on my forehead, which I'm sure is going to turn into a beautiful, sickening shade of yellow and green before long. I'd wear a ball cap to at least hide it under the shadow of the brim, but my forehead is too swollen. It would only end up hurting—not to mention looking weird.

"Well, now you can rest up a little. Maybe it'll look better by Monday." Her endless optimism is sweet. Something tells me it's going to take a little longer than that.

What we need is a couple of days spent recuperating, though. She's right about that. And when we get home, I'm more sure than ever. Nix is sprawled out on the sofa, looking pissed. He doesn't even brighten up when Leni comes in. "Finally. I thought I'd be sitting here alone all day," he mutters, scowling like we're the ones who dictate when our classes land during the day and how long they last.

"We got back as soon as we could." She glances at me, frowning like she's worried, before going to the bedroom to leave her book bag there. I hear her kicking off her shoes, then sighing as she sits on the bed. She's definitely feeling it, even if she pretends not to since I'm the one who was more seriously injured.

"I'm going to fucking lose it if I have to sit here like this for the rest of my life." He says it in a quiet voice, like he doesn't want her to hear. That's one thing we can agree on: keeping things as easy for her as we can. She's gotten a few more messages since Tuesday, all through social media instead of via text. Whoever is doing this probably doesn't want to run the risk of getting another phone call.

I wish I had been awake when Nix called that number. Maybe I could've recognized the voice, even if he swears I wouldn't have been able to. There's still a chance. But since then, the number they used has been disconnected, along with all the others we went through.

"Try to deal with it without making it her problem," I remind him, since all we have in front of us now is a weekend spent together. The three of us, all in the same apartment, and I don't need him throwing his attitude around. She's doing her best to be strong, but neither of us can afford to forget how she broke down on Monday. It feels like it was so long ago.

It's obvious when Leni wanders into the kitchen, moving slowly, that she's hurting. "I'm really all right," she insists when she catches us watching her. I can only guess Nix looks as worried as I feel. "I just got a little stiff sitting in class. You know how it is. It's easier if you can keep moving."

"You should probably soak in a hot tub," Nix suggests. "That's always the best way to loosen up when you're injured. I could go run you a bath, if you want? Don't you have all that smelly bubble stuff?"

She stares at him, blinking. "You mean bubble bath?"

"Yeah, whatever it's called." He's just fucking around to make her laugh, which she does. The sound makes me feel warm inside.

He's already off the sofa and on his way to the bathroom —he's moving a little slow, too, but he's trying to play it off. "Make sure you don't add too much," she warns.

"I think I can handle it."

"You couldn't remember that it was called bubble bath," she reminds him, giggling, but one look at me cuts off her laughter before she takes on a guilty expression.

"It's okay," I murmur, standing and wrapping my arms around her waist when I return to the kitchen. "You're allowed to laugh at his jokes. You have my permission."

"I'm sorry. It's just after that talk we had on Tuesday, in the hospital—"

Whatever she's about to say, I cut off with a kiss. It's not like I needed to hear it, anyway. I know what's going on in her head.

"Listen to me," I tell her once I let her up for air, noticing how she looks a little dazed and unsteady. "The only way we can make it work, the three of us living together, is if we loosen up a little. We're here to take care of each other, and that's what we need to do, because we are all we have. Do you know what I'm saying?"

"Of course, you're right." She clicks her tongue, shaking her head at herself. "I need to lighten up. I just want to make sure you aren't feeling weird about it or anything."

Right now, it doesn't matter what I feel. She is what matters. How can I get that through to her?

With the water running in the tub, I lead her toward the bathroom. Her eyes widen when we find Nix lighting a couple of candles. "That's so nice," she whispers, beaming. "Like going to a spa."

"Sorry we don't have cucumber water or any of that shit," he jokes.

"Let me help you," I offer, raising her arms over her head from behind and lifting her sweater. It's not easy to touch her like this without my desire exploding in the most undeniable way, but that is not who she needs me to be right now. Loving her means taking care of her without always thinking about myself.

Even though her warmth and softness, and her sweet scent make me rigid, I unclasp her bra without copping a feel of her tits. And even though Nix can't keep his eyes off her as I peel away one layer of clothes after another, he keeps his hands to himself. Somehow, he understands the way I do without us needing a discussion. Monday was only four days ago. She still needs time.

I can't help staring at her body's perfection before taking her by the hand and helping her into the tub, now full of fragrant bubbles. "Did I do a good job?" Nix sits on the edge of the tub, close to her head, while I sit near her knees.

"Perfect," she tells him with a grin, resting the back of her neck against a folded towel, releasing a deep sigh as her eyes close. I couldn't be happier to see her letting go, allowing herself to feel good. She's done too much worrying lately, on top of everything else that plagues her.

We don't have to talk about it, Nix and me. It's like we're moving in sync, connected by some psychic bond that guides us. When I run a hand over her knee, poking out from a mountain of bubbles, he strokes her hair back from her face with a gentle touch. I didn't know he could be that gentle.

"That's nice." Slowly, her legs part, her breathing going deeper while Nix massages her temples, and I explore her smooth, slick skin. I could touch her forever and never get tired of it—I'm addicted to her, plain and simple. Not just to her body, but to her spirit.

Right now, though, it's her body I'm most concerned with, the soft sighs that now accompany my slow, careful stroking of her inner thighs. Her chest and neck are starting to flush, and I don't think it's just from the warmth of the water.

Nix moves from rubbing her temples to massaging her shoulders. "That feels so good," she moans, and my cock might snap in half if this keeps up. The soft sounds of her pleasure slowly grow louder, and louder still once I up the ante by stroking her bald, plump lips under the water's surface.

"You like that?" Nix whispers, and I watch as his fingers press into her flesh until she moans again "That's right. Just relax. Just feel it."

"Don't stop," she begs, her lips parting so she can breathe, so she can moan.

"Not until you're a good girl and come for us," I whisper. Her hips move when I start running a finger along the length of her slit, teasing without touching her clit. Not yet. Not until she begs me to. I want to see how far we can take her. How much pleasure we can make her feel.

"You like when he touches you that way?" Nix's hands slide over her chest, grazing the tight nipples that peek out over the surface of the water.

Her back arches in a sharp gasp that fills the air. "Oh, god," she moans, and her hips move faster. Nothing in the world matters more than this, right here, this moment. Building her up, working her body.

"That's right," I tell her. "Let it out. Show us how good you feel."

"I do," she rasps, then moans when Nix pinches her nipple and rolls it between his thumb and forefinger.

That's when I decide to drag a finger through her folds, stopping at her clit and moving in slow circles over it. Her eyes fly open, her moans echoing in the room. "Oh... Oh, yes... Yes," she pants.

"What do you want him to do next?" Nix is breathing faster, grunting softly. His tongue glides over the curve of her ear until she moans again.

"I..." She shakes her head, whimpering.

"I won't know what to do unless you tell me," I warn, easing up on the pressure against her engorged clit, knowing it'll drive her wild with frustration when I do. She needs to know she can control this. All we want is to give her pleasure.

Her frustrated groan makes us both chuckle darkly. She's ours. She'll always be ours.

"I want you to... fuck me with your fingers." Moving her hips, she whimpers, "Please."

"Like this?" I work one finger inside, then a second, still thumbing her clit as I massage her slick walls. She's whimpering, almost sobbing, the water splashing with every desperate jerk of her hips.

"Yes, just like that." Her voice is tight, strained. "I love it. Yes, don't stop."

"How's that pussy feel?" Nix asks me.

"Getting tighter," I announce, working faster, going deeper as my knuckles hit her swollen flesh with every stroke. Her cries rise in pitch and desperation until she's squealing, almost shrieking, humping my hand until finally, she clenches tight and goes still with her mouth hanging open, her eyes squeezed shut.

And then it breaks with an ecstatic cry before she sinks back into the tub, panting weakly. I still feel her pulsing around me, fluttering in the aftermath, and I help her ride it out as long as I can before she relaxes with a happy sigh.

I don't know why, but there's a sense of pride that rears up in me as I look down at her, crashed out in the tub, dizzy and breathless after what we made her do. "Wow," she sighs, her lips curving in a satisfied smile.

Nix presses a kiss against her temple before standing up. The sight of his bulge sticking out in front of him tells me he's going through it the way I am, wanting to do more, holding himself back. It's for her sake, and I can't imagine anyone else I'd suffer this kind of discomfort for. Self-control has never been my thing, and I sure as hell know that's true for my brother.

But she's worth it. I'm starting to wonder if she has what it takes to turn us into the men we're capable of becoming.

I keep my thoughts to myself, pondering the idea while Leni finishes her bath. Once she's done, we help her from the tub and dry her off before wrapping her in a fluffy robe.

"What else would you like to do tonight?" I ask with a wicked grin that makes her blush.

"Right now, I feel like I could go to sleep—but I don't want to," she adds when I'm about to tell her to do that. "Maybe we could finish watching the show we started on Tuesday?"

"You know, I was just wondering how the contestants did during bread week," Nix muses. The funny thing is, I can't tell if he's serious or joking. He did seem sort of into it.

"Then I guess that's what we do," I decide. "Let's order some Chinese from the place around the corner. It's been a while since we've gotten it from there."

It helps that she likes it so much and that her face lights up the way it does. What is it about her that leaves me scrambling around, trying to come up with ways to make her happier?

She's Leni. It's as simple as that.

Within the hour, we're back where we started a few days ago, watching TV together, now sharing food from the takeout containers arranged on the coffee table.

"I don't understand why they can't give these people air conditioning when it's hot outside," Leni mumbles around a mouthful of lo mein. "They want them to sculpt chocolate, but everything's melting. How are they supposed to compete under these conditions?"

I have to grin at how serious she takes it, and Nix is smiling when he meets my gaze over the top of her head.

And just like back on Tuesday, before all hell broke loose, I wonder if we could make this last. The three of us here, living together, sharing each other's lives. Me and my brother focused on making her happy. Could we make it work?

Feeling the way I do right now, I hope we do. I really hope we do.

26. LENI

I don't wait until the water turns all the way hot before I step under the spray of the shower. My body jolts in shock and a shiver shoots down my spine as the cool water hits my skin. I breathe through the urge to get back out until the water turns warm and then slowly hot. My muscles relax, and I sigh into the steaming air.

The last few days passed in a blur. I feel like a robot going to school and participating in classes, while a threat continuously looms over us. I try to act normal, but I must be a bad actress because both Colt and Nix constantly ask me if I'm all right. I tell them I'm fine, but we all know it's a lie.

How can I be fine when our lives are a complete clusterfuck right now?

I wet my hair and wash it with my favorite shampoo before I shave my legs and armpits. Lathering my body with shower gel, I massage it into my skin while remembering how the guys gave me a bath the other day. They have never been that gentle with me before and though it has been nice to see this softer side of them, something about it feels off.

I feel like the guys are not being themselves around me. It's like they are pretending to be someone they are not.

Are they trying to change who they are for me?

While I rinse off, I let the question run through my mind. What if that's exactly what they are doing? Somehow that thought makes me sad. I don't want them to change. But why? Why in the heck would I not want them to change?

The answer lies on the tip of my tongue, but I'm too embarrassed and disappointed in myself to even think about it. But of course, now I can't stop thinking about it.

I like their darkness. I crave that depraved part of them, and I want them to hurt me sometimes. I shake my head at the realization. Something in me wants them in a way I shouldn't. Or at least that's what it feels like. It feels wrong to want this, yet thinking about them pushing me to my limits and beyond has my pussy clench.

Yes, there is definitely something wrong with me.

Turning the water off, I step out of the shower and wrap myself in a large, fluffy towel. I use a smaller towel to dry my hair while I look at myself in the mirror. My cuts and bruises from the accident are all pretty much healed now.

Only some faint yellow spots remain on my arm, but I guess even those will be gone by tomorrow.

I wonder if my marks are the reason for the guys treating me like I'm made out of glass, or was it the freak out I had last time we had sex? My guess is the latter. How can I tell them that I'm ready to have sex again, sex without them holding back? Because I can handle it, right?

Staring at my reflection, I let all my questions, doubts, and fears run through my mind until my hair is almost dry.

Taking a deep breath, I straighten my spine and reach for the edge of the towel to tuck it free. It falls into a heap around my feet, and I step out of it to walk to the door. My hand is trembling slightly as I reach for the handle to open it.

Ignoring my shaking fingers, I walk down the hallway and into the living room, where Colt and Nix are watching TV. They both look up almost at the same time. Their eyes go wide, and Colt's jaw actually drops.

"Hi," I say dumbly, while standing completely naked in front of them.

"Hi." Nix grins back, sitting up a little straighter.

"What are you doing?" Colt asks while his gaze roams my body lustfully.

What am I doing? Trying to seduce them, I guess. Which I'm apparently pretty bad at. What if they don't want me anymore?

Doubt weasels its way into my mind, but I don't let it take hold before clarifying, "I was thinking we could have sex."

"Okay." Nix is on his feet a moment later, reaching for the hem of his shirt to pull it over his head.

"Hold on a second." Colt stands up as well, grabbing Nix by the arm before he can get to me.

My heart sinks. Colt doesn't want this. He doesn't want me.

"It's fine if you don't want to," I blurt out. Crossing my arms over my chest, I suddenly feel as naked as I am.

"What? No, it's not that. I just want to hear that you are sure about this. A lot has been going on and last time..." Colt trails off, probably not wanting to bring up the past. He runs his hand through his hair before continuing. "I guess I'm just surprised. You never initiate, that's all."

"Oh..." I guess I didn't think about it that way. "It's just you haven't initiated anything, and I feel a little... I don't know... neglected."

"We didn't mean for you to feel like that," Nix chimes in. "We thought you needed some time."

"And I did, but I also need you—both of you." My voice falters into a whisper as I admit it out loud. My cheeks heat, and I look between Nix and Colt, scanning their faces, trying to figure out what they are thinking. Both of them stare at me like they don't know what to say, so I tell them what's on my mind. "I don't want you to treat me like

I'm breakable, either. I can handle you... both of you," I say, keeping my voice laced with confidence.

"Are you sure about that?" Nix asks with a smirk.

I nod and smile at them. A moment of silence passes before Colt's lips finally turn up, and I know he is on board. I almost sigh in relief.

Unfolding my arms, I wrap them around Colt's neck as soon as he is close enough. His lips find mine in a searing kiss as he picks me up and carries me into the bedroom, with Nix following us close behind. I wrap my legs around Colt, loving how the rough material of his jeans rubs against my bare pussy.

He drops me onto the bed, where I bounce a little on the mattress. Before I can recover, Nix is on me. He must have gotten undressed on the way because his naked body is covering mine. He spreads my legs and positions himself between my thighs. Then he enters me with one harsh thrust.

I groan at the rapid intrusion, thankful that I'm wet enough to take him like this. My eyes squeeze shut and my nails rake over his back as he stretches my walls almost painfully. He doesn't wait for me to adjust and get comfortable. He simply starts fucking me like a starving man having his first meal.

He snakes his arms around my torso, hooking his hands over my shoulders so he can hold me against him while he thrusts into me violently. His face rests in the crook of my neck, his mouth opens, and he presses his tongue against my sensitive skin. He licks me softly before sinking his teeth into my flesh.

I yelp out in surprise, more than pain. Instinctively, I try to wiggle away, but Nix has me in an iron grip. He chuckles darkly, fanning hot breath against my wet skin. Goosebumps pebble over my arms and a shiver runs down my back as my pussy clenches down on Nix's cock.

He snickers again, before roughly sucking on the spot he just bit. Pain and pleasure courses through me, all of it rushing between my thighs, where Nix's cock impales me with every thrust.

I'm so overwhelmed with what Nix is doing to me, I'm only vaguely aware of Colt's hand wrapping around my ankle. He moves my leg up, spreading me open for his brother to go even deeper.

"Fuck, how does this cunt feel so good?" Nix grits out while fucking me into the mattress. "I feel you clenching down, slut. You like when we fuck you like this. Like you're our sex doll. We can do whatever we want to you. Use all your holes until you bleed and there is nothing you can do about it..."

His depraved words should have me revolting, instead it sends jolts of pleasure to my core.

"You're nothing but a filthy whore, a cum dumpster for us to use. Just keep your legs spread so we can have your pussy and ass whenever and however we want..."

He keeps grunting vile things into my ear while his thrusts become more erratic. His fingers dig into my shoulders as he pushes me down onto his cock. He is so deep inside of me, I can feel the tip bumping against my cervix.

Nix shoves his cock into me a few more times before I explode. A tidal wave of pleasure washes over me, taking my breath away. My whole body shudders while an intense orgasm ripples through me. My heart races in my chest as I try to get my breathing under control.

Nix doesn't stop fucking me through my release, which only makes it last longer and feel stronger.

When I'm finally coming down, my body goes slack in Nix's hold, and he slows himself at last. He is breathing heavily too, and I can feel the sheen of sweat between our bodies.

Now that he is going slower and the high from my orgasm is fading, I can feel my pussy is already getting sore. Each of Nix's lazy pumps sends tiny ripples of pain through my core. Nix was anything but gentle, which was exactly what I asked for. But I can't help but wonder how much is yet to come?

Nix suddenly pulls out and untangles himself from me. My eyes fly open to see him and Colt switching places. Colt is also naked now, his muscular torso flexing with each movement. His cock is rock hard, pointing straight at me.

I lick my dry lips and look up at Colt through hooded eyes. When I see the way he stares at me, I swallow hard. His pupils are dilated, his eyes looking almost black. His shoulders are tense, and his hands are balled into fists by his side. He looks unhinged, almost mad, and for a moment, I think I might have done something wrong.

"I want to do things to you, Leni... devious things. I want to hurt you." He admits through clenched teeth. He looks like he is holding on by a thin string, and I'm not sure what he is going to do next. Right now, he is unpredictable.

I'm lying in front of him, naked, with my legs spread, and he is telling me he wants to hurt me. But this is not anyone. This is Colt who is saying these things to me. My boyfriend who loves me, and I have to trust that he would not take it too far again. I have to believe that he only breaks parts of me he can rebuild after.

"Are you sure you can handle more? Your pussy is already red and puffy," Colt says, glancing between my legs. He looks back up at my face, and I can see the worry flickering in his eyes.

"I can handle more," I assure him, though I'm not one hundred percent sure myself.

He must be able to see the hesitation in my face. "How about a safe word?" he suggests.

"A safe word?" I repeat.

"Yeah, when you say it, we know you can't take any more," he explains, like I don't know what it means. "We'll stop when we hear it."

"Okay," I agree, nodding before looking at Nix standing behind Colt.

He looks less than amused with a safe word, but he nods back at me regardless, letting me know he will also respect this boundary.

"Let's go with the classic." Colt grins, probably remembering the time I made him watch *Fifty Shades of Grey* with me. "Your safe word is red."

I nod again. Feeling a little less nervous, I relax back into the mattress.

"What are you going to do to me?" I ask curiously.

"You'll see," Colt tells me with a mischievous grin. "Nix, hold her down for me," he orders his brother, who gleefully obliges.

Nix climbs on the bed and slides behind me. He grabs me under my arms and pulls me between his legs until my back is resting against his chest. I lean back, relaxing against him when he grabs my wrists roughly. With a little too much force, he crosses my arms over my stomach and pulls them down so I'm tightly hugging myself.

Colt gets up from the bed and stands by the dresser. He digs into the top drawer for something, before getting out a bottle of lube. He closer the drawer and walks back over to us.

He gets onto the bed where he kneels between my legs. He spreads them apart with his thighs as he scoots closer. His gaze is on me, his eyes dark and predatory. He looks at me like I'm his prey, and he is the hunter going in for the kill shot.

My breath hitches and real fear creeps up my spine. Colt's face darkens further as a chilling grin pulls on his lips. He can see I'm scared, and he likes it. It turns him on.

I wiggle in Nix's hold, which only makes him tighten his grip on me.

Colt pops open the bottle of lube before pouring a healthy amount over my pussy. Enough that some runs down my slit and over my ass. I shudder at the coldness while wondering what Colt has planned for me.

He throws the bottle aside and brings his hand to my center. His fingers slide through my folds with ease, teasing up and down before he shoves two fingers into my tight channel. I throw my head back against Nix's shoulder at the sudden intrusion.

Colt pulls out his fingers just to push them back inside a little more forcefully. He thrusts all the way in until his knuckles are pressed against my pussy lips. He turns his hand while bending his fingers inside of me. The intense feeling makes me moan softly.

"You like that, don't you," Colt says, his voice low and rough. "Let's see how you feel with another."

I'm about to ask him another what? When I feel Colt adding a third finger into my pussy. I'm glad for the excessive lube now, because it seems to ease the stretching sensation as he forces a third digit into me.

It takes him a moment to get all of them in before he starts fucking me again. Each of his strokes stretching me further. I feel really full and since I'm already a little sore, there is some slight pain as well but nothing I can't handle. Matter of fact, I welcome the small sting of pain. A pressure begins to build in my lower belly, and I know if he would just touch my clit right now, I would come apart for him.

"You are taking three pretty well. Can you take four?" Colt rasps out.

"I don't know," I say without thinking, because I really don't know. I feel pretty maxed out already and though he would only be adding his pinky, it's still a lot to take.

"Let's find out," Colt grits through his teeth before he enters me again with all four of his fingers.

I squeeze my eyes shut at the sharp pain of being stretched. When I open them again, I find Colt smirking while he looks between my legs. "You are so tight. I want to know how much you can take. How much can we stretch out this little cunt?"

"Fuck yeah," Nix murmurs behind me, his hard cock pressed against my lower back. A constant reminder of what is still to come.

It takes me a few strokes to adjust, but I finally breathe through the discomfort of being stretched to the fullest. It's not until I see the mischievous glint in Colt's eyes that I realize he is still not done with me. He meant what he said. He wants to know how much I can handle. And right now, what it means is if I can take his whole fist.

"I don't think I can take more than that," I admit, but Colt is already grabbing the bottle of lube again, pouring more over his hand.

I shake my head and wiggle in Nix's arms, but there is no budging. He holds me down with ease while his brother brings his hand between my legs once more.

"Wait," I beg, trying to close my legs. Colt pries them apart, using his body and free arm to keep me spread.

"Relax, or this will hurt." Nix is breathing heavily in my ear while my own chest is heaving.

I swallow hard and squeeze my eyes shut as I feel Colt's fingers enter me. His fingertips feel fine, but the deeper he goes, the wider his hand gets. I grind my teeth together as he forces his hand into my aching pussy. The pressure is enormous now and the pain almost unbearable.

Short and shallow breaths are all I can suck in at the moment, which makes talking a little hard. "I can't..." I grit out through clenched teeth.

"Yes, you can," Colt quips. "You can take my fist like a good little slut."

I groan. His cruel words egg me on, reigniting the fire I felt earlier.

"I'm almost in all the way, just a bit more." Colt's voice is filled with excitement as he continuously works his fist into me.

Every time I think I can't take any more, he pushes in another inch, the fullness ever growing and the pain slowly rising.

I grind my molars together. My safe word is sitting at the tip of my tongue, ready to be blurted out when something rubs against my clit. The sensation is so intense, I shudder.

"I think you can come with my fist inside of you," Colt says roughly. "Come for me while I have your little pussy stuffed to the brim."

I shake my head. Unable to believe that I can come, but as Colt rubs his thumb over my engorged clit, pleasure builds in my core, spreading like a wildfire without rain.

"Come for us," Nix growls into my ear, his tone demanding.

Colt pinches my clit—pressure and pain come together in a crescendo of pleasure. My whole body tightens as an overwhelming orgasm rushes through me. The fullness in my core makes my release different, more intense, and definitely longer. My mind goes blank, my thighs quiver, and I make a wonton sound I've never heard before.

When I eventually come down from my high, I relax back against Nix, who still has a tight hold on me. Colt moves his fist inside of me, and I shudder again.

"Knew you would like this," Colt admits.

"I hope you don't think we are done with you yet." Nix chuckles behind me.

"I didn't think you were," I quip. The only question is, how much more can I handle?

27. NIX

This must be the sexiest fucking thing I've ever seen. My cock is so hard it hurts, and my muscles ache from being so tense. My hands are wrapped around Leni's wrists tightly enough to leave bruises, and I have to force my grip to loosen so I won't actually hurt her.

Not that she is complaining much. Quite the opposite. The sounds coming from her mouth are sweet little moans and sexy small gasps while Colt moves his fist out of her pussy.

I look down, enjoying the perfect view of Leni's stretched out cunt. Her pussy lips are forced apart, red and angry looking as Colt's lubed up hand slides out of her tight channel at last.

Leni is completely still in my hold, her body relaxed and limp from her intense orgasm. I let go of her wrists and her arms fall to the mattress beside us. Grabbing her by the hips, I pull her up into my lap until my dick is lined up with her pussy.

I enter her in one deep thrust, enjoying how wet and hot she is. We both moan as I push into her a few more times before pulling out. I don't want to fuck her cunt right now. I want her ass.

Lifting Leni up slightly, I position her tight back entrance over my cock while pushing my hips upward. My tip forces her narrow hole open a little too fast. I hiss in pleasure as Leni screams out in pain.

"Nix!" she says in a warning tone, but I'm too far gone to stop.

I push my cock in a little deeper, making Leni groan like I'm hurting her. Hot pleasure races through my veins, and I almost come again. The intense feeling of having her asshole squeeze my cock while seeing her in pain and hearing her little whimpers will be forever in my spankbank.

I really hope she doesn't use that fucking safe word, because I honestly don't know if I could stop.

Another few inches, and I'm seated inside of her tight ass. My fingers dig into her skin as I hold her against me tightly. I hold still for a moment, letting her adjust before I start to rock my hips in and out of her slowly.

Leni's whimpers turn into moans just as I loosen my hand on her hip and bring it up to her throat. I wrap my fingers around her slender neck, putting slight pressure on my thumb and fingertips. I don't press hard enough to make her pass out, but firm enough to pose a threat. She can still talk, still use her safe word, but she doesn't.

Her pulse races under my touch, and I can feel her swallow just before I squeeze hard enough to choke her. Leni's hands come to my arms, where she grabs hold of me. Her sharp nails dig into my skin, making me hiss out in pain.

I release my hold on her throat, and she sucks in a deep breath. For a moment, I fear she is about to say red when Leni relaxes back into my hold.

The corners of my mouth pull up as I take in her actions. She is okay with me choking her. She trusts me enough to let me do this, to control her breathing.

Looking over at Colt, I find him staring at us in awe. He can't believe she is letting me do this to her. I'm surprised myself, to be honest. Leni is letting me take control more than she ever has, and I intend to take all she gives me.

"You look so fucking hot," Colt tells Leni before scooting closer to us. "I'm going to fuck your pussy while Nix is in your ass," he continues.

Grabbing her thighs, Colt spreads Leni's legs apart further, giving him better access. He grabs hold of his cock and lines it up with her puffy cunt. He pushes inside, making Leni groan.

She throws her head back against my shoulder, and I take

the moment to squeeze her throat again. Leni makes a choking sound, and my cock hardens further.

I pump into her ass while Colt thrusts into her pussy. I can feel my brother through the thin skin. With each push inside of her, my balls tighten almost painfully. I want to come again, I'm so close to blowing another loan.

Leni rakes her nails down my arms, and I loosen my grip on her once again. She gasps for air, her chest heaving, but she still hasn't used her safe word. Thank fuck for that.

I don't let her breath long before I choke her again. She fights in my hold, scratching my skin and shaking her head, but every time I let her go, she stays quiet.

I fuck her ass and choke her out like that until I feel her ass clamp up on me, and her thighs quiver with her release. Only then do I let my own orgasm free. With a loud groan, I force my cock deep into her ass one last time before I come undone. Ropes and ropes of my cum paint the inside of her walls as I come so hard my vision goes black for a few seconds.

By the time I come back down from my intense release, Colt is grabbing Leni and pulling her off me. My sensitive cock slips free, and I immediately miss her heat around me.

I watch as Colt makes Leni turn around and get on all fours. The next moment, he enters her from behind. Leni slumps forward, letting her head lull to the mattress while keeping her ass up.

Colt grabs her hips and fucks her until he comes himself with a loud groan. Then he slumps over too. Leni and Colt both straighten out, moaning in pain with each move.

For a few minutes, we all just lie there, calming down from the experience. My breathing returns to normal, and my heart rate is back down. My throat is dry, and my muscles ache with exhaustion, but I'm not worried about myself right now. I'm worried about Leni.

Was I too rough with her?

She hasn't moved an inch, and she doesn't even when Colt slowly sits up. Leni's long red hair is in a messy halo around her, hiding her face.

Colt places his palm on Leni's shoulder. "Hey, you okay?" he asks gently.

When she doesn't respond, I sit up and move closer to her so I can swipe her hair from her face. Her eyes are closed, her mouth slack. She looks like she is peacefully sleeping. I sigh in relief.

"I think she is fine," I murmur, more to myself than anyone.

Colt doesn't seem satisfied. He shakes her shoulder slightly. "Leni!"

"Mmmhhh," she finally answers with a moan, then adds a single word, "Tired."

"All right, go to sleep. We'll clean you up," Colt coos before getting up from the bed.

He grabs some boxers and puts them on before disappearing into the bathroom. I get up and grab some underwear and shorts myself. By the time I'm dressed, Colt returns with a wet washcloth and a dry towel.

I take the warm washcloth and carefully clean between Leni's legs. Her pussy is red and angry and small whimpers fall from her lips as I wash her. When I'm done cleaning her up. Colt comes after me with a dry towel.

Once she is all done, we gently position her in the center of the bed so her head is lying on the pillow. I take the folded up comforter and cover Leni up with it. A smile crosses her lips as she cuddles deeper into the bed.

My own lips curl up as I take her cute form in. My chest swells and something warm spreads inside of me. A feeling I've been trying to suppress for a long time. A feeling I'm not supposed to feel, not for her, my brother's girlfriend.

As if Colt can read my mind, he shakes his head at me. "It's okay to love her."

I'm about to deny loving her, but the words get stuck in my throat. I can't lie to him, not now, not ever.

"We can't both love her," I whisper, not wanting to wake Leni up.

"Why not? She wants us both." Colt doesn't even bother keeping his voice down. I look down at Leni, who is still passed out.

"She doesn't love me," I quip, letting the pain of that realization slice through me. She loves Colt, and that's not going to change. Jealousy burns a hole in my chest. I lift my hand and rub the spot as if it could alleviate the hurt.

"I think you are wrong," Colt muses, but I ignore him.

"There is no way Leni loves me, not after what I've done to her." Jealousy fades and guilt settles in my bones. Why do I have to be so fucked up? Why can't I keep the darkness inside of me in check, hidden from the world? Hidden from her.

"We both did fucked up things to her, and she forgave me. She'll forgive you too," Colt tries to assure me.

"I killed her mom," I point out, letting the whole weight of that dire mistake rest on my shoulder.

"By accident. You didn't know she was in the house." Colt tries to make light of the situation, but there is no sugar coating what I did.

"Accident or not. It's my fault she is dead and then I killed again…" I let my head hang low in shame. I'm not sorry for killing Dennis and Deborah, but I shouldn't have done it in front of Leni.

"For her. You killed them to protect Leni, and she knows it."

I'm still standing next to the bed, looking down at some spot on the carpet when Colt climbs into bed and settles next to Leni. I glance up at them, realizing in shock that

Leni's eyes are open. She doesn't say anything, but I know she heard everything we talked about.

Her eyes are soft and her smile sweet when she lifts an arm and holds out her hand to me. "Come on," she whispers, bending her fingers to motion for me to lie with her.

I climb into the bed, lying down next to her, I place my hand into hers. She wraps her slender fingers around mine and pulls me closer.

Colt is cuddling her from behind, being the big spoon, but I'm face to face with her, which I like even better.

She grabs hold of my other hand, bringing both of them to her chest, where I can feel her heart beating softly. She closes her eyes again and cuddles into the pillow before murmuring a sleepy, "Goodnight."

I can't help but smile as I take her in. She looks so fucking adorable. I want to take a picture. Her hair is a mess from sex, her skin is glowing, and her pouty lips are slightly parted. I could count the freckles on her nose right now and be completely content with just being here with her.

The irony is not lost on me. How can I want to hurt and control her, but also like watching her go to sleep? Less than thirty minutes ago, I wanted nothing but to degrade her and fuck her any way I wanted to, but now I want nothing more than to keep her safe and happy. How can I want both?

Fuck me, I think Colt is right. I think I'm in love with Leni.

28. COLT

LENI: CLASS RAN A FEW MINUTES LATE, AND I HAVE TO PEE. I'll meet you at the car.

Leni's text reaches me as I'm walking across campus, ready to meet her and head home. Every day that passes without any mention of our late classmates makes me feel a little more secure. Is it unnerving that there hasn't been a big uproar over their disappearance? More than a little. But I'm not going to look a gift horse in the mouth. If nobody's concerned about them going missing, I'm not going to worry myself about it. Why waste time making problems? It only means you can't enjoy what's going on around you.

The parking lot is half full at this time of day. I cross it, heading to where I parked Leni's car earlier. She still hasn't driven it, but at least it's getting some use until my insurance shit gets ironed out. I wonder if there will ever come a day when she'll get behind the wheel herself.

Maybe I bought myself a car when I meant to buy one for her.

I'm too busy thinking about that to notice an engine revving behind me until it's almost too late. Reflex takes over. I turn my head to look over my shoulder, then leap out of the way, narrowly avoiding getting hit by a black BMW.

From the corner of my eye, I watch the car swerve like the driver is trying to follow me and make sure they get the job done. They're determined to hit me. Only they end up driving up onto the concrete median and sideswiping a light pole before coming to a stop.

Did that just happen? It takes a second or two for me to pull my thoughts together and catch up to the present moment while I crouch on the ground in shock. But as soon as it clears, I take off after the fucker. That was no accident. They aimed for me.

And now they're going to find out the consequences.

The car is still sitting where it came to a stop and shocked cries ring out behind me by the time I reach the passenger-side window, banging on it with both palms—before I recognize the driver.

And he knows me, too, glaring at me with hatred in his eyes. "George?" I whisper in disbelief. Bradley's dad. Dennis's dad. The realization and the implications that come along with it make my heart drop.

"We fucking warned you!" he shouts from inside the car, sweat beading on his bald head, his eyes narrowed in rage. "You're gonna die for what you've done. And your girlfriend, too!"

And then he's gone. Tires screeching. The smell of burned rubber hangs in the air.

"Colt!" Leni's voice reaches through the fog of confusion in my head, reminding me what needs to happen here and now. I go to her, wrapping her in my arms and shuttling her to the car, waving off the questions and concern from random witnesses.

"We have to go home," I whisper to her on the way, careful not to be overheard. "I know who's been doing this."

∼

"ALL THIS TIME, it was their dad behind it." Nix's head bobs slowly as he processes everything that happened earlier. "Probably encouraging Dennis to go after Leni and you. Yeah. I believe that."

"What, you think I was lying?"

"Of course not, dickhead." He gets up from the sofa, punching his palm. I know how he feels. I've only been able to keep it together for Leni's sake. "It makes perfect sense."

Leni's been quiet through all of this, choosing to listen carefully, tucked into a corner of the sofa. Her voice is soft when she asks, "What do you mean?"

"Why they would keep it all a secret and try to handle it themselves. Both of them—George and Cecilia—all they ever cared about was their image and how they looked to other people. They wouldn't want the rest of the world to find out something that could turn into a scandal."

"What about Deborah's parents?" she asks.

"Who knows? Maybe they're in on it, too. Maybe they're not. But I know George," I mutter, remembering the rage burning in him. The fucker came close to taking me out today. "I'm not letting him get away with it."

I look at Nix. Nix looks at me.

"What are you going to do?" Leni asks. She's right to sound nervous—even if she's not the one who's going to suffer tonight.

"How do we do it?" I ask him. There's something hot pumping through my veins—bitter, satisfying.

"I'm not sure." He shrugs, a smirk playing over his mouth. "But I'm good at blowing up houses."

"Wait. What?" Leni scrambles onto her knees, clutching a pillow in front of her like a shield. "No. You're not serious, right?"

Of course, she would hate this. But I can't worry about that now. Certain things are more important even than her ideas of right and wrong. Like her safety.

"He said he was going to kill us. Me and you." I watch as

understanding sinks in. "This is the only way to make sure that doesn't happen. We get rid of him and this is over."

"This is what we have to do for you," Nix tells her. I can sense the anticipation he's feeling—it's in the air, crackling like a thunderstorm is about to hit.

"We're not in any danger." I don't know if that's true, exactly, but it's what I need to believe. I can't let the little doubts stop me. Nix and I won't have any trouble getting into the house. I'm sure of that.

I only hope I get a little time alone with George before the place goes up in flames.

Her face falls, eyes darting back and forth between us. "What if this is what they want you to do? They could be waiting for you, you know? What happens then?"

"I guess we'll just have to deal with it," I decide. "We can't go right now. We'll have to wait until later. After dark."

She blurts out a laugh, but there's an edge to it—panic, fear, disbelief. "We're just going to sit around, knowing what's going to happen later?"

That's exactly what we do.

We go through the motions of watching TV, eating dinner. I barely pay attention to anything on the screen and hardly taste a bite. All I can focus on is what's going to happen tonight. And I can't stop wondering if George is thinking the same thing. He could be waiting outside for all I know—plotting, planning, waiting until it's late enough that he can get away with sneaking up here.

There's an uneasy energy in the air, and the hours pass almost silently. Every once in a while, I look at Nix, and I know he's planning, running through the steps in his head. He's a lot more familiar with the house—he was always closer with Bradley than I was.

It feels like time is stretching on forever, but before I know it, it's almost eleven. Nix and I exchange a look, and he nods before I get up and go to my bedroom closet, opening the safe inside.

Leni's footsteps sound on the floor behind me, and she gasps as she watches me pull a pair of Glocks from inside. "When did you get those?"

"They're mine." Nix joins us, takes one from me, and makes sure it's loaded. "I picked them up one day while you guys were at school. One of the perks of the shit neighborhood I stayed in."

"On second thought, here." I take the third from inside and turn to her. "Take this."

"Wait. What? What am I supposed to do with it?"

"Usually, you point it at someone and pull the trigger," Nix murmurs.

She doesn't think his joke is funny—in fact, she scowls at him. "I've never fired a gun." She even hands it back to me, shaking her head.

"It's easy." I check to make sure the safety is off before pressing it into her hand. I don't let go of her wrist until she looks up at me with wounded eyes. "I'll feel a lot better if you have this, okay? If someone tries to get into this apartment who isn't Nix or me, you fire. Don't waste time trying to aim for anything in particular. You just point and shoot."

After taking a deep breath, she nods slowly. "Okay. Just do me a favor and come back, okay?"

"You don't have to worry about that." Still, I take my time kissing her. When I'm finished, Nix kisses her forehead. He doesn't say a word—I can tell he's locked in, ready to do what needs to be done.

We take his car, where he gets behind the wheel without a word. Finally, I have to ask, "So that's the plan? We go in, we take them out, we burn the house down?"

"Do you have any better ideas?"

"No. Just making sure we're on the same page." There's not a doubt in my mind that this is what needs to be done when I remember George's furious glare. He's going to kill Leni if we don't take care of him now.

We are half a block away from the house when Nix parks. "You ready for this?" he asks, staring straight ahead, where the house sits at the end of the cul-de-sac, on top of a hill. The gate sits open, almost like George is inviting us in. Maybe he's waiting.

The gun in my waistband feels heavier than it should as we get out of the car and go the rest of the way on foot. We walk side by side, being careful to stay in the shadows of the trees lining the driveway.

There are cars outside, but the house is dark.

"Going through the kitchen," he murmurs. "I remember the code for the security system. It's Bradley's birthday. Guess which one was the favorite son?"

"No wonder George was riding Dennis to get answers." Not that I have even a shred of sympathy.

The back patio is overgrown, unused. Like the people living here haven't been paying attention—busy worrying about one son and covering up the death of another. The weeds and dead leaves add an eerie feeling as I keep watch while Nix forces open the back door.

Once it's open, we wait for the sound of a siren inside, but there's nothing. Only silence. We exchange a glance before he leads the way into the kitchen.

"I can't see a fucking thing," I whisper after tripping over a stool. It's pitch black in here.

"Let me help you with that."

Before I can process the strange voice, the lights go on, revealing not only George and his wife but also Deborah's father, Mike.

And they're all armed, just like we are.

Shit.

The three of them are just as surprised by the presence of my brother by my side. Cecilia gasps while Mike makes a horrified, choking noise. George finds his voice first. "You're dead," he whispers, eyes bulging. "You're fucking dead."

"This isn't the first time a resurrection happened." Nix reaches behind himself like he's going for his gun.

"Don't move," Mike growls, aiming his pistol at me. "Or this one says goodbye."

"How is this possible?" Cecilia looks back and forth between us. I remember her as always being so put together, but times have changed. She's looking rough—roots grown out, circles under her eyes, pale skin.

"It's easier for me to answer questions when there's not a gun in my face," Nix mutters.

"Too fucking bad." George moves first, stepping closer, eyeing us warily. "Keep your hands visible. Don't fucking move." He steps up behind us, taking our guns while Cecilia and Mike hold us in place with their weapons.

How the hell are we getting out of this? Three against two. Granted, one of them is a woman and probably wouldn't take much to overpower, but she's armed.

And once George is through with us, we won't be.

His gun's muzzle presses against my lower back. "Now, into the basement. One of you tries anything, the other one gets it first. Got it?"

We don't have a choice, even though I know we're only making it easier for them to do whatever they have planned. They fucking lured us here. Are we that easy to predict?

"And what are you going to do to us down here?" Nix asks as he steps through the open door and starts down the stairs to the finished basement. It's a pointless question—the further we go down, the more I can see. There's plastic on the floor and a pair of chairs side by side.

"Have a seat," George mutters, and this time he stands in front of us while Cecilia and Mike bind our wrists behind the chairs, cinching the ropes tight enough that I grind my teeth while glaring at the man facing us.

Just like earlier today, he's sweating, making his head glisten. His eyes hold just as much cold hatred. "Now that we're all together, it's time to start telling the truth. What happened to my son?"

"Would that be Dennis, or the one you really cared about?" Nix chuckles, smirking at the way Cecilia's mouth falls open.

Without saying a word, she pulls her right hand back and slaps him across the unscarred side of his face. "How dare you? You killed him, too, didn't you? You murdered my boy! You're a monster!"

"Why are you here and my son isn't?" George's voice shakes with rage, but it's the way his gun trembles that concerns me. He's unstable, capable of anything. What is he going to do?

"Do you want the truth? Fine, I'll give you the truth." Nix spits out blood—Cecilia hit him that hard—before continuing. "Bradley is dead. It's his body in my grave."

"You killed him!" Cecilia wails, turning to her husband, forgetting to aim at us. "I told you! I told you he did this!"

"We set the fire to my dad's house," he continues, speaking over her like she doesn't matter. "I got out, but he didn't. That's the truth. But your little boy was in it with me," he sneers, staring at Cecilia. "Don't forget that. He thought it was a great idea to burn the place down."

"Liar!" she shrieks. I don't think I've ever seen anybody completely lose it the way she is right now. With her eyes bulging, she jabs the gun in his direction. "That is a lie!"

"Whatever you need to tell yourself," he replies. "Either way, he's dead. And so are Dennis and your little girl, thanks to them abducting Leni and holding a knife on her," he continues, looking at Mike.

Mike's been quiet through all of this, but now his face darkens, his chin trembling, his nostrils flaring like an animal ready to attack.

"I am the one responsible," Nix concludes. "My brother didn't have anything to do with it. Only me. So if you want your revenge, I'm the one you kill. Let him go unless you want more trouble."

"From you?" George asks before barking out a laugh edged with insanity. "Right. You'll be dead, remember? How will you give us any trouble?"

"I never said the trouble would come from me. It'll come from the cops," he reasons.

"Don't do this," I mutter, but he ignores me.

"Remember, I'm already dead," he says. He sounds so casual, matter-of-fact. "So if I disappear, who will care? But if Colt disappears, that's when you'll have a problem. And according to what he already told me today, George had a little bit of a problem steering his BMW in the school parking lot. I wonder how long it would take for security footage to be pulled up. I bet they got a really nice shot of his plates before he tried to run Colt down."

The fact that he doesn't take the time to think any of this out in his head tells me this is part of what he was mulling over during the hours we spent waiting until it was safe to come out here. He spent the time running through potential scenarios, while all I did was fantasize about how satisfying it would be to end George's life. If we get out of this, I'll have to thank him.

But we have to get out of it first. I will not let my brother sacrifice himself for me—and there's something else, another aspect he hasn't mentioned, but I know must be on his mind. What about Leni? They're not going to let her go.

"Don't listen to him." George looks at his wife, then at Mike. "We all know the police won't fucking care. They sure as hell didn't when it came to confirming whose body was in the kitchen. This one's car was parked at the house; they were satisfied he was the one who got blown up. Even when we asked them to confirm, they couldn't be bothered. They won't go out of their way to find out what happened to Colt when it hasn't even been a year since his father and brother died in a tragic accident." He sneers. "Maybe he was feeling unstable. They'll believe what they need to believe to file their reports and move on."

He's probably right about that.

"That's why we have to do this," George insists. There's something fanatical in his voice, unhinged. He reminds me of a preacher trying to convince his congregation to handle a snake. His breathing is sharp and grasping, and now sweat is practically pouring down his head and the sides of his face. "If we want justice, we take matters into our own hands, right? That's where all of this started. We do not give up now. For our kids, for all of our kids."

"I'm sure the cops would never suspect you." Nix almost seems like he's enjoying himself, almost laughing. "If you've been raising shit with the police over what you think they should have been doing for your kid, who do you think will be the prime suspect? So let's pair that up with the footage of you trying to run Colt down—which there were witnesses to, by the way—and you have an open-and-shut case. They would be happy to put you away quickly just to close the case and move on. Is that justice? It's not like it would bring Bradley back. Or what's his name? The one you don't give a shit about."

"That is enough!" Cecilia shrieks. "Do not talk about my boys! You nasty, evil, disgusting thing!"

Mike looks at me, then at Nix, before looking at George. "You know, it could be true."

Yes, but will that be enough to convince George to change his mind? Or have things already gone so far there's no turning back? There's nothing to do but sit here and wait to see what our fate will be.

29. LENI

This is ridiculous. Am I supposed to sit here all night, worrying myself half to death, jumping every time there's a tiny noise outside?

Because that is exactly what I'm doing—ready to jump out of my skin, pacing my apartment like a crazy person as minutes turn to hours. Before long, it's almost 12:30, and I haven't gotten a text from either of them to let me know they're still alive.

What are they doing? What's happening? What if I'm right, and George was waiting for them? What if this is exactly what he wanted Colt to do? Because he didn't know Nix is still alive, so he wouldn't be expecting him. What if he hurts them both?

What if he does more than hurt them?

My heart seizes when footsteps in the hallway outside the apartment get louder. The gun sits on the coffee table—I haven't been able to touch it since I left it there after the guys left. Do I need it? Should I grab it? Holding my breath, I listen as the sound gets louder, and louder… and softer as whoever it is keeps walking.

I can't take this anymore.

Colt's laptop sits open on the kitchen table, where he looked up the address earlier while we were waiting for pizza to be delivered. We actually sat and ate pizza while waiting for the right time for them to leave and do things I don't want to think about. Like this was an ordinary night. The house is still pulled up on Google Maps—I type the address into my phone, shaking with fear but filled with determination. I'm not going to let them do this on their own, not when I'm part of the reason they went in the first place. Maybe they need my help.

Even if I wonder whether I would be able to shoot somebody if the time came. I guess that's the kind of thing you just have to do in the moment. You can't think about it beforehand.

Colt will be so happy to know I am finally driving my car. I guess this is as good a reason as any to get behind the wheel. The house is a short drive from the apartment, but that still gives me plenty of time to worry like hell and hope I'm not making the wrong choice by coming out here. *Let them be okay. Let it already be over and let them be okay.* Colt will probably be annoyed with me for taking a risk, but that is nothing compared to the terrible things that could possibly be happening.

Right away, I notice a car parked down the block from the end of the cul-de-sac that definitely does not belong here. Nix's car. They must have left it here to keep from being noticed. I park in the next empty spot near the curb, kill the engine, and sit in silence for what feels like forever. Am I seriously doing this? I can't turn back now.

It's a cool night, and the air hitting my skin once I step out of the car makes me shiver. I shove my fists into the pockets of my hoodie and tuck my chin close to my chest, walking quickly the rest of the way to a set of open gates at the end of a wide driveway leading up to a house that sits above the others.

The grounds around the house are covered in trees, giving some privacy and cover for me to sneak up there without worrying about being spotted. There are no lights on in the front of the house, and I walk as quietly as I can around the outside, listening hard for anything coming from behind the walls.

The first beams of light I see comes from windows just above ground level, telling me they're in the basement. Something inside me is almost too afraid to let me get any closer—my feet are rooted to the ground, and I'm shaking so hard it's tough to walk a straight line. But this isn't about me, it's about them, and thinking about what they might be going through keeps me moving until I reach the window and lower myself to one knee, peeking inside.

I have to clamp a hand over my mouth to hold back my gasp. There are three people in there, two men and a woman, and the men take turns punching Nix while a bloody, bruised Colt watches. Nix spits blood onto his T-shirt and lifts his head, saying something I can't hear with the windows closed. Whatever it is, it enrages the woman holding a gun on them—she shrieks something and motions with the gun like she wants to fire. One of the men has to be George, though I don't know who the other one is. Not like it matters.

They're going to kill them. Why else would they have them tied up like they are? I can't just stand here and let that happen.

Now I rush, jogging to the back door with the gun tucked in my waistband, the way I saw Nix and Colt do it before they left. The back door is broken—that must be how they got in.

The kitchen is large but cluttered, messy, like it's been neglected for a while. I hear voices coming from downstairs. The basement door is open next to the fridge, and I tiptoe toward it, careful in case there's a squeaky floorboard or something else that would give me away. They're obviously too busy down there to notice anything up here, though. Shouting, accusations, and pained groans from the sounds of flesh hitting flesh tell me the beating is still going on. I have to stop them. But how?

Footsteps ring out. Somebody's coming up. With my heart in my throat, I tiptoe away, rounding a graceful archway separating the kitchen from the room beyond it. Everything is dark—not that I would care about the decor if the lights were on.

"Maybe it's time to use the knives." It's the woman of the group, now standing in the kitchen. Knives? It's enough to make my blood run cold. She's puttering around in there, doing something at the sink—before coming my way.

I have to do something. I have to stop this!

She walks past the archway and doesn't notice me standing in the dark—at least until she hears me draw the gun from my waistband and click the safety off and point it at her. All at once, she turns around, her mouth hanging open, and the light coming from the kitchen illuminates her eyes as they widen in understanding.

"Don't say a word," I warn through gritted teeth. I barely recognize my voice. "I want you to turn around and get on your knees, hands behind your head. Do it," I go on, aiming at her head.

"If I scream, they'll come running," she whispers.

"Then I guess it's a good thing I have all these bullets. Do it." Who am I? Oh, right. I'm a girl trying to save the men she loves.

She turns in a circle, lowering herself to her knees. "You're going to regret this, you little slut. You're going to be sorry."

When she's kneeling, her hands behind her head, I step up close behind her and touch the metal to her back. All I have to do is pull the trigger. That's it. It'll be so easy.

I can't. I just can't. How am I supposed to take a life?

"Don't have the guts, do you?" she asks with snide laughter in her voice. "You only think you do."

She's right. I don't have the guts to kill her.

But I do have the guts to pick up a lamp from a table close by and bring it down on top of her head.

It's not so much the breaking of the lamp that's loud. It's the way her unconscious body hits the floor with a heavy thud that sets off rapid footsteps coming up the basement stairs.

"Cecilia?" a man asks. "What happened?"

I don't think—I react, spinning in place and meeting him in the kitchen by the time he reaches the top of the stairs. All it takes is our eyes meeting from across the room for me to know who he is. Deborah looked a lot like her dad.

There's a second that might as well be an eternity when we stare at each other. Time stops. There's nobody but the two of us, locked in a staring contest.

Before he lunges.

And I fire. Like magic, a wound appears on his thigh, which begins oozing blood that soaks into his jeans.

"Shit!" he barks, stumbling backward, pressing a hand to the wound, not stopping until it's too late. Until his eyes bulge even wider, his mouth falls open, and he reaches out to grab the doorframe to keep himself from tumbling backward down the stairs.

He's too late.

The sound of him falling is loud enough to make me cringe and wince as he hits every step on the way down. When I work up the guts to go to the top of the stairs, I look down at where he landed and stare in sickened disbelief.

He's lying on his stomach but looking up at me. His head is twisted in a way it shouldn't be.

He broke his neck. He's dead.

It's like I split in half on the spot. One half of me is horrified, ice filling my veins, nausea twisting my stomach. He wouldn't be dead if I hadn't shot him. I am responsible for his death when I look at it that way.

The other half stares down in triumph. Grim satisfaction tugs at the corners of my mouth until I'm smirking down at the bastard who was beating Nix when I first looked through the basement window. I wouldn't have shot him if he wasn't doing this, if he hadn't made a move like he wanted to hurt me. He got what he deserved.

When the other man—who I'm now guessing is George—rushes to him and stands over his body, I train the gun on him.

"Don't move!" I shout. Again, I don't recognize the voice coming from me, just like I don't recognize the thrill of watching disbelief play over his face when he looks up at me.

"What do you think you're doing?" He's almost laughing,

like he doesn't believe what he sees. "Making our job easier? Because you're next. Don't think you aren't."

"I don't know who you're talking about when you say 'our job,'" I reply, slowly walking down the stairs, watching his every move—every twitch of his jaw, every direction his eyes travel. "Because it looks like he's dead, and the woman upstairs is unconscious. Maybe even worse—I hit her pretty hard."

"Cecilia?" His voice has a note of desperation that only grows louder when he calls her name again.

"I told you. Back away," I warn, and I have to force my hands to be steady as I reach the basement floor, stepping over the body lying at the foot of the stairs.

"Leni," Colt grunts.

I don't dare look his way. I don't trust this guy in front of me. He looks unhinged, and now he knows he's in this alone.

"Untie them," I demand, jerking my head in their direction while staring at the sweating man who tried to run Colt down. "George, is it?"

"Yeah," he grunts. "And you can get fucked, bitch."

"Things not to say to a woman holding a gun on you," Nix quips, because even now he has to be a smart-ass and pretend there's nothing seriously messed up about this situation.

"Fine. I'll do it myself. But don't you move," I warn, backing away from George toward the chairs where the guys are tied up.

"There are knives over there," Colt tells me, nodding toward a small table under the window. I couldn't see it from where I was looking in earlier—there are a few of them lined up in a row, telling me how tonight was supposed to end before I got here. I grab one at random, holding the gun in one hand while using the knife on Nix's ropes.

"How's it going there?" George asks.

There's a crazed look in his eyes. He has sweat through his shirt, big dark stains under his arms and around his collar. My gaze keeps moving back and forth between him and the ropes, since I'm afraid I'm going to cut Nix in the process. "Not that easy, is it?" he asks with a snide laugh.

"That's right, keep talking," Colt tells him. "Wait until I cut your fucking tongue out."

"Her hand is shaking. The gun is shaking," George taunts while I saw at the ropes as carefully as I can, while also trying to move fast. The longer I take, the more of a chance this will end badly.

The damn rope is so tough to saw through, like it's defying me the harder I try.

"Stop!" Colt barks, making me train my full attention on George, who has crept a little closer.

"Shoot the fucker!" Nix shouts. "Fucking kill him!"

I have to, don't I? I know I have to.

"She won't do it," George predicts, scoffing. "She doesn't have it in her. She's a stupid slut, but she's not a fucking psycho like you two."

"Do it!" Nix urges.

He's right. I have to.

But George is too fast. He throws himself across the room, startling me into dropping the knife and fumbling with the gun until it's too late. He's already on top of me, knocking me to the floor.

The gun slides away, out of my reach, but it's the hands he wraps around my neck that are the bigger problem.

I hear Nix and Colt shouting and struggling while I claw at George's hands, desperate for air as he presses hard against my windpipe. My eyes bulge, and an ugly, croaking noise comes out of me when I open my mouth, fighting desperately to suck in a breath.

His crazed face fills my world when he leans down over me. "Was it worth it?" he demands while the world starts to go out of focus. "Was it? You don't know how I have dreamed about this! Die, die like my boys died!"

I think I'm going to.

Colt shouts my name while I kick and claw, but it's no use. I'm too weak. He's too strong.

He's killing me.

I'm dying.

Life is slipping away while he shakes me, crushing my throat.

Mom. I'm coming.

All at once, the pressure eases, and I suck in a gulp of air.

The world comes back into focus in time for me to watch Nix hook his hand under George's jaw and pull it back sharply—before he drags the knife across his throat.

A sudden rush of warmth sprays across me.

I barely have time to feel it before I realize what it is—the same dark red, sticky liquid pouring from the wound, pumping with every beat of George's heart. His eyes bulge, his hands cover the slit in his throat, while Nix holds him in place wearing a look of triumph. "She doesn't have it in her, but I sure as fuck do," he announces to the dying man.

The world goes fuzzy again, and this time, there's nothing to stop me from succumbing to the darkness when it rushes in all at once.

If anything, I welcome it.

30. NIX

I'M MESMERIZED BY THE THICK DROPLETS OF RUBY RED blood dripping off Leni's cheek and onto her collarbone. My eyes are trained on that single drop, leaving a track on her delicate skin before soaking into her blue shirt and turning it into a dark purple stain.

I force my gaze away and look up into Leni's bloody face. She is still a little out of it, her eyes unfocused, her stare blank. I lift my hand and cup her cheek.

"Hey, are you still with me?" I ask gently, running my thumb over her quivering bottom lip, just as Colt enters the bathroom behind us.

She nods slightly, but I'm not convinced. Her body language tells me she is not okay. Frowning, I let it go for now and concentrate on getting us out of these clothes.

"We need to get cleaned up before we leave," Colt points out the obvious.

Leni nods again but makes no move to undress. I reach for the hem of her shirt and carefully pull it over her head. She lifts her arms to help me, then wraps them around herself like she is cold when the shirt is off.

Colt is already turning the shower on, letting the water get hot while I continue to undress Leni. When she is completely naked, I can't help but stare at her in awe. She looks like a fucking warrior princess returning from battle.

My cock was already semi hard before, but seeing her completely bare has me rock solid. How fucked up am I to get turned on right now? Leni is in shock, covered in blood, and we just killed two more people. Yet, my dick can't think about anything else besides fucking.

Colt ushers Leni under the water spray while I start to take my own clothes off. I discard them onto a pile on the floor before I step into the large shower stall.

"Really?" Leni shakes her head while looking at my hard cock.

"You know I'm fucked in the head," I tell her unashamedly. "Of course this is a turn on for me."

"I shouldn't be surprised, I guess," Leni murmurs while turning to look at Colt's dick, who, to my relief, is also hard. "Both of you, huh?"

I shrug. "What can I say? You always make me hard."

"Me too," Colt chimes in, and suddenly the whole situation seems a little lighter.

I'm just glad Leni is talking again. She seems to have snapped out of her shock. Maybe a little distraction wouldn't be so bad after all.

A grin tugs on my lips before I place my hand on Leni's shoulder and gently push her down. "Get on your knees," I order, watching her lower herself until she is kneeling in front of me.

Colt adjusts his stance, so the spray is not in Leni's face. I cup her cheek and look into her hungry eyes as I bring my cock to her waiting mouth. She parts her lips and sticks out her tongue. I groan at the sight of her eagerness to please me.

Precum beads at the tip of my mushroom head as I push forward into her hot mouth. A moan slips from my lips as I shove deep enough to touch the back of her throat.

Leni makes a gagging sound, and my balls draw together, wanting to shoot a load early. I pull myself together, not wanting to come yet. I slowly move in and out of her mouth, enjoying how wet and hot she is.

I look down at her with hooded eyes, admiring how beautiful she looks with my cock in her mouth. She closes her lips around me and hollows out her cheeks, sucking me in. A guttural groan rips from my throat as she presses her tongue on the underside of my cock.

"Let me have a turn," Colt blurts out with an urgency that almost makes me laugh. I'm usually the out of control one, but looking over at Colt's impatient face tells me he is the unhinged one today.

Before Leni can move on her own, Colt grabs her by the hair and half drags her over to him. Pleasure bursts through me and swirls in my gut as Colt holds her head in place so he can fuck her face.

He isn't gentle, making Leni gag every time he thrusts into her roughly. I wrap my fingers around my cock, wishing it was her cunt around me instead. I run my fist up and down my shaft while watching my brother fuck Leni's face like he doesn't love her.

His hands tighten in her hair as he pauses mid thrust; buried inside her throat, he holds himself there for a moment. Leni makes a gagging sound, her back rounds and her hands come up to push against Colt's thigh. He releases her, and Leni slumps over, gasping for air.

Colt grabs her hair again, pulling her up by it to bring her mouth back to his cock. Leni opens her mouth, and Colt thrusts in until his balls press against her chin.

Seeing him lose control with her is such a fucking turn on. Even worse, it makes me want to lose control of myself. I squeeze my cock tight enough to make it hurt, but I welcome the pain. It's the only thing keeping me sane right now.

"My turn," I announce when I can't wait any longer.

Following Colt's suit, I don't ask. I simply grab Leni by the hair and drag her to kneel back in front of me.

She glances up at me with glassy eyes, and her lips are red and puffy, spit dripping from the corner. There is still blood on the side of her face and through her hairline, making her look like the sexiest fucking thing I've ever seen.

"Open," I order. My pulse races as she parts her lips for me. "And keep your eyes open too."

She nods before I cup her face between my hands and thrust my cock deep into her throat. Though she just agreed not to, she closes her eyes on me. I miss that contact between us immediately.

Without thinking much about it, I pull my right hand back slightly and slap Leni's cheek. Her eyes go wide in shock as she looks up at me, bewildered. I glance over at Colt, who looks turned on. The same darkness that I'm feeling reflects back at me.

Leni has my dick still in her mouth, and she didn't pull away or slap my leg, so I go in and test the water. Pulling my hand back again, I slap her cheek a second time, this time slightly harder, but still not hard enough to actually hurt her.

She groans, the vibration of the sound going directly to my balls.

"You like this," I state while keeping eye contact with Leni. I can see she is struggling. She looks a bit confused by her own feelings, but she doesn't disagree either.

I rub her cheek before striking her a third time. She groans again, and that's all the restraint I have.

"Get up," I order gruffly while pulling her up by her arms. I need to be inside of her tight cunt. And it needs to be right now.

As soon as she is on her feet, I spin her around so she is facing away from me. "Hands on the wall," I demand, and she complies immediately.

I position myself behind her, letting my cock run through her wet folds before I enter her pussy in one deep thrust. We both moan, the sound echoing through the bathroom as I start fucking her.

Her cunt feels so good, like it was made for me. Her inner walls squeeze me so perfectly. I don't want to stop, but too soon I do so Colt can have at it. Pulling out and stepping aside so my brother can have a turn is torture, but I have to share, even now... especially now.

For a few minutes, I watch Colt fuck Leni, waiting patiently until it's my turn again. When Colt finally moves, I'm back inside Leni in the next instant. Keeping my right hand on her hip, I snake my left hand around her body and grab a hand full of her breast. I roll the perk nipple between my thumb and index finger, drawing a loud moan from her.

Her inner walls squeeze me, and I know she is about to come apart. I lower my free hand to her pussy and find her clit. It only takes a few circles over the tight bundle of nerves before I feel her thighs quiver and her core tightening.

Leni's back arches as she comes all over my cock. I groan at her cunt clamping down on me, my own orgasm approaching rapidly, but I don't want to come yet.

Pulling out, I let Colt have another turn. He takes it eagerly, pumping into Leni like his life depends on it. He comes with a roar, grabbing onto her hips with bruising force while Leni holds onto the wall for dear life.

When Colt is done, he straightens up, and Leni spins around to slump against the wall for support.

"You okay?" Colt asks, sounding seriously concerned. He reaches for her, but I'm faster.

"I've got her," I tell them both before grabbing Leni and picking her up.

She wraps her arms around my shoulders and her legs around my waist before burying her face in the crook of my neck.

"I don't think I can stand right now," she whispers in my ear while clinging to me like a monkey.

"Good thing you don't have to," I answer. "Just keep your legs spread for me and your pussy wet."

I push Leni's back against the tiled wall as I line myself up with her entrance and push into her to the hilt. We both groan, and her sharp nails rake over my shoulders as I rock her whole body up and down against the wall.

Hot water cascades down our naked bodies, washing away the final remainders of blood while I fuck my brother's girlfriend against the wall. The thrill of it all is making this ten times more exciting.

My fingers dig into her upper thighs where I hold her while hers dig into my shoulder. We cling to each other, making me feel a connection between us I haven't felt during sex, not like this, not so intimate.

Leni lifts up her head and presses her forehead against mine so our faces are only an inch apart. Then she crashes her lips against mine in a searing kiss. I part my lips and so does Leni. Our tongues meet, and I enjoy the warmth of her inviting mouth.

I keep fucking her while passionately kissing her. Our tongues dance while my chest is pressed against hers so tightly I can feel her heartbeat through our skin, and it's beating just as fast as mine.

We come apart together, her orgasm egging mine on, making it last for what seems like minutes. My release is so strong, my knees threaten to give out.

"Can you stand?" I ask when I don't know if I can hold Leni up much longer, my muscles weak and relaxed.

"I think so," Leni answers, and I carefully lower her legs to the tile floor.

I hold onto her until I know she is stable before letting her go. I'm just about to step out of the shower to grab a towel when Leni grabs my hands and interlaces them with hers. She brings them to her chest, right above her heart.

"Nix, I think I'm in love with you," Leni tells me, like it's the most normal thing in the world. "I know I shouldn't, not after everything you did, everything that happened between us. I know, but I can't help it. I love you, and I hope you love me back."

I stare at her dumbfounded, my tongue heavy and my throat dry. I open my mouth, but nothing comes out. Then I see it in her eyes, the fear of being rejected. She blinks away some tears threatening to fall from the corner, and I finally snap out of it.

"I love you too," I say, the words feeling foreign but true.

"You do?" she asks, giving me a shy smile.

"It's about damn time you two admit it," Colt chimes in. Fuck, I forgot he was still in the bathroom with us.

I turn off the water and open the shower stall. Colt is already dried off and partially dressed when I grab a fluffy towel from the rack and hand it to Leni before grabbing one for myself.

"And you are okay with this?" I ask my brother while stepping out of the shower to dry off.

"Yes, I already knew you guys cared for each other, so there is no surprise here. I don't particularly like sharing Leni's love, but I'm willing to try. I don't know how we're going to make it work, but I'm sure we can figure it out."

Colt's words have a weird effect on me. It's like there is a weight lifted off my chest that I never knew was there. I suck in a breath, and somehow it feels lighter to breathe than before.

"You look relieved," Colt points out. "Were you worried I would punch you again?"

"Wait, when did you punch Nix?" Leni questions as she steps in between us, wrapping a towel around her body.

"When I first saw him again, right before we came to rescue you," Colt admits before adding, "he deserved it."

"It's all right, it barely hurt," I lie. It hurt like fucking hell. Colt didn't hold back in his swing.

Leni shakes her head and frowns, but lets the subject go. "We need to get out of here."

"I couldn't agree more," I say as we all get dressed quickly.

Colt and I already arranged the bodies to make it look like they were in bed sleeping. I set everything up to start a fire and let it appear to be an accident. Now that we are somewhat clean and dressed, it's time to blow this joint. Figuratively and literally.

A few minutes later, we are all downstairs and out the back door. We walk around the house in an eerie silence. I think we're all holding our breath, waiting for someone to jump out at us. I scan the area continuously, looking in every dark corner, behind every bush and tree we pass until we finally get to the cars.

"I'll take your car. You can ride with Nix," Colt tells Leni before leaning down and kissing her on the lips. She briefly hugs her arms around his neck, pulling him in closer before releasing him. He gives me a nod before getting in Leni's car to start the engine.

Leni and I get into my car. I push the key into the ignition and turn it, making the car roar to life. Leni buckles up beside me as I reverse the car back into the street. As soon as I'm on the road, I hit the gas. I don't want us anywhere near the house when it goes up in flames.

I learned my lesson the first time.

31. COLT

For the second time in two weeks, there are fresh bruises on my face that will take time to fade. Just when the horror show on my forehead started to disappear, I had to go and get myself tied up and beaten.

Staring at myself in the mirror, I examine each one. Some might cringe at the sight, but to me, they're like a badge of honor. The visual proof of what I was willing to do to protect Leni, to protect all of us. Proof of what some people are willing to do for revenge, and how that drive for vengeance can drive them crazy.

I run a hand over the glass to wipe away the steam from my shower, getting a better look at my hard, glittering eyes. Yet another tragic house fire claimed three victims—that's the story on the news. Maybe George had a point about the police not giving a shit, since they seem satisfied with taking things the way they appear on the surface. A tragedy. The kind of thing that happens all the time.

Ugly images flash through my mind as I shave carefully, wincing when I have to work around the colorful patches across my jaw and mouth. I might let it go and deal with the grow-out if I could stand the scratchy feeling of my beard coming in. Leni doesn't like the feel of whiskers against her cheek, either. I'll deal with the discomfort. It will pass.

Just like interest in George, Cecilia, and Mike will pass. The explosion of reports in the day or two immediately following the fire died down in no time. That's the thing about a twenty-four-hour news cycle: there's always another story to catch people's interest. It's like the whole world has turned into an infant who needs a rattle shaken in front of their face to keep them entertained. At least it works in our favor right now while we lie low, waiting to see whether there's any further investigation into the so-called accident. A tragedy that wasn't tragic at all.

By the time I'm finished, the smell of bacon has started to creep under the bathroom door. It makes my stomach growl, and now I'm in a hurry to get dressed. If I don't grab my share as soon as it comes out of the pan, I might not get any—unless my brother suddenly doesn't like bacon anymore.

I still feel like I have to pinch myself. I have no idea how long this arrangement is going to last or how we're going to make it work. I only know I want to enjoy it as long as I can. I want to soak up the simple ease we've found together—at least when it's just the three of us, without the rest of the world getting in the way. It's a shame we can't shut them out for good.

I'm finishing pulling a T-shirt over my head when I reach the kitchen, where Nix is already sitting down with a piece of bacon in one hand and a cup of coffee in the other.

"Shit. I was hoping you'd take your time so I could get more of this." He holds up a piece of crispy bacon before taking a big bite.

"I made more than enough for everybody." Leni smiles at me from in front of the stove, and it takes a second for me to catch my breath. Sunshine pours in through the window next to her, making a halo effect around her head. I could drop to my knees in front of her delicate beauty.

But there is a solid core of strength running through her, like steel. She proved that when she followed us to George and Cecilia's. Even if I wish she hadn't risked herself, she saved our lives. There was no way we could've gotten out of there without her.

"Looking pretty good, brother." Nix runs a hand over his bruises and the swelling in his jaw. "Colorful."

Leni runs a hand over her throat but doesn't say a word before turning back to the stove to finish scrambling a bunch of eggs. When I shoot Nix a look, he cringes. We might be able to joke about our injuries, but she's not ready to do that and probably never will be. Her sense of humor isn't as dark and twisted as ours.

"So what's up today?" he asks, trying to change the subject for her sake. "We've already run through every season of that baking show—I'm pretty sure I could be a competitor at this point."

"I know you must be bored to death watching all of my shows." She sits down with us, heaping scrambled eggs onto her plate from the platter, which she sets in the middle of the table, and adding a couple of pieces of bacon. "We should watch something everybody is into."

Nix and I exchange another look. It's incredible, really, the way we can have an entire conversation without speaking. That's what no one else understood during those months we were apart. We're not twins, but we're close enough to understand each other without a word. It's the sort of connection that doesn't fade. I would have known if he was really gone.

And that's why I know now what he's thinking—it's the same thing that's been on my mind. We can't stay locked up like this forever. There will have to come a time when we can start fresh, and that means all of us. Nix included.

I need to find the right words, which is not exactly something I'm great at. "It might be time to start talking about where we go from here," I murmur, glancing up from my plate to check Leni's reaction.

She sets her knife and fork down with a soft, resigned sigh. "I'm glad somebody finally brought it up. I didn't know how to do it myself."

She always finds a way to surprise me—not that I'm stupid enough to think she's blindly happy about being cooped up here with us every day. She's a smart, thoughtful person. Of course she's already wondered how long things can continue this way.

Sitting back in her chair, she looks from me to Nix and back again before lifting her shoulders in a shrug. "I'm open to any ideas."

"When did this turn into a business meeting?" Nix asks, making her crack a grin.

"In a way, it is sort of a business meeting," she retorts, sticking her tongue out at him. "We're talking about the business of where we go next. There's a lot that needs to be considered."

Folding her arms, she hits him with a serious look. "For starters, are you sticking with us, or are you going off on your own? Now that George and the rest of them are gone, you don't have to stay close for our protection."

"Are you kicking me out?" he asks around a mouthful of bacon. "Aren't you supposed to get thirty days notice when you're being evicted?"

She's not smiling, and the way her face goes still must change his mind, since he puts down his fork and gets serious. "Sorry. Trying to lighten the mood. It's been pretty fucking dark around here lately."

"I'm not trying to evict you. That's not what anybody wants," Leni tells him, shaking her head. She looks sad—

so sorrowful. "But if you want to go live your own life, I don't want to stop you. And I don't think it would be right if Colt tried to stop you either," she adds with a look at me, like she's warning me to stay quiet. I would normally be irritated by that, but the opposite is true. She wants so much for Nix to have what he needs.

He doesn't say anything right away, like he's really thinking about it. What is there to think about? It's enough to make me wonder if he does want to go. Maybe he finds it too hard to be around us together. Maybe he doesn't want to share.

"Do you want me to stay?" he asks, going from looking at her to looking at me. "Don't feel like you have to say yes. You know I've had my reasons for staying away."

Leni doesn't know about our conversation; about the things we've confessed to each other. "And you remember what I told you," I counter.

"I'm lost," she admits with a soft laugh.

"You remember who we came from," I murmur, staring at him. "Both of them. You can be whoever it is you decide to be. It's up to you. And we'd be here for you," I add.

"I don't want you to go, Nix." I'm happy to hear her say that, and I can tell he is too. I keep my mouth shut, since they have their own shit going on. It's one thing that he accidentally killed Dad, but he also killed her mother. I can't step in and get in the middle of it. One of the hundreds of things Leni has taught me without trying.

"All right," he announces before grabbing another piece of bacon. "I'll stay. You're welcome."

He can fuck around all he wants, but I know the truth. He's happy. He's relieved. Because I am, too. "That's done." I look around the table and ask, "But what now? We can't keep you locked in here all the time."

"Glad you see it that way, because I'm sick of this place. No offense or anything."

"So what do we do?" Leni asks. "Do we stage a miraculous return from the dead?"

She's kidding, of course, but her confusion is real.

There's only one answer that works. It's not easy to say it out loud, since there's nothing simple about it. "We would have to leave town. Start over."

"Go someplace nobody knows us," Nix agrees.

If there's one thing about Leni, it's how realistic she is. She's not one of those girls who's going to get all emotional and throw a fit over what needs to be done. Instead, she chews thoughtfully, eyes narrowed as she stares out the window. "You're right. That's what we would have to do. Just to be safe."

"And you would be okay with doing that?" I can tell Nix feels bad—that's why he's so unsure.

But she isn't. "I mean, I'll miss Piper, but there's FaceTime, and I can always visit her. She couldn't really come visit us, though," she concludes with the closest thing to sadness I've seen so far. "But it would still be a lot easier than going around making sure I never mention Nix. Starting fresh is the only thing that makes sense."

Scanning her face, he asks, "And you would be willing to do that? It wouldn't be hard for you?"

"Honestly? I have some good memories, but there are a lot more bad memories around here. It's time to start a new life—as long as I'm with you two, it doesn't really matter where we go. That sounds corny, doesn't it?" she asks, wincing.

Maybe it does, but it also sounds like the best thing I've heard in a long time.

"Wait," Nix blurts out. "What about Mom?"

Of course. "I guess we'll have to work backward."

"What does that mean?" Leni asks, glancing at Nix. He only shrugs.

"We find someplace with great facilities for her. One where she can get everything she needs. When we find it, that's where we move."

It feels right because it is right. I see it in my brother's grin and the light that comes into Leni's eyes. It's time to start over—the three of us.

No. Four.

"Let's go tell Mom," I decide, shoveling the rest of my food into my mouth. Now that I have a plan, a goal, I can't wait to get moving.

"Mom?" I rap my knuckles against her doorframe, and she turns her head slowly from where she was looking out the window, sitting in a wheelchair. She can't move around much, can't get in and out of bed or wheel the chair from one place to another, but it's still great to see her like this. She looks more like herself—like I remember her.

Her smile is just the same as it used to be. With a slight wave of her fingers, she motions for me to come in, then looks over my shoulder like she expects Leni, who follows close behind.

"I brought somebody else to see you today." Because George got in the way last time. First, though, the way her face changes reminds me of the way I look. "It's nothing. It doesn't even hurt." Leni could at least wear a scarf to cover up the marks George left on her neck.

Something tells me bruising is going to be the last thing on Mom's mind once Nix comes in.

And he does—before I have a chance to warn her—because he's never been very patient.

"Mom?" he whispers, his face mostly hidden by the hood he always uses when we're in public.

Even though she can't see much of him, her smile is joyful. He steps in front of her chair, then kneels in front of her, taking her hands. "Mom. Colt told me he found you. He told me you woke up. I've even seen you while you were asleep. But looking at you like this... I didn't think it would make me feel this way."

Her brows draw together as she reaches out, touching a hand to the side of his face—the side that will always bring the memory of what he did to end our father's hold over us. Her mouth opens, and something like a choked whimper makes me cringe.

Nix covers her hand with his and shakes his head. "I am fine. There was an accident, but I made it out okay. Just a little marked up." He presses his lips to her palm and releases a deep breath.

"We're all together again," I remind her, since she still looks worried. "That's all that matters. And we came here to tell you we're all going to move."

"Including you," Nix adds. "It's time for a fresh start. They take good care of you here, but there are other places in other cities that are even better. We're gonna get you back on your feet. You'll be running marathons in no time."

"Let's leave all the bad stuff behind." Kneeling next to Nix, I watch as Mom looks at me, then back at him. Tears fill her eyes, but I know they come from happiness. I know because I understand the feeling. Just the idea of never coming back to this town, never seeing places where I have memories of my father, is good enough for me.

Leni stands behind us, one hand on each of our shoulders, and I get the feeling life is never going to get more perfect than this. Everyone who matters, all together, nothing but the future ahead of us.

32. LENI

"I do wish we had been able to spend more time together." Dr. Miller looks like she actually means it, putting her notes aside with a sigh. "But it makes sense that you would want to move on and make a fresh start. Do you feel like you're ready for that?"

Right away, I want to fire off a quick response—yes, of course I am. I'm ready to put everything behind me all at once and never look back.

And that is true. But it would be an empty answer, in a way. The kind of answer that makes people raise their eyebrows and purse their lips and keep their thoughts to themselves because they don't want to hurt your feelings by telling you you're delusional.

"It's time for something new," I reply. "I'm looking forward to living somewhere where there aren't any ugly memories. I want to make some good memories now. And I don't want to be the girl whose mom died in an explosion."

"That's only natural. You're a young woman. You have so much ahead of you. It will be good to start again." Then she pauses, because of course she does. It's her job to look at both sides of the situation. "And you're secure in this arrangement you have with these two men in your life?"

That is still an easy question to answer on the surface, but just like the first question, she'll want to dig deeper. I might as well give her the full answer she's looking for. "I know it's unconventional. I know it won't be easy all the time—it's not easy with one of them alone, much less two of them at the same time. They're both stubborn and super protective and competitive. But... I don't know. Together, we make sense."

"How so, do you think?"

"It's tough to put into words. It's like they balance each other out. They have this shorthand they can use. Sometimes, they don't even need to speak out loud—they just understand each other. If one of them is acting like a jerk, the other one calls him on it. If anything, it sort of makes my life easier."

She chuckles softly. "Twice the help around the house, too."

"That's true."

Her smile fades before she asks, "What about the other things we've discussed? This darkness you've mentioned —is that something you're sure you can handle? Because —and this is my role as your therapist to remind you— you're leaving behind everything you've ever known and moving to a new state with these two. A pair of men whose darkness has frightened you in the past. Are you sure you're secure in this?"

Part of me wishes I hadn't been quite so honest with her, but it's really not my problem whether or not she believes me. All I can do is tell the truth.

"Yes, definitely. It's not going to happen overnight, but they're both learning to control it. They were just as affected by their life in that house as I was—only they had years and years of it."

"It could be they would both benefit from therapy. Maybe you should suggest it to them. It'll be a lot easier than trying to do it all on their own."

It's not a bad idea, and if I thought they would listen, I would suggest it. Maybe I'll ask them to do it for me, since they would never come up with the idea otherwise. It's fine to encourage me to get help, but for them? They've come a long way on a lot of things, but there's still a long way to go. "What's most important to me, though, is that they know I love them no matter what."

"Both of them? You can say that now?"

"Yes." That one I don't need to explain. I know it's true. I just needed to give myself permission to say it. I had to remember it doesn't matter what the world thinks. The world doesn't come home with us. The world isn't in our bed or our kitchen in the morning. The world doesn't know how they make me laugh. How safe I feel when I'm with them. Safe to be me.

"I wish you the best of luck, Leni." Before I leave the office for the last time, she places her hands on my shoulders and holds me in place in front of her. "It's time for you to rewrite your story. You're strong enough. You have the tools you need. Now use them."

"I will. Thank you."

I carry her kind words in my heart as I leave the building, stopping for a second to let the last of today's sunlight warm my face. A deep breath of fresh air fills me with hope.

And a light tapping of a horn makes me smile. Always so impatient, both of them.

Jogging across the street, I shake my head the whole way. "What, did you think I forgot you were here?" I ask Colt, leaning over to kiss his cheek while Nix snickers from the backseat.

"I told him you were, like, having a girl moment or something." When I stick my tongue out, he laughs. "I was waiting for you to close your eyes and spin in a circle with your arms stretched out."

"Maybe that's what I would have done if I wasn't interrupted." After nudging Colt with my elbow, I buckle in, and he pulls out onto the street. This is another area I won't be sorry to never see again. I don't ever want to look at the place where Dennis drugged me. That's in the past.

Like Dr. Miller said, I'm writing a new story now—one that involves packing boxes and tape and conversations about downsizing and decluttering and how there's no way two people should have so much stuff. Wrapping every plate and glass, asking myself if we can just leave everything in the apartment and buy new things after we move. Somehow, it all got done without more than a few arguments.

But there's one more thing I have to do before we leave tomorrow.

My heart gets a little heavier the closer we come to the cemetery. I know Mom isn't here—not really. Her spirit is all around me. If I want to talk to her, all I have to do is talk. It doesn't matter where I am.

But there's still something sad and emotional about leaving the place where she's buried. We are the only people who will know who she was. That she was a person. That she existed, and she was real. That she had a hard life with a lot of rough breaks. That, she honestly thought, at least in the final months of her life, she had finally made it. That all of her worries were over.

She never knew, until it was too late, exactly what she had found in James. That new beginning was what led to her ending.

For years to come, people will walk past her headstone and know nothing about the woman the words etched in marble represent. I hate the thought, but I guess that's what happens to all of us. Just another part of life.

"Go ahead," Colt murmurs once we park in the familiar

area we have visited so many times. "We can wait here so you can have some privacy."

Taking the bouquet of roses from Nix's hands, I set off for the grave. The last bouquet I left is long gone, a handful of weeds in its place. I get on my knees without thinking about it and pull them, knowing I'm doing it for the last time.

Who will do it when I'm gone?

"Hi, Mom," I whisper. "I'm sorry to say goodbye like this. I know this is stupid, but I feel like I'm leaving you all alone. I have to believe you wouldn't want me to stay here just so I can pick dandelions off your grave. You would want me to have a fresh start, right? Isn't that what you would want for me?"

I hate how much I wish she could answer. I wish there was more than the whistling of the wind through the trees as a response.

Taking a deep breath and letting it out slowly, I murmur, "I know you could never have imagined things turning out this way. Me being with Colt and Nix—that's not how it was supposed to be. But none of it has been the way it was supposed to be. And I guess if there's one thing I've learned, it's that you can't really predict life. It's going to do what it wants to do. All we can do is try to grow and learn and adapt. I'm trying to do that now. I want to make the best of my life. And even though James hurt me so much, he brought me his sons, and they make me happy. They really do."

Sudden footsteps nearby make my head snap around while my heart lurches, then takes off at a sickening speed —until I see it's only the two of them. With a hand on my chest, I whisper, "I didn't think you were joining me."

"There was something I thought I had to say." Nix steps up to the foot of the grave. I watch as his eyes move, taking in the name and the dates under it. "I'm sorry. I didn't mean for you to die that day. I wasn't thinking. I hope wherever you are, if you can hear me, you can forgive me."

Looking down at me, he adds, "I want you to know Leni is in good hands. I'm going to do whatever it takes for the rest of my life to watch over her for you. That's all I can give you now, and I hope it's enough."

"I think it is," I tell him, smiling as I stand, wrapping my arms around his waist and touching my head to his shoulder. He releases a shuddering breath that I think holds sadness and relief at the same time. I don't want him to spend the rest of his life blaming himself.

"We'll both take care of her," Colt agrees, and I put an arm around him with the other still around Nix. I'm going to need to lean on both of them, just like they lean on me. That's what it's all about.

A warm breeze washes over me, and I smile, hoping this is Mom's way of saying she understands—and that it's time for all of us to move on together.

"It's getting dark," Colt murmurs, lowering his head until his lips press to my temple. "You ready?"

"Just about."

They start back toward the car, giving me an extra moment to go to the headstone and run my hand over it one more time.

"I love you," I whisper, closing my eyes, imagining her standing with me. "Thank you for everything you did for me. I hope you're at peace now."

A tear leaks out from under my lashes before my eyes open. Only one last thing to say once I back away.

"Goodbye," I whisper.

And now it's time to go.

Away from the past, which I leave behind me with every step I take toward the car.

Toward the men waiting for me inside.

Toward the future, which is mine to create.

EPILOGUE

Leni

One year later

Together, the three of us sing, "Happy birthday, dear Mom, happy birthday to you."

"Make a wish, Mom," Nix urges, standing on one side of the birthday cake.

"I already have everything." She speaks slowly but clearly after a year of speech therapy. "I'm only worried I won't have enough breath. Thanks for adding a candle for every year."

"Here!" I urge as I lean closer. "Do you want help blowing them out?"

"Let me try." Closing her eyes, she takes a deep breath, then blows out every single candle on the first try.

"Way to go, Mom!" Colt leans down to kiss her cheek while Nix kisses the other.

"Hold it, hold it! I have to get a picture of this." Grabbing my phone, I snap a shot of the three of them—two very happy sons and their deliriously happy mom on her birthday. There's a twinkle in her eyes now, a brightness to her smile.

"Thank you, Leni," she beams. "Now let's cut into this cake. It's almost too pretty to cut, though."

"I remembered you always liked cakes with lots of flowers and icing," Colt tells her while I pick the candles out.

"That's sweet of you to remember, my sweet boy. Both of you," she adds, smiling at Nix. "I didn't think I would ever be able to do this again with you after I woke up."

"You worked your ass off. That's why you're able to do it." Nix practically glows with pride when he looks at her. He's right, too. Over the past year in her new facility, she has completely outpaced even the most optimistic predictions.

When she stands—cautiously, but smoothly—she shakes her head at the help Colt offers. "I need to do it myself. We forgot to set out napkins."

It's very sweet, the way the guys hover, wanting to help her, but she is determined to do everything she can on her own. It's a stubborn streak she definitely passed on to her sons, which is why I think it's so funny when they get frustrated at her for doing the exact sort of thing they would've done.

"So, tell me, how is school?" She sounds like any typical mother on her way back to the table, where I slice the cake.

"I'm loving it." She gets the first slice, and I make sure to include as many of the frosting lilies as possible. "Classes are going great."

"It's so wonderful that you want to help others by becoming a therapist. And sports therapy, too—it's a perfect fit. Helping athletes develop their mindset and turn their setbacks into strong points."

"That is exactly what I want to do."

Because if there's anything I've learned in the years since I was a competitor, it's the importance of mindset. Being able to pivot when necessary. Turning your greatest pain into your greatest asset. It only sounds corny to someone who's never been through it.

"And here I was, thinking we could just get free therapy out of you." Nix smirks while I roll my eyes.

"How do you put up with him?" his mom asks.

"Sometimes I wonder," I reply, and we share a grin while the guys groan.

"I never make you roll your eyes at me, do I?" Colt asks, hugging me from behind.

"Oh, no," I tell him with a smirk while his mom laughs. "Usually, you make me grind my teeth. Big difference."

There's a particular expression a mom wears when she's happy for her kids, and I'm glad to see that now. Our arrangement isn't typical, but she doesn't seem to have a problem with it—if she does, she keeps it to herself. After everything she's been through, I guess certain things just aren't worth getting all worked up about. Life is too short for that.

After eating cake, and setting up the new laptop the guys bought for her, it's time for us to go. "We'll be back next week," Colt promises.

With a happy smile, she says, "You know how much I look forward to it."

Before we leave, I bend down to give her a hug, and her lips brush my cheek before she whispers, "The best gift is seeing them so happy. Thank you."

I'm a little choked up as we leave. Somehow, she knew exactly what I needed to hear.

∽

ON OUR WAY HOME, I try my best to act normal, but I can't help getting antsy. I have big plans for tonight, and the guys have no idea what I've been up to. I grin to myself, thinking about the toys I stashed in the bedroom closet.

"What are you smiling about back there?" Colt asks, looking at me through the rearview mirror.

"Nothing," I say a little too fast, clamping my hands together in my lap. "I'm just happy. It's been a great day."

I'm not sure if he buys it completely but, even if he doesn't, he lets it go. "It really has been a great day. I can't believe Mom's improved so much already."

"She looked genuinely happy today," Nix says from the passenger seat.

"You guys looked happy too," I point out.

"'Cause we are," Colt agrees, just as he pulls the car into a parking spot in front of our apartment building. I open the door as soon as we're parked, sucking in a deep breath of fresh, cool air.

It's dark outside, but the neighborhood is well lit with street lights scattered along the walkways. I shut the door and make my way to the front door, with Nix and Colt falling into step soon after. Together we walk in and up the stairs, where Colt unlocks the door.

We pile into the apartment, and I flip on the lights.

"You sure you're okay?" Nix questions, scanning my face.

"Actually, I have a surprise for you," I admit.

"For me?" Nix wiggles his eyebrows.

"For both of you," I clarify, looking between the two brothers.

"I like surprises," Colt says, before adding, "Actually, I don't, unless they come from you."

"What is it?" Nix asks impatiently.

"It's in the bedroom," I explain.

"I definitely like where this is heading." Colt grins at me, setting butterflies loose in my stomach.

I'm nervous as I lead the guys through the hallway and into our bedroom. Opening the door to the walk-in closet, I grab the bag I stuffed behind the hung up clothes. Nix and Colt stand patiently in the center of the bedroom when I turn around.

I carry the bag to the bed and pour the items inside out onto the mattress. There is a blindfold, a ball gag, a pair of handcuffs, and a small paddle for impact play.

Biting my bottom lip, I look between Colt and Nix, who are both gawking at the pile on the bed with piqued interest.

"Those look fun," Colt speaks first. He reaches for the handcuffs, picking them up to inspect them. "You didn't go cheap. These are sturdy."

"You won't be able to say your safe word with this," Nix says, picking up the ball gag.

"I know," I answer a bit nervously. "But I trust you not to take it too far."

Nix meets my eyes, his pupils are already dilated, making

him look dark and dangerous. My breath hitches when he suddenly eats up the distance between us.

"What are you waiting for? Take your clothes off and put your hands behind your back," he orders in a gravelly voice.

Excitement fills my veins as I start to undress quickly under the guys' watchful eyes. When I'm completely naked, I turn around and let Colt cuff my hands behind my back.

"Open up," Nix demands, holding the ball gag in front of my face.

I part my lips, and Nix forces the rubber ball in my mouth before fastening it at the back of my head. Then Colt puts the blindfold on me. My vision goes black, and I'm left at their mercy.

One of them grabs me by the upper arm and guides me back to the bed. My thighs make contact with the edge of the mattress just as a strong hand pushes me down so I'm bent over. I turn my head, so my cheek is pressed up against the cool sheet.

I can't see or speak, but I can hear zippers being lowered. I gasp against the gag when someone kicks my legs apart roughly. Fingers find my center, running up and down my slit with ease.

"She is wet for us already," Nix says behind me.

"Of course she is," Colt agrees.

Something smooth and cool is dragged up my thigh. I recognize it to be the paddle a second before someone lifts it up and brings it down on my ass with a harsh smack. I jolt forward and yelp against the gag, more from surprise than pain.

The guys chuckle behind me before I'm smacked with the paddle a second time. I'm prepared now, so I don't jolt as much, but the third impact is hard enough to rip a deep groan from my throat.

The paddle leaves my skin and is replaced with a warm large hand. A palm rubs over my sore spot, taking the ache away immediately.

After I get the same treatment on my other side, my whole ass feels hot.

Someone positions himself behind me to line his cock up with my wet pussy. He enters my body with one hard thrust. I squeeze my eyes together under the mask and bite onto the gag in pain as he stretches me too quickly.

"Fuuuuck," Nix groans behind me as he grabs my hips to pull me closer to his groin. His thick cock impales me, filling me so deeply I can feel him bumping against my cervix. "This is truly the best day ever."

The bite of pain is gone quickly and replaced with a deep pleasure. Nix fucks me like this for a few minutes before Colt's impatient voice rings out. "My turn. Quit hogging her."

Nix buries himself one last time while giving me two harsh smacks to my ass. He pulls out, leaving me empty and wanting for more. Colt replaces him quickly. Filling me to the brim with his hard cock.

His fingers dig into my hips as he fucks me like a madman. Each bruising thrust burrowing inside of me with force.

My first orgasm hits me out of nowhere. I moan against the gag as Colt brings the paddle down on my ass midst my release. The pain breaks through my orgasm, merging into white hot pleasure. I moan around the gag as my pussy spasms around Colt's dick.

"Fuck, you squeeze my cock so tightly when you come," Colt murmurs.

He slows down his pace, lazily fucking me while my sensitive pussy pulsates around him.

Suddenly, he slips out and steps away. I whine in displeasure, making the guys chuckle again.

Nix takes his place a moment later, but instead of his cock, I feel his fingers enter my pussy. He gathers my wetness from there and brings it to my asshole. His fingers rub around my tight hole before he shoves two digits inside me.

I bite down into the leather ball at the harsh intrusion. I wiggle my butt away from him, but he simply places a flat hand on my lower back, pushing me into the mattress until I can't move.

He fucks my ass with his fingers until my asshole is stretched out enough to take his cock. He pulls his digits free and a moment later replaces them with the smooth head of his dick.

He shoves his hips forward, breaching my tight ring with his thickness. We both moan in unison as he fills me up. His palms grab my ass. He pulls my cheeks apart with his thumbs and thrusts deeper into me.

His gravelly grunts fill the room and mix with my low moans, creating a symphony of pleasure as he fucks my ass without restraint. The rhythmic sound of our flesh slapping together is the music in the background.

At some point, Nix switches with Colt, who is just as rough with my ass as his brother. They take turns fucking both of my holes until I'm sore everywhere.

I lose track of who is inside of me and who is slapping my ass when I come apart again. My release coating someone's cock as an orgasm rips through me.

Both my pussy and my ass are sore and feel raw, but the guys keep fucking me until I come a third time. By then, I'm whimpering in pain. I'm spent and so sensitive between my legs.

Nix groans behind me, his fingers digging into my hips painfully as he finally comes deep inside my ass. I can feel his thick cock pulsating with his release, and I slump against the bed as he pulls out of me slowly.

Colt takes his place once more and before I know it, he is buried in my aching asshole. I yelp out in pain as he forces himself into my swollen hole.

"I know you must be sore," Colt's deep voice meets my ear. "Your asshole is all red and puffy, but your pussy looks even more beat up." He thrusts into me deeply, tears dwell in my eyes as the pain intensives.

"You can take it, though, my little slut. You can take the pain. Let me fuck your tight little ass with my fat cock." His deviant words send zips of pleasure to my core. He leans over, his weight pressing me into the mattress as he fucks me even harder. Every time I think he can't get any deeper, it feels like he does.

Just when I think I can't take any more, he buries himself a final time before coming deep inside of me with a loud grunt. He pulls free a moment later, leaving me breathing heavily from exhaustion. My legs quiver and my knees threaten to give out when I feel someone's hand back at my pussy.

I shake my head and groan, mumbling no against my gag.

"You are so hot like this," Nix murmurs. "Your pussy and ass look used. You must be tired, but we are not done with you yet."

A shiver runs down my spine. I don't know if I can take any more.

"You can come one more time for us," Colt promises, but I'm anything but convinced.

A moment later, I hear the familiar sound of the vibrator wand. I suck in a quick breath when I feel it on my over-stimulated clit. I try to squeeze my legs together, but someone is wedging them apart.

I groan in frustration and try to get up, but strong hands push me back down onto the bed. I squirm under their touch, overwhelmed by the feeling between my legs. I try to wiggle out of their hold, but it's laughably futile. The more I fight, the more of the vibrator I get. It's pushed against my clit in an onslaught of sensations.

"You can take it. We know you are tired but this is going to feel so good," Colt coos. "We promise. Just be a good girl for us and take it.

I try to close my legs again, which earns me a hard slap against my butt cheek. I yelp out in pain as a weird feeling overcomes me. It feels like an orgasm, but stronger and more unhinged. Pleasure creeps up my spine and explodes in my core like I've never experienced before. I'm barely aware of a liquid squirting from my pussy and running down the inside of my leg.

"Fuck," Colt groans. "That's new." He finally removes the vibrator from my clit, and I breathe out in relief.

My whole body goes limp as I recover from the most intense orgasm of my life.

"I didn't know you were a squirter," Nix tells me as he climbs onto the bed next to me and undoes my gag.

He pulls the ball from my mouth so I can answer him. "Neither did I." My voice comes out raspy and tired.

Colt uncuffs my wrists and rubs my skin while Nix unties the blindfold. My eyes remain closed, even with the silky fabric above my eyes gone. I'm just too tired to open them. My whole body is exhausted, even though technically I was just lying here, I feel like I've just ran a marathon. Every fiber in my being is exhausted.

I don't move when the guys clean me up, and I don't say a word when they move me around in the bed so my head hits the pillow. Someone drapes a blanket around me, the cool fabric covering my heated skin, making me shiver.

"I love you," Colt whispers, before placing a kiss on my forehead.

"Love you," Nix murmurs from the other side before nuzzling my neck.

Two strong arms pull around me, and I slowly drift off, knowing that I'm safe, happy, and loved.

The End.

Thank you for reading The Locked Duet.
For more dark bully romance, check out my Corium University Trilogy or my Wicked Falls series of standalones, starting with Hateful Vows.

About the Author

Born and raised in Germany, Cassandra attended business school in her home town before immigrating to America when she was only eighteen. At nineteen, she married her husband who was active duty military at that time. Together, they traveled the country for years, before finally settling down. Now, she lives in the mountains of North Carolina with her husband of sixteen years, their three children, two dogs, and one hairless cat.
With a love for reading, that love slowly transpired into writing she put her fingers to the keyboard and started writing about the dark side of romance.

C. Hallman is a USA Today Bestselling Author who wrote her debut Novel in 2018 and has since published over 100 books in various romance sub genres. Her works have been on numerous bestseller lists and have been translated into 8 languages around the world.

www.authorchallman.com

Printed in Great Britain
by Amazon